Bent Tree
Bride

Denise Weimer

SMITTEN
HISTORICAL ROMANCE
LIGHTHOUSE PUBLISHING of the CAROLINAS

Smitten Historical Romance is an imprint of LPCBooks
a division of Iron Stream Media
100 Missionary Ridge, Birmingham, AL 35242
ShopLPC.com

Cover design by Hannah Linder Designs

Iron Stream Media serves its authors as they express their views, which may not express the views of the publisher.

This is a work of fiction. Names, characters, and incidents are all products of the author's imagination or are used for fictional purposes. Any mentioned brand names, places, and trademarks remain the property of their respective owners, bear no association with the author or the publisher, and are used for fictional purposes only.

All Scripture quotations, unless otherwise indicated, are taken from the Holy Bible, King James Version.

Library of Congress Control Number: 2021932252

ISBN-13: 978-1-64526-295-4
Ebook ISBN: 978-1-64526-296-1

Printed in the United States of America

PRAISE FOR *BENT TREE BRIDE*

Bent Tree Bride offers a rare glimpse into the hidden history of the past where larger than life, unlikely heroes helped forge our nation in remarkable ways. Well done!

~Laura Frantz,
Christy Award-winning author of *The Frontiersman's Daughter*

Romance. Intrigue. Honor. *Bent Tree Bride* is all that and more. An action-filled historical depiction of a time of unrest in our nation, when tensions were high and so were the stakes. And if that weren't enough, the love story between Susanna and Sam is positively swoon-worthy! I heartily recommend it.

~Michelle Griep,
Christy Award-winning author of *Once Upon a Dickens Christmas*

Be transported to the eastern frontier of Tennessee and the Cherokee Nation in this slice of lesser-known history. Denise Weimer weaves a heartrendingly sweet love story against the backdrop of an intriguing and enlightening account of native involvement in the War of 1812. You'll find yourself rooting not only for Susanna to grow in strength to match what her heart already wants, but for Sam to know that he is indeed a man of honor and worthy of his beloved. This author is fast becoming one of my must-reads!

~Shannon McNear,
2014 RITA finalist and author of *The Cumberland Bride,*
#5 of Daughters of the Mayflower

Bent Tree Bride is an intricate weaving of history and fiction. Denise Weimer takes her readers on a perilous and emotional journey, leaving me to wonder where history left off and fiction began. With richly drawn characters who capture your heart and imagination, *Bent Tree Bride* is a page-turner I highly recommend.

~**Ane Mulligan,**
Bestselling author of the Chapel Springs series and the Georgia Magnolias series

Denise Weimer weaves tales rich in history and populated with characters deserving of the stunning settings in which she places them. Don't miss this one!

~**Terrie Todd,**
Award-winning author of *The Silver Suitcase, Maggie's War,* and *Bleak Landing*

Bent Tree Bride is an intriguing story of love and family set against the backdrop of the War of 1812. Susanna, daughter of a white captain, is promised by her father to wed a man she doesn't love. Sam, a mixed-blood Cherokee, struggles to understand his ancestors' long-held customs. When Susanna and Sam fall in love, they are forced to grapple with clashing cultures that threaten to keep them apart. Denise is a masterful storyteller who weaves fictional characters with historical events to touch readers' hearts while presenting enlightening glimpses into our nation's past.

~**Pat Nichols,**
Award-winning author of The Willow Falls Series

Bent Tree Bride is an exquisitely complex, compelling, intriguing dive into colonial history. Real-life characters such as Davy Crocket, General Jackson, and Cherokee and Creek Indians, and well-researched details set the reader in that time. Weimer captures the sights, sounds, and drama of Susanna and Sam in Indian Territory so well that it came alive as I read the story. A must-read for history lovers ... or anyone!

~**Susan G Mathis,**
Author of *Devyn's Dilemma* and *Katelyn's Choice*

DEDICATION

This novel would not have come about but for an idea sowed by Pegg Thomas, so Pegg, this book is dedicated to you. You've been my coauthor, my coeditor, and the best possible mentor in the world of publishing and editing. May God bless you richly.

ACKNOWLEDGMENTS

Ever since I began my stint as a regular contributor to Colonial Quills blog, I've come to realize a special breed of authors and readers exist whose ideal trope of novel is the Early American frontier romance. Slowly, you sucked me in, and now I'm one of you! While this book was originally conceived as part of a series that didn't come to fruition, I'm so glad it was written … because I truly believe it pulled my best writing out of me! I'm also thankful for the opportunity to continue Sam's story from *The Witness Tree*. Thus, I'd like to begin by conveying my appreciation to the supportive community of authors and readers who share my deep love of heart-pounding Colonial- and Federal-era yarns chock full of action and romance. You've interacted on historical blogs, attended Facebook parties, served as beta readers and launch team members, and offered valued endorsements. You know who you are.

Special thanks also is due to my agent, Linda S. Glaz of Hartline Literary Agency, who has continued to encourage and place my writing, whether it be historical or contemporary.

Barbara Curtis, my general editor for *Bent Tree Bride*, you stepped up to the plate when I asked, and you knocked it out of the park. Your keen eye and questioning mind made you a huge asset for this project. Thank you for being willing to work with me, and I hope this proves the first of many partnerships.

CHAPTER ONE

Autumn 1813
On the Tennessee-Cherokee Nation Border

The smell of books—leather and dusty pages mingling with the burnt ash of the morning fire—stirred Sam's blood as war cries stirred some men. Despite the commission in the inner breast pocket of his swallow-tailed coat, Sam saw the way forward in words, not wars. The library was left wanting in comparison to his father's, but for a white man like Captain Gideon Moore living in Indian Territory, 'twas not poor.

The house, however—a massive, white-washed rectangle flanked by chimneys and facing the Hiwassee River—had given him pause. Only for a moment. Still, he was rather glad Moore had a visitor in the parlor when he'd arrived, giving him time to acclimate … and browse.

Where to start? Laying his top hat aside, he faced a polished bookcase inlaid with some kind of wood he'd never seen. His gaze danced over the titles. *The Federalist. A Survey of the Roads of the United States of America.* His index finger grazed the spine. He'd never been farther north than the Indian Agency a few miles and a ferry ride across the Tennessee River.

On the shelf above, a volume with a German title drew his attention. A warmth, a comfort, filled his chest as he opened the book and smoothed a hand over the pages. Even Cherokee chiefs like his father's friend The Ridge marveled that people and ideas lived in books like this, but Sam knew truth when he saw it. Had since the missionaries came, bringing that truth when he was a child.

The library door flew open. A figure in olive green darted inside, not turning, but closing the door with stealth and speed. He'd seen a fox move that way once, slinking out of range of his blowgun into the cover of thick woods.

Sam opened his mouth to alert the woman to his presence, but with three rapid steps, she backed into him. The volume toppled from his hands, and she whirled.

"Wha—" He didn't get to complete the word.

She clasped her hand over his mouth the same moment she used the force of their bodies coming together so suddenly to secure the book between them. Sam could only stare.

The muslin of her raised collar trembled with her breaths. Her nostrils flared. The girl smelled of outside—the crispness of September flaming into October—the wool of her riding habit, and expensive soap. Intoxicating. It made his heart race. But in her eyes was pain.

She addressed him in a tremulous whisper. "Please, do not speak." Her glistening brown eyes searched his. Indeed, the eyes of prey when cornered. But not by him. No, the plea in those eyes grabbed his heart as surely as her hand had grabbed his mouth.

To show his agreement, Sam exhaled. His breath on her fingers—such soft fingers—must have jolted her to awareness, for she dropped her hand, and if possible, the flush on her cheeks grew even rosier.

"I'm sorry. But no one must know I'm in here."

He was almost reading her lips. She still stood so close, he could lower his face and …

As the fringe of her lashes swept down, Sam gave his head a brief shake. He was not here for women, even one as young and lovely as this one. He straightened.

Her gaze snapped to his again. "Please." At the sound of voices coming from the parlor, she tilted her head, with a puffy, brimmed bonnet—like a *u-lo-que*, er, mushroom—atop her hair, toward the door.

"Very well." He used the same volume she did. Only then did she step back, and Sam could breathe again. "Are you the daughter of Captain Moore?" He'd thought the children of Gideon and Polly Moore all younger.

She nodded, her fingers fluttering to the chest of her short, cropped jacket, trimmed with ridiculous braid. With the movement, the train of her skirt swept forward. A loop connected it to her left hand. She had been riding.

Despite her fair skin, she possessed the dark hair and eyes that could mark her as the offspring of Moore and his one-half Cherokee wife. But even Peggy Vann, the wealthiest mixed-blood woman in the territory, didn't dress like this. "Forgive me. I heard ... what I heard ..." Her lashes batted rapidly as her focus skittered to the corners of the room as if she searched for escape.

"Sam Hicks." Clasping the tome to his chest, he executed the type of bow he made to the American officers who frequented the Hiwassee Garrison. Then he waited.

But no recognition lit her expression. In fact, she asked, "And you are here ...?"

"On business to your father."

"And waiting where I am hiding. While reading ..." She turned the book in his hand. "*Idea Fidei Fratrum?*" Her full lips twitched, raised brows betraying skepticism. "You know German?"

The familiar resentment pricked Sam's chest, but he kept his face passive. "It's the English translation, but yes, I do. This is, in fact, the book that brought my father to faith."

The dark brows winged higher. "Not the Bible?"

Sam dipped his chin in acknowledgment. "The Bible too. But it was this account of Moravian theology which explained to him what he read in the Bible."

She studied him, something elusive flickering behind her eyes.

"You sound very proud of him."

"I am." Wasn't she proud of her father? The son of a famed Revolutionary War colonel, himself a captain in the Tennessee militia, wealthy, respected by whites and Indians alike?

"That's good. Because despite one's efforts to become one's own person and make one's own decisions, fathers so greatly influence their children." With a swish of the olive train, she paced toward the front window, drew a fancy curtain aside to reveal a shiny buggy, and jerked back. "He is still here."

"Your father?"

"No, the doctor." She sank onto a leather wingback chair.

He knew only one doctor, but he belonged at the fort. Maybe, like Moore, the man had purchased acceptance into Big Springs with the acquisition of a Cherokee wife.

Sam approached her. "Why are you hiding from this doctor?"

She jerked her chin up. "Because I cannot marry him." So much for Sam's theory. A tear plummeted down her cheek so fast it looked as if it fled from the hand that chased it. Dashing it away, she made a soft growling sound. "What you must think of me."

"Only a dead man—or woman—has no weakness." And for some reason, he wanted to understand hers. It could be because he glimpsed more solid granite than crevices in the way she straightened her spine, this daughter of a soon-to-be-colonel. He tugged his handkerchief from his pocket and offered it to her as he sat on the ottoman nearby. "What I think is, what kind of man must this doctor be if he brings you to tears?"

"That's just the thing. He is a good man." She blotted her cheek, then extended the white square of fabric back to him.

Flicking his fingers, Sam shook his head. "In case you cannot escape this good man."

In the girl's face, panic hardened to determination, and her voice firmed past her previous whisper. "I must. I will. But thank you." She stuffed the handkerchief through the pocket slit in her skirt, then squared her shoulders. A dimple appeared in her right cheek when she pressed her lips together. "Normally, I am an optimistic person. I'm sorry you caught me in a pucker."

"Please, do not apologize. You came across a stranger in your home."

"I'm still mortified. Father would scold me for such a display in front of one of his business acquaintances. Are you here about our family's trading post?"

She thought him a white man. It was not the first time Sam Hicks had passed as one, despite his high cheekbones and black hair. He'd learned to turn such situations to his advantage. Amazing, the political and military intelligence he gleaned from merely nursing a drink with men who fancied him a citizen of Tennessee, a simple clerk. But if Moore's daughter was a mixed-blood like him ...

"I come from the Hiwassee Garrison. I carry an important missive for your father from my superior, Colonel Return Jonathan Meigs."

"I've been away at school until recently, yet ..." Her gaze swept his hair, cropped in the latest European fashion, then his finely tailored coat, waistcoat, breeches, and Hessian boots. "You do not look as though you're in the army. Or, in fact, like any men around here."

"People have told me that as many times as they've told my father that he has no need for all his books." Sam swept his gaze around the room. Matter-of-factly, not with pride. "Many more books than this."

Her eyes widened, then narrowed.

He couldn't tamp down the hope that she shared the bittersweet tang of being different. With a house like this, with clothes and manners like hers—like his—she must.

His heart surged, a reaction he didn't want, didn't need, because he was looking at a woman, not his land. Now of all times, on the eve of a war men couldn't prevent with words.

She tilted her head. "I know Colonel Meigs, but you, I have never seen."

"Nor have I seen you. For I would remember." Why did that last come out raspy, as if he'd spent the night patrolling with The Ridge's Cherokee Lighthorse company, drinking dust? Sam held the gaze of Moore's daughter. Frustrating, how he possessed not an ounce of desire to snap the unseen thread stretching taut between them. "But I still don't know your name."

"Oh, I am—"

The door banged open, and Gideon Moore's substantial frame filled the threshold. "Susanna! There you are."

Susanna shot to her feet like a Tennessee militia volunteer. If only ramrod posture, polished boots, and a snappy salute were all her father required of her. The weight of his hovering brows and the darkening of his smoky-gray eyes as they shifted to his guest, who also rose, promised a private storm later.

"And with Mr. Hicks."

"Good afternoon, Captain Moore." The intriguing Sam affected another bow, this one managing to convey genuine humility. "Your houseman bid me wait here in the library."

Father gave a curt nod. "I can meet with you now. And you, Susanna, Dr. Hawkins would like to see. He brought his buggy on this fine day in hopes of taking you out and speaking to you about some rather important matters."

A knot the size of a sycamore ball and just as prickly obstructed Susanna's throat. Beneath it, from somewhere in her rapidly beating chest, pressure built. A sudden picture of that panic expanding until it caused the imaginary obstruction to pop out of her mouth and fly into her father's frowning face resulted in a dreadful reaction. A hysterical giggle escaped instead of a sycamore ball.

Father's glower deepened. "You find that amusing?"

She clapped her hand over her mouth, heat spreading over her cheeks as Sam Hicks' dark, studious eyes moved to her with something akin to concern. Probably for her sanity. "No, Father. It is just that, well, you see that I have returned from a ride and am not presentable."

"Then pray tell what you are doing closeted in my library with Colonel Meigs' emissary."

"I was—er—"

In two long strides, Sam took up the theological tome and showed it to her father. "I'm afraid I detained your daughter with my interest in *Idea Fidei Fratrum*."

"With the door shut?" The buttons on the captain's brocade waistcoat strained as he looked between them.

Was he wheezing? Susanna lived in fear of a return of her father's lung sickness. She sided with Dr. Hawkins when it came to discouraging Father's drinking and smoking.

"Please forgive me, sir." Sam bowed his head and laid the book on the mahogany end table. "I do not think clearly when there is a chance to discuss religion or philosophy."

Susanna's lips parted. This gentleman, who had already captivated her by the intelligence shining out of the eyes in such a handsomely boned face, who had not brushed aside her uncharacteristic emotional breakdown as female hysterics, was taking the blame for her.

The lines on Father's forehead relaxed. "Yes, well, we share a deep appreciation for the work of the Moravians at Springplace. It was they who gifted me with that volume."

At the mention of the mission school located southeast on the estate of the late Chief James Vann, Sam's face lit. "I figured that might be the case. I love to stop in and encourage the students there. I am due for another visit. I haven't seen them since Good Friday."

"The day your father was baptized?" Father extended a hand,

indicating Sam should precede him into the hallway. "I heard about that."

"Yes, that was it."

"Come with me to the parlor. You must know Dr. Nathaniel Hawkins, physician to the soldiers at the garrison."

Sam paused, casting a glance back at Susanna. A flash of surprise crossed his face. Like everyone else, he'd wonder what she found objectionable in the steady nature of the hardworking doctor. She dropped her attention to the tips of her boots peeking out from her hem.

Sam's hesitation seemed to cause Father to realize that they were abandoning her in the library. "Since you find yourself unprepared for a buggy ride, Susanna, go upstairs and dress for dinner. I will ask the servants to lay a place for the doctor at the table."

"Yes, Father." Her stomach sank.

The words she'd overheard earlier between the two men agitated in her head. Dr. Hawkins had asked to court her, and her father had agreed. Then a wild hope stirred. Wasn't Sam Hicks also an educated Christian whose attire suggested his family possessed considerable wealth? Handsome. So handsome, her mouth had gone dry when she'd stood inches from him. And young. Only a couple years older than she, if she wasn't mistaken. Not twice her age and responsible for three motherless, rambunctious children. Susanna snapped her gaze up. "And Mr. Hicks? Will he be staying too?"

Father's eyes widened. His mouth tightened as he angled to study the man at his side. He got that same look of veiled displeasure when her stepmother, Polly, made Cherokee corn and bean bread, so Susanna didn't hold out much hope when he said, "We shall see."

CHAPTER TWO

Polly Moore did not share Susanna's hope that Sam Hicks would stay for dinner. In fact, she expressed the wish that he'd never come.

"I have seen this cloud on the horizon." Her stepmother stood looking out the window in Susanna's bedroom with such intense scrutiny one would think she spied an actual storm brewing over the Hiwassee. "Meigs sends a message that will lure your father to war. You watch." Her dark gaze shot to Susanna's.

Susanna tied the strings of her royal blue, drop-front dress at her stomach. "So you have been saying since the Fort Mims massacre."

"From before then." Polly gave her head a firm shake. "Before Burnt Corn Creek. When Tecumseh and the Prophet came south to visit the Creek Indians, spreading their visions to those who were unhappy when the deer hides ran low. Only by the wisdom of chiefs like The Ridge were they kept from our lands."

"The Ridge knew their command to destroy everything the Cherokees have learned to use from the whites would lead to war."

"Still, the Tennessee militia and the Cherokees will be dragged in, did I not say?"

The urging of the Shawnee chief and his brother for American Indians to unite might have seemed noble had they not been allied with the British. And no real peace had been achieved with the Crown since the Revolution. The Royal Navy had blockaded ports, fired on American ships, and sometimes even forced American sailors into service.

"Tecumseh's message seems to have done more to divide the Creek people than anything." Susanna raised the square bib of her dress and began to hook it into place.

Polly left the window and came up behind her, smoothing the sleeves of the muslin fabric. Her touch soothed Susanna's taut nerves. "My sister, who lives south and west of here in the Cherokee village of Turkey Town, says they have many refugees. The Red Stick Creeks who follow Tecumseh and have painted their clubs for war have turned on any who refuse to join them. The loyal National Creeks and the Natchez Creeks have, since summer, called on their brothers the Cherokees to help them."

"Yes, I heard Father say back in August that even Colonel Meigs suggested raising two companies of Cherokees." Susanna drew a blue paisley silk scarf from her dresser, and her eyes met her stepmother's in the mirror. "You think now it has happened? And they want Father as an officer?"

"I would say so."

Susanna tried to maintain steady breathing. What if he did not return? Even though she and Polly could inherit Father's property since it lay in Cherokee Territory, what was a thin layer of land when a void gaped beneath? Father was the bedrock under Big Springs Bluff's seven hundred acres. As much as she loved the massive gardens, the fields of river-bottom corn, the horses in the meadows, smokehouse, kiln, blacksmith shop, and spreading orchards of peaches and apples, without him, she would feel little security here. Have little desire to push down her roots.

Polly spoke again. "If we are quiet at dinner tonight, we may learn much."

And that was one of her subtle prompts meant to persuade Susanna. Tugging her brush through her long, dark, wavy locks, she hit a snag and flattened her mouth.

Her stepmother gathered information by a submission often bordering on invisibility. Maybe she could do this because she'd grown up secure in her rights in a matrilineal society. When Polly had caught Susanna reading *A Vindication of the Rights of Woman*, she had required an explanation. Then, with a *humph*, she had said a Cherokee woman would have written such a book better. The whites had much to learn from her people. Father never suspected the subtle but ingenious ways his second wife machinated outcomes to her favor.

Susanna admired her humble cleverness, but smiles, laughter, and wit were the best-worn tools in her own arsenal. And they usually worked until she said what she really thought and messed things up for both herself and Polly.

Polly picked up Susanna's hairbrush and leaned over, her warm smile glowing. "Need help?"

Susanna nodded, not trusting herself to speak as tears pricked her eyes. Polly's gentle strokes smoothed both her hair and her anxiety. She blinked several times as warmth rose in her chest for the woman behind her—her ally, the closest thing she had known to a mother since her own had died birthing her. It had taken Gideon Moore five years to find Polly.

Susanna picked at a hangnail. "When you first met Father, after your husband had died and left you to run the trading post here in Big Springs, how did you know? That he was the one, I mean. You said you had lots of suitors."

"Oh yes, many … most, more interested in my business than me. Your father was the only one who offered more than he would take." He had, in fact, not even taken the trading post, as Father encouraged his wife's continued oversight of the business she had inherited from her previous spouse.

Susanna focused on Polly as her stepmother began to pin up her hair, weaving the scarf among the layers. "So that was what made you decide? What he brought to the match?"

Polly pressed her lips together, a sure sign she didn't want the full truth to escape. "Dr. Hawkins is much as Captain Moore was."

"Yes, but I doubt Father made your stomach sour."

Polly didn't chide her, but neither did she laugh. Or so much as crack a smile. "Why does he have this effect on you? Like the captain, he is a good man. A good provider. A good father."

"To three children! The oldest five years younger than myself." With a smack, Susanna flattened her palm onto her dresser, sending a puff of nefarious powder rising from an open pot. "Close to George's age. And we both know, my dear half brother thinks himself quite the little man."

"To care for her family is a woman's highest duty." Polly's even tone reminded Susanna that she was but fifteen years Susanna's senior. She'd never sounded more English, but Susanna couldn't jest. The last thing she wanted was to disrespect this woman who shouldn't speak of duty, but grace. Grace was what she had given five-year-old Susanna, and for the twelve years since.

"I am sorry. I know." She snaked her hand behind her head to grasp Polly's hand.

"You are good with your little sisters. And you have an interest in healing ways."

"*Your* healing ways."

As a girl, she'd been eager to learn Polly's skillful uses of herbs, roots, and barks—but more as a means to bond with her stepmother than out of medicinal curiosity. And without sounding terribly selfish and petulant in view of all Polly had done for her, how could she explain that mentoring her half sisters, Sally and Molly, in no way resembled taking on the full care of three children not her own?

At the agitation in her tone, Polly's face softened. "I try not to convince you, Susanna. Only to point out good things. Because I know your father wants this."

"My head sees the benefits. But my heart rebels. Was there ever a more phlegmatic man alive?" Falling back on her habit of making light of a serious situation, Susanna rolled her eyes. "If alive is what one can call him. He scarcely twitches an eyebrow at my funniest jokes."

Not that Polly did either. But when she gave a soft grunt as she did now, joy swelled within Susanna that her humor had penetrated her stoic stepmother's guard. One day, she'd finally make Polly break into a rib-grabbing chortle. Polly tipped her chin down. "Is that any wonder?"

Susanna allowed a rueful smirk. "Well, no, but nothing seems to rattle him. Not good. Not bad. Even if the Red Sticks invaded, I doubt he would get excited. I would imagine such a demeanor makes him an excellent surgeon but a dismal husband."

"And Sam Hicks? You think he would laugh at your jokes?" One of Polly's brows rose. She tugged her hand free to complete her ministrations to Susanna's coiffure.

Susanna cocked her head. Her brief meeting with Sam had crackled with intensity rather than mirth, stirring unexpected awareness of a nature that did anything but make her want to joke. "I don't know, yet … somehow, I think he would. At least, I would like to find out."

"Do not set your heart on it." Polly bent closer again, her hand on Susanna's shoulder. "Your father will never allow you to marry a man like Sam Hicks."

To question why not was on Susanna's tongue when a servant rapped on the door, bidding them descend for dinner.

She was beautiful, this daughter of Colonel Moore. It was all Sam could do not to stare as she descended the stairs before Moore's wife, also a beautiful woman. They were like the *du-di*, birds of winter in bright blue and deep red, their hair and eyes nearly black, Susanna's skin nearly as white as snow. But he had no right to admire.

Nathaniel Hawkins stepped forward to take Susanna's hand, the colonel taking Polly's. Sam was left to trail the party into the dining room with the Moores' son, George, a boy of around twelve. Sam was under no illusions as to why he was still here. While Moore had accepted the commission, dinner had been announced before he had satisfied himself about all the military details surrounding the appointment.

Still, the invisible thread remained. What should he do about it? The subtle tug toward the colonel's daughter upended him, but awareness flowed like sap through his veins, sweet and heavy. The fire behind him added too much warmth, crackling beneath a mantel decked with urns displaying pheasant feathers. He drew his chair closer to Susanna's than was needful because she'd stiffened the moment the doctor had taken her hand. In the man, he sensed no danger, but he could liken such a match to The Ridge riding an old nag ready to be put out to pasture.

"I have an announcement," Moore said to his family as the first course on china dishes printed in a cheerful blue was served by black servants. His wife and children listened with hands in their laps, faces polite, tight. "With the rising tide of Creek aggression, we have suspected that I might be called to Camp Blount in Fayetteville, Tennessee, where the majority of the militia will muster. But today, Mr. Hicks brought a commission from Colonel Meigs."

"A commission? To do what?" Susanna twisted her napkin in her lap.

"To serve as colonel of a Cherokee Regiment raised right here at Hiwassee."

George's coat strained against his bony shoulders as his fist shot into the air. "A Cherokee Regiment! Whoo-weee! Can I join up?"

"No." His mother smacked his hand down.

"Son." Moore fixed him with a constraining stare. "You will behave with the decorum befitting a young man if you wish to remain at table with adults."

"Yes sir." The boy snapped off a salute, making Sam suppress a smile. George reminded him of himself back in his mission school days, always eager for an adventure. His father's frown didn't squelch another question. "And who shall your commanding officer be, Father?"

Even the colonel sat a little straighter with his reply. "Brigadier General James White of Knoxville."

George's dark eyes rounded. "The one who founded the city?"

"Good memory. Yes, back when it was White's Fort. I am glad you have attended to me when I've spoken of the history of the region. And White will serve under Andrew Jackson from Nashville. Well?" He turned to the women. "What say you?"

"Congratulations, Father." Susanna lowered her gaze to her soup, moving her spoon around in her bowl.

Polly laid her hand on his sleeve. "To lead warriors in battle is a great honor, my husband. How many men will you command?"

"There will be five hundred to seven hundred organized into seven companies." Moore glanced at Sam as though he doubted the total Sam had related earlier.

He nodded. "The Ridge is already recruiting. He will bring the men. It was his influence that convinced the council to support the war."

"That and the Cherokee woman who was killed by Red Sticks near Etowah." Dr. Hawkins sipped his drink, the green gaze in his lantern-shaped face on Susanna. When she continued to click the sides of her bowl with the listless movements of her spoon, tender concern weighted his brow.

Blast it. The man had feelings for her. Although why that realization should stab Sam with dismay, he couldn't figure.

"True." Shrugging off the unwelcome emotion with a roll of his shoulders, Sam sat back for the servant to take his bowl. The butternut squash soup had been delicious, but he imagined plentiful cows and hogs foraged in the woods and fields around the farm in the Cherokee style of grazing livestock. Hopefully, the next course would prove hearty. "The woman's murder did make thirst for revenge burn, but many Cherokees were already eager to sharpen their tomahawks. They are long dull."

"Not too long," Dr. Hawkins muttered under his breath.

Sam leveled his attention on the man despite the servants bearing silver-domed plates to the sideboard.

"Yes. I wanted to ask you about that, Hicks." Moore patted his mouth with his linen napkin. "As Indian agent, is Meigs concerned about how the militia will react to fighting alongside the very men who tried to kill them at the close of the last century?"

Sam lifted a shoulder. "I admit, he is." He had recorded those very sentiments in his superior's letters to other officers. "There will be much suspicion between the two, but it is our hope they will learn to fight as brothers."

"Will you enlist?" The unexpected question came from Susanna.

"As my father does, so will I." That was a yes. Ridge would not rest until his good friend Charles Hicks took up the hatchet.

He held her gaze. He wouldn't show his fear. While he'd been raised like all Cherokee boys to hunt, fish, and split a melon with a tomahawk tossed from thirty feet—had even served a couple of stints as a regulator under The Ridge—the most violence he'd witnessed had been the whipping of an adulterer. He'd heard of harsher sentences. Torture. Burnings at stake. But his father had kept him from the worst of it. How would he react when the men he knew as brothers rallied as warriors? Would he shame himself? His father? That must not happen, any more than Susanna should shame the colonel.

She watched him. Sam swallowed and continued. "Many signing up are former Lighthorse—the regulators started five years ago. They are capable of covering large distances rapidly, even over rough terrain. Those with former combat experience will be put in charge of the companies. One company will be formed under the chief of the Natchez Creeks taking refuge in Turkey Town."

"Mmm." Colonel Moore sounded none too pleased about that. "Can we trust their loyalty?"

"Since the revolt against the French failed in their western lands, they have become one with the loyal National Creeks. Portions of their people joined the Cherokees. I would say yes." If Moore had a protest to lodge, he could lodge it with Meigs. Sam might as well produce the other news sure to ruffle Moore's feathers. "Path Killer will receive a commission as well."

"As colonel?" Moore's customarily deep voice rose along with his heavy eyebrows.

"Meigs is determined it will be so."

Polly Moore spoke for only the third time, though that was more than the doctor, whose attention since the main course had arrived had scarcely left his plate. "He may be principal chief, but he is an old man. Too old to ride to *da-na-wa* … war."

Hawkins chewed his beef as noisily as if a tributary of the Tennessee threatened to chase the morsel down his gullet. Beside Sam, Susanna stiffened. Sam cut a glance at her. As she returned it, the furrow between her brows gave way, and her lips softened.

Clamping his jaw, Sam cut into root vegetables oozing with some sort of glaze. He feared the clever girl had noted his struggle to keep his face straight. A moment of shared amusement could land him in a whole heap of trouble. He firmed his voice in reply to Mrs. Moore. "Doubtless, he will remain at Turkey Town, but he will be given the commission, nonetheless."

Flicking Sam a disdainful glance, Dr. Hawkins leaned forward to murmur to his host. "An honorary title. The Indians need men like yourself to command them lest they give way to their baser nature and resort to brutalities."

Sam froze with his knife poised over his plate, staring at the doctor. Better the man had remained silent. Or chewing. Good thing for Hawkins he'd not been raised like the warriors of his people.

Sam exhaled, relaxing his grip as regret stole over him. And to think he'd boasted but an hour ago about his faith. Well, that was the problem. Boasting. Pride. Still, he didn't have to give Hawkins the satisfaction of hearing him relate the nature of the orders Meigs was drafting, commanding no scalpings or mutilations.

"Dr. Hawkins, is everyone going but you?" Susanna blurted the question, her hands in her lap. She refused to lower her gaze even under the incredulous stare of her father. And to Sam's grudging admiration, she said more. "Perhaps you should be on hand for the aftermath, in case the red man refuses restraint."

A flush stained the sandy-haired physician's jaw, and he set down his own knife he'd been using to cut his beef. "I told your father in our earlier conference I felt the call to enlist. The men on the battlefield will be sorely in want of experienced surgeons."

Moore cleared his throat. "But I told him forts like Hiwassee will remain staffed as part of our supply line. We will need to establish another base between here and Turkey Town, don't you agree, Hicks?" When Sam nodded, the colonel resumed. "I asked Dr. Hawkins to remain here for the time being. He has agreed to check on you regularly at Big Springs Bluff. In my absence, you are in his care."

Susanna lowered her head. The bodice of her blue dress moved up and down, and her fingers again twirled in her napkin. Everything in Sam strained to reach out and take her hand, to draw her out of the house and steal her away on his stallion. But he had no business imagining such fanciful things. He had no say over Susanna Moore.

In response to her silence, Colonel Moore straightened. "I expect you to make Dr. Hawkins welcome. I have given my permission for him to court you, Susanna."

Her chin jerked up, and her gaze speared the doctor across the table. "You did not ask me!"

"It was my intention to do so today, Miss Moore, had you joined me for a buggy ride." To his credit, regret strained the faint lines around Hawkins' mouth and eyes, and he laid a hand on the table as if to reach out toward her.

"Well, now it is settled." Colonel Moore sawed off a big bite of roast and held it up on his fork, his expression almost jolly. "Shall we enjoy our meal?"

Even as Polly Moore focused on Susanna and gave the slightest shake of her head, the young woman made a small choking sound. She turned her face toward Sam, but he wouldn't look at her. Couldn't. The eyes of his commanding-officer-to-be pinned him to his carved mahogany chair.

Navigating this war to benefit the Cherokees trumped involvement in any lesser disagreements.

Susanna leapt to her feet. "Please excuse me. I do not feel well."

She seemed to yank something from Sam's chest as she fled the room. But he remained seated, chewing the vegetables that now tasted as dry as drought dust. What else was he supposed to do? Regardless of the fact that she was the first woman who'd captured his interest—regardless of the fact that he began to share her aversion to the doctor—he'd never see Susanna Moore again. She must be strong enough to make her own way.

CHAPTER THREE

The two white feathers in his hair had bedeviled him since he'd signed up at Hiwassee. All members of the Cherokee Regiment were required to wear them to mark themselves as friendly to the Americans. Most men added a deer's or at least a squirrel's tail to their long, dark locks. But keeping the blasted feathers attached to his short hair had been trouble enough for Sam. He'd finally secured them to a beadwork band he wore around the crown of his head. But it felt nothing like a top hat. Like nothing he would wear of his own accord. So much had changed in the month since he'd delivered Moore's commission that it felt a lifetime ago.

Today, a creeping sickness in his gut told him the feathers would prove the least of his discomforts. It started with the fog in the early November air. Or was it smoke? Hard to tell, judging by the gray mist that had hung low ever since they'd ridden out of Turkey Town. They'd been told that a sizable enemy force had gathered at the village of Tallushatchee, about twenty-five miles south.

It was the stench that told him that the Tennessee militia must have found the foe first. As they drew nigh, the horses of the men in his unit snorted, while the riders unsheathed their weapons. Eyes glowed. Spines stiffened. Tawny faces strained for a glimpse through autumn's glorious canopy.

Sam's empty stomach knotted.

What was he doing as an officer in such a company, a mounted spy company, each member hand-selected from the other units to ride ahead and reconnoiter?

He might be here as a translator and scout rather than under

Charles Hicks because he spoke four languages—including that of the Creek people—and had traveled extensively at his father's side, but right now, someone needed to keep the men in check. Who knew what they were riding into?

Sam spurred his stallion up near David McNair's. The thirty-nine-year-old Cherokee captain from Tennessee extended his arm with a bird-like whistle. Halt. He spoke in a low tone in their native tongue. "Look up ahead, Lieutenant."

He'd seen the buzzards circling from a mile back, so he assumed McNair referred to the thinning woods. "The trees are charred."

The touchy first sergeant—aptly named Nine Fingers for the loss he'd suffered in an adolescent fight—gave a low growl. "We missed it."

The hairs at the back of Sam's neck prickled. "Yes, but who won?"

"Ride ahead and find out."

McNair was looking at him. Sam's mother, Nancy, was the daughter of a chief, and her blood made him Wolf Clan, warrior, protector. He'd been taught how to fight by the best warrior chiefs in the nation. But did the commander know that in Sam's nineteen years, the toughest foe he had ever taken down had been a wild hog—with a blowgun? Quite a feat, considering how enraged the hog had been, but nothing compared to a potential ambush by a town full of Red Sticks. McNair's company spearheaded the rest of the Cherokee Regiment. And now, he was to spearhead *it*?

He thought he was as good as any Indian at keeping his face impassive, but a challenge ignited in McNair's eyes. With a jerk of his chin, he tossed Sam a bone. "Take Nine Fingers."

Wonderful. The fight leading up to his potential death had just been prolonged.

"At a walk," he whispered in Cherokee to the buckskin-clad sergeant, earning a glare in return.

Not that his efforts at a stealthy approach proved effective. As the trees thinned, their mounts tossed their heads, snorted, and whinnied, protesting what Sam saw as they rode into the clearing— mounds of mangled bodies topped by the flapping black shapes of birds of prey.

"Red Sticks." Nine Fingers fought his shying horse.

A half glance sufficed to confirm the crimson paint and lack of clothing but in that half glance … a lifetime of nightmares. Some of the warriors had been scalped and mutilated. By the white men? Those had been the units present in the conflict.

Nine Fingers rose in his stirrups, bloodlust in his eyes. "Signal for the men."

"After we check the village."

What was left of it, that was. They found militiamen dragging more bodies into additional piles. Others fanned out in the woods, searching for survivors. Smoke curled from the remains of blackened cabins. When they rode close enough, it was everything Sam could do not to heave up the contents of his stomach, for not only men but women and children had been burned inside those cabins.

A tall, dark-haired man in buckskin stood near the smoldering ashes of a large structure where a number had perished. Something in the hunch of his shoulders as he leaned on his rifle spoke of regret, making Sam stop and address him.

"What is your name, sir?"

The militiaman removed his floppy, wool felt hat, revealing a fairly young face with soulful eyes and a long, narrow nose. "David Crockett, Second Regiment of Tennessee Volunteer Mounted Riflemen. You with the Cherokee Regiment? You speak good English."

"Some of us do." With a creak, Sam shifted in his saddle. "First Lieutenant Sam Hicks, McNair's advance company. Just arrived."

"How do, Lieutenant?"

A movement by Nine Fingers caught Sam's eye. He was using the muzzle of his rifle to lift a bow from the side of an old woman who'd been shot an obscene number of times. "Have mercy." He prayed the bile wouldn't come up. Why were there women and children among the dead? "Go. Get Captain McNair."

Nine Fingers rode off with a whoop, and Sam turned back to Crockett. "What happened here?"

The soldier shook his head. "At first, I thought things would go easy. But about four dozen Red Sticks took cover in this buildin'. General Coffee sent his dragoons in. And here was this old woman, sittin' on the ground, stretchin' that bow there with her feet. I reckon she was too weak to pull it with her arms. But she fired an' hit an officer, which sent everyone into a murd'rous rage. It all went downhill from there. The Indians would fire with their guns, then their arrows. We had to burn 'em out. You can be proud, though. The few Cherokees who were here under Colonel Brown fought good."

Proud. Yes. The ground rumbled under the advance of many horses as Sam struggled to form his next question. "Why did they kill civilians—against orders?"

Crockett replaced his hat and ran a hand over his stubbled jaw. "It's a shame, that's for sure. I heard Coffee say their braves shouldn'ta taken refuge in the cabins."

"Thank you ... private?"

"Private Crockett." He nodded. "Here on the three-month enlistment like everyone else."

A scream sounded behind them, and Sam turned his horse. Like an overturned hornets' nest, his regiment swarmed into camp. The cry issued from a young Creek woman struggling in the arms of a mounted Cherokee as a militia infantryman pulled on her leg.

"She's mine!" The Tennessee recruit shook the musket in his other hand. "I claimed her before she ran off into the woods."

With a stony, blank glare displaying his incomprehension, the warrior holding the captive jerked his horse's bridle to edge the animal away.

"Bring the girl here." The authoritative Cherokee command of The Ridge boomed out as the hulking first lieutenant rode up on his equally massive horse. With a nod at Sam, he swung a leg clad in homespun breeches over the saddle holding his army-issue blanket roll and rifle. "All prisoners will be taken back to camp and cared for." He extended his arms for the Creek woman, and with a sneer, the Cherokee soldier shoved her off in front of Ridge, then urged his horse away.

Steadying the woman by her shoulders, Ridge addressed Sam. "Tell her, Hicks. She is safe with me."

Sam dismounted and, using the Muskogean tongue of the Creeks, quite different from their own, repeated the assurance of the man he admired. Her eyes widened, and she allowed Ridge to lead her to a huddle of women and children under the guard of The Ridge's Cherokee captain, Alexander Saunders' company.

Chaos akin to battle had broken out around them. Warriors hunting captives they might take as slaves. Warriors hunting the spoils of jewelry and weapons. Warriors hunting scalps, even though they had to settle for the scalps of the dead.

"Stop!"

The booming voice of Gideon Moore snatched Sam's attention. The colonel rode toward a group of marauding Cherokees, his new adjutant, John Ross, at his side. The younger man—only four years older than Sam, and like him, a mixed-blood educated at a mission school—dismounted and planted himself, arms extended, between his brethren and a pile of dead warriors.

With a sick sensation twisting in his gut, Sam looped his horse's reins around a sapling and hurried toward the scene. But before he could come to Ross' aid, a middle-aged, bare-chested Natchez Creek, roached scalp lock flying, seized the hair of a Red Stick boy. The reddened tomahawk that lay inches from the youth's hand testified that he'd fought bravely even though he'd not yet reached manhood. When his eyes flew open, horror snatched Sam's breath.

Sam launched his weight into the Natchez warrior before his

knife drew blood. He landed on top of him in the dirt.

The man shoved Sam off and sprung into a crouch, fists balled for a fight. "Are you crazy?" The warrior's demand issued from a clenched jaw marked by a jagged scar.

Sam crouched also, answering in the man's native tongue. "In this army, we do not take scalps without honor."

"Where is the lack of honor? The boy took up the war hatchet."

A movement from that boy caught his eye—fingers curling around the handle of his tomahawk. Blood staining his bare torso, the young warrior raised up on his knees. Drew the weapon back. John Ross stood within range, facing the other way.

"No!" Sam snatched his long knife from the sheath on his belt. No time for a tackle, only for a throw. With a quick jerk of his arm, the weapon sailed end over end and plunged into the boy he'd just saved.

The youth grunted and released the tomahawk. Its weakened arch landed short of Ross, skidding to his feet. Ross turned as Sam reached their foe and drove him to the ground. His fingers closed over the handle of his knife, the blade embedded between two ribs. The boy toppled facedown again, the sounds of his death nothing like that of a deer or a hog.

He'd drawn first blood, and his stomach wrenched.

Sam sucked in air, a gray haze fogging the edges of his vision. A small tug, and with a sickening lessening of resistance, the weapon slid free.

A horse's legs appeared in front of him as he sat on his knees. Colonel Moore bent into his view. "We owe you our gratitude, Hicks."

He nodded and the colonel rode away. But then he saw it—faint breaths still gyrated the boy's bony shoulders. No. Oh no.

The Natchez Creek strode over and jerked his foe's head back. "Aren't you going to finish him?"

It would be a mercy to do so. The boy was gutshot, and now,

backstabbed. But Sam could only stare as a tear rolled down the youth's crimson cheek.

"Coward." The warrior growled the insult in the Creek tongue, then completed the job. Dropping his victim at Sam's feet, he glared. "The white officers may think you saved them, but I know the truth. Your cowardice almost killed them."

Susanna ducked back into the root cellar for one more bag of apples. Good thing she knew right where they were, for the early November pre-dawn barely illuminated the earthy-smelling room. She hastened back outside for her father's head man, Solomon, to secure the canvas sack on the pack mule. One of two pack mules, actually … in addition to the three horses she, Polly, and George would be riding.

She still could not believe Polly was allowing her to go to Turkey Town. Actually, to Armstrong, the fort near the Cherokee village where her father garrisoned his regiment. Her stepmother hardly required her assistance to nurse the colonel back to health. But ever since Father's adjutant, John Ross, had written privately, asking Polly for recommendations to counteract the effects of cold and damp on Colonel Moore's weak lungs, and Polly had declared that only her personal ministration of her own remedies would strengthen her husband, Susanna had begged to accompany her. If Polly left, Dr. Hawkins would set up camp on the front porch. And she couldn't abide that.

"Where is Mama?" George shifted impatiently atop his gelding.

"Packing her medicinal chest, I suppose. She went last night to collect extra goods and spices from the store." Susanna skimmed the supplies. Did they have enough? Adjutant Ross had said the army requisitioned from the nearby Cherokee villages but still lacked food and medicine.

"I made a level spot for it right here." With his dark-skinned, wrinkled hand, Solomon indicated a folded blanket padding the mule's back between the sacks of apples and potatoes. "We tie it on real tight."

"Thank you, Solomon. Leave room for the eggs." Her stepmother had wrapped each one individually in rags and straw inside a wooden box. "They're imperative to Father's diet."

Her half sister Sally ran down the steps of the back porch and up to Solomon's side. Standing on her tiptoes, she strained to place her favorite rag doll on the spot he'd cleared. "Lulu will go with you."

Her heart constricting, Susanna knelt in front of the nine-year-old. "Sally-love, we talked about this. You're to stay with Solomon and Mammy Kate and help watch after Molly."

"I know." Sally nodded, her dark braids sliding over her calico-clad shoulders. "I will send her without me."

"But what if you need her?" She frowned. Her younger sister slept with her favorite doll every night. She was sure to feel less secure with both parents and older siblings gone.

Sally jabbed a finger onto the chest of Susanna's long, woolen pelisse covering her dress. "*You* will need her more. In case you get scared."

"Oh, Sally." Susanna drew her into an embrace. She couldn't tell her sister that while yes, Creek braves on the warpath should scare her, the idea of adventure, of encountering new lands and people—and hopefully, Sam Hicks, whom she hadn't been able to put out of her mind since he'd brought Father's commission—flooded her limbs with tingling excitement. Father had let drop that Sam had signed up. Maybe, too, she could finally show her father that she didn't need a proper life in a fancy home to be happy. She was bred to thrive on the frontier, just as Father was. "That is so sweet of you. I will take her, but only so she can say hello to Father for you. Mama will make him well, and we'll be back before you know it."

Sally gave a firm, jerky nod as Susanna released her.

George tipped his head toward the horizon where the rising sun split the low bank of clouds. "We'd best be on our way." All man, with his rifle riding a strap on his back.

"Let's go see about Mama." Susanna called Polly "Mama" to her little sisters but used her given name otherwise. It was as her father had wished. When she'd been young, she'd longed to call Polly "Mama" herself, but now she'd grown accustomed to the Christian name. And rather liked it. It was like having a big sister and a mother rolled into one.

Susanna offered Sally her hand, and together they hurried to the kitchen.

The smell of baked bread mingled with the smoke from the big, open fireplace as Solomon's wife, Mammy Kate, transferred hot, steaming rolls into a basket. Polly stood by the rough-hewn table with her medicine chest open, the flame of the oil lamp flickering high and bright. Her deft hands poured finely ground, golden powder into a packet labeled *mustard* while seven-year-old Molly clung to her skirts.

"Check my list again, Susanna."

She rounded the table. As she read aloud from her stepmother's parchment, Polly pointed to ingredients in different slots. "Pleurisy root. Mullein. Bark of wild cherry and white pine. Linseed. Garlic. Pepper. Cinnamon."

"And mustard powder. Yes, that should be it." Polly patted the air over her precious store of medicines before closing and locking the lid.

"Good, because George is ready to ride off and face the entire Creek Nation all by himself."

Polly shook her head. "It will be all we can do to keep him from sneaking off with the army."

A whimper sounded from the folds of Polly's skirts. She knelt to reassure her youngest child, but Susanna moved to the window. "Horse hooves? What? Is he leaving us already?" Her hand fell from the muslin curtain. "Dr. Hawkins! Why is he here?"

"Maybe he comes to say goodbye." Polly looked up from smoothing Molly's hair.

"How does he know we are leaving? Who told him?" Susanna cut a glance at Mammy Kate, whose eyes rounded and lips puckered in a gesture of such contrived confusion it roused all her suspicion. She shook off a frown long enough to bend and hug her smallest half sibling, then hastened back outside, where her ire deepened as she surveyed their unexpected guest, who now waited beside her brother. Dr. Hawkins' saddlebags bulged, his own medical chest behind him, and a caped overcoat draped his slender shoulders.

George turned to her with a frown, confirming that he shared her irritation. "Dr. Hawkins says he is going with us, Susanna."

She marched up to Solomon and stared the old man in the face. "I wonder how he knew we were going anywhere."

"Doan ask me, Miss Susanna." Solomon turned to fiddle with the girth strap of her mount.

Mm-hmm. Father had a snitch.

She planted her hands on her hips and faced the doctor. "Thank you for your kind offer, Dr. Hawkins, but we would never dream of taking you away from your patients at Hiwassee. There is no need to worry. As you know, there's no more effective healer than my stepmother."

Hawkins stiffened in his saddle. He was always trying to ferret out Polly's secrets, even though he'd never admit they might be superior to his traditional methods. "I was more concerned about your safety as you travel."

"We appreciate that, but we know the owners of the inn we'll stay at tonight. And of course, Polly has family at Turkey Town."

"What if you are set upon by ruffians? Thieves?" Hawkins drew his mount closer to her, his forehead creasing.

George cleared his throat and patted his rifle. "What do you think this is for?"

Hawkins didn't take his eyes off Susanna. "The boy would not be able to withstand a party of ne'er-do-wells. You need a man's protection to get you safely to Fort Armstrong."

"Pardon me." Her little brother drew himself upright, his voice squeaking with indignation. "I can bark-chip a squirrel out of a tree at sixty paces and not lose an ounce of meat."

Finally, Hawkins' gaze cut to George. "Squirrels don't fight back." He swung out of the saddle, leading his stallion until he stood inches from Susanna. He extended his hand, which she ignored, crossing her arms. "Miss Moore ... let me do this. I made a promise to your father to keep you and your family safe."

"My son is right. We will be safe, Dr. Hawkins." Polly spoke from behind her. As usual, Susanna hadn't even heard her approach. And the doctor had been so intent on her, he didn't seem to have noticed either. Her stepmother hefted her wooden chest to Solomon, who worked to secure it on the mule. "No one will harm the family of Colonel Moore. They know if they do, they will pay."

Susanna looked back at Dr. Hawkins, firming her jaw. He couldn't argue that.

But he did argue. "Then let me do this for myself. Guilt and regret have eaten me up since Colonel Moore left without me. Staying back at the Hiwassee Garrison for me is cowardice. You would not deny a man's right to tender his skills where they are most needful, would you?"

As Polly's expression wavered, softening with Hawkins' bid for bravery, Susanna considered her options. She was leaving to get away from the doctor. Now he intended on following her? He was sure to press his emotional advantage on the trip. But if she stayed, would he insist on staying as well? And she would miss seeing her father ... and Sam. Assuring herself that they were well.

Why the fortitude of that particular Cherokee volunteer was any of her concern, she had no idea. She'd been addle-pated to hope he might somehow help her evade the doctor's pursuit when they'd first met, and she'd heard nothing from him in the weeks following. But she'd never met a man like him, and if they knew each other better …

Susanna sighed and led her mare to the mounting block. It would be worth Dr. Hawkins trailing her to Indian Territory to see him again. *Him* meaning her father, of course.

CHAPTER FOUR

"What do you think, eh?"

Polly had taught Susanna enough Cherokee that she could make out her cousin's question—although she didn't really have to. Nokassa's expression as she slid aside the woven partition in her family's cabin said it all. Glowing. Like a star, the meaning of her name. Her round, expressive face made her easy to read. Susanna had taken to her from their first meeting in Turkey Town several days ago.

The girl swept a hand down her own slender frame, proudly sporting Susanna's blue muslin dress—the same one she'd worn to dinner the night Sam Hicks had visited—while Susanna, Polly, and Polly's sister, Walani, oohed in delight.

"In that, you will be sure to catch the eye of Culsowee." Walani paused in stirring the rabbit stew to offer her daughter an encouraging smile, and then she turned to Susanna. "But are you sure you will not need it?"

Polly translated in case Susanna missed something. Susanna patted the homespun dress Nokassa had lent her. "This makes much more sense for Fort Strother. That is … if Dr. Hawkins will ever let us go." She released her breath in a little huff as she squatted next to the glowing fireplace embers. Grabbing a short poker, she shuffled aside some of the ashes covering the first loaf of bean bread she'd ever made that was now baking in a corn husk.

Walani clicked her tongue and rushed forward, seizing the metal implement and scolding in English. "Not ready. You mess up!" She hastened to re-cover the bread.

"Susanna, you must be patient. In this, and in all things." Polly sent her a pained expression as she placed a wooden bowl at each table setting. "There is a time and place for everything."

Susanna couldn't be sure if her stepmother quoted Cherokee or biblical wisdom, for the woman had a love of finding where the two intersected and endlessly repeating the advice she internalized. But neither would have diffused the growing pressure in her heart. "I have been patient. After that horrible journey in the rain, we got to Fort Armstrong, if you can call it a fort." The small barricade of rough-hewn poles north of Turkey Town on the Coosa River had still been under construction by a skeleton crew of Tennessee militia. "Where they informed us the Cherokee Regiment had just left to go attack some enemy villages! And who knows how sick Father is, riding around in this cold and damp. We have been here for days—when we well know they will return first to their outpost farther down the river."

"You saw the conditions at Armstrong. We do not know what waits at Strother. Dr. Hawkins is right. We should not go until we know your father will be there."

Nokassa came over, swishing her skirt like the belle of the ball, and offered Susanna a hand up. Then she sat on the trestle next to the fire and patted the spot beside her.

Susanna lowered herself with a plunk. "One would think Dr. Hawkins would wish to go where the sick and wounded are." More than once, she'd contemplated leaving the lanky physician behind.

Walani tilted her head, regarding her as though reading her mind. These Paint Clan healer-women seemed to have an extra sense about them. She spoke in simple enough Cherokee that Susanna could understand. "My husband, Bold Hunter, agrees with the doctor. He says you must not travel until the time is right. Too many dangers."

One of the warriors of the Wolf Clan who helped protect Principal Chief Path Killer, Bold Hunter possessed undeniable credibility. And not just because of his impressive physique. The man knew the terrain and its occupants well. Each day since they'd been here, he'd lived up to his name, bringing home fresh game, while many families shared a single bowl of corn mush. Susanna had been thankful … until she'd gotten detailed tutelage on preparing that game for stew. My, the Cherokees wasted nothing.

Nokassa reached for her hand. "Great Spirit will keep your father safe. He leads many warriors to glory."

"I pray so." Susanna squeezed her cousin's hand, amazed at the affection she'd so quickly found in her heart for the winsome girl. The other day, she'd explained about God the Father being the Great Spirit. Much of what she'd said seemed to have made sense to Nokassa. In fact, their lack of actual relation did not appear to deter Nokassa's openness. She seemed fascinated by her "white cousin."

Susanna's gaze fell on the ecru strings tied in a neat bow beneath Nokassa's chest, and she chuckled. "These are supposed to go under the blue material." She snagged the bit of underpinning with her index finger, then made a weaving gesture toward the slit of the dress.

Nokassa covered her mouth with her hand. "Oh. I thought the bow look pretty."

"So will the white soldiers coming through. Here, let me help you." Laughing along with their mothers, Susanna assisted Nokassa in unpinning the drop front and retying the slip beneath. "At least, I am not the only one who messes up new things." They'd all laughed at her earlier when she'd turned pasty whilst handling rabbit innards.

The door burst open right before they finished, and the men—Bold Hunter, Dr. Hawkins, and George—clamored in, smelling of the smoke of the meeting house. Giggling with Nokassa, Susanna hurried the last hook into place. When they stood, Dr. Hawkins' disapproving stare swept the two of them. She lifted her chin. He found her unappealing in homespun Indian attire? Well, good.

Walani hurried forward to take the long, fringe-trimmed great shirt her husband wore as an overcoat. Susanna let her mother collect Dr. Hawkins' similar woolen garment. He focused on her again, even as he spoke to Polly.

"Mrs. Moore, we will depart in the morning to meet the colonel at Fort Strother."

A small gasp escaped Susanna, and Nokassa grasped her sleeve.

"What has happened?" Her eyes round, Polly folded his coat over her arm.

George popped around Hawkins' elbow. "A runner came to the meeting house. One of the Deer Clan. He'd run all night and all day." He sounded as breathless as if he'd kept pace with the messenger.

Bold Hunter shooed the boy to the periphery. Polly translated her brother-in-law's words. "The Cherokee Regiment attacked the Hillabee villages south of here and have taken many captives. A decisive victory. It is safe to journey to the army camp to give welcome and honor to Colonel Moore."

And hopefully, to save him from himself.

Sam could hear Colonel Moore coughing from thirty yards behind. The man bent over his horse, hacking, water dripping off the brim of his hat. John Ross caught Sam's eye and spurred his mount forward to catch him at the rear of McNair's group.

"The colonel wants you to join us in the fort to report on the scout your men captured." He spoke in English, for his Cherokee was halting.

"With all due respect, the colonel sounds fit for nothing but a hot foot bath and a toddy."

"I know." Ross' slender shoulders lifted in a sigh. "Before we left Armstrong, I posted a letter to his wife without his knowledge. I heard she is a healer of the Paint Clan. I asked about her treatments, but she said she will only administer them in person."

Sam jerked to attention. "You think she might have come to Strother?"

"So I hope ... and fear. The colonel might have my head if she is waiting there."

Sam brushed off the skittering hope that Susanna might accompany her mother. Foolish. Doubtful even that Moore's wife would venture into hostile territory. He lobbed Ross a grin. "Probably only your scalp." Then his grin faded.

Ross noticed and shook his head. "Too much of that already. Our regiment killed sixty warriors in twenty minutes. Animals too."

"Something was wrong." The ache that had haunted him for a week, ever since General Cocke had ordered General White to ride against Hillabee from Armstrong, returned to Sam's gut. They had expected to be sent to aid General Jackson, who was operating out of Strother. The whole thing stank of something foul. "I heard them fire only one gun."

"Yes, something was very wrong. It was as if they thought we were allies."

Yet the string of burned buildings and dead they'd left behind, as well as the hundreds of prisoners in tow, said otherwise. Even The Ridge had taken captives this time. The Cherokees would take them to their camp on the parade ground outside the fort before receiving leave to deliver their new slaves home. More would come of this, of that Sam felt certain.

For now, it was a small comfort that at least one man shared his repugnance for the slaughter of the past several days. The things they'd seen, they'd no wish to discuss. But they'd spoken enough to establish a bond of understanding, he and Ross.

The surging of the shallow shoals at the *Oti Palin*—Ten Islands— alerted them of their approach to the fort before the woods thinned. Smoke rose from the huts of friendly Creek nationals near the trading post of Chief Chinnabee. Across the ford, at the base of Hines Mountain, the hundred-foot-square stockade, more substantial than Armstrong last he'd seen it, squatted near the Coosa's junction with Canoe Creek.

The heads of sentries observing the regiment's river crossing dotted the blockhouses. Hogs grunted from pens, and mostly empty corrals awaited their horses. Relief would have swept Sam if a better place than a flimsy canvas tent and a hard pallet on the ground waited to welcome him. Still, he could rub down his horse in the stockade, and then, in the spirit of home, maybe the colonel would offer him some hot tea.

"Do you see what I see?" The question from Ross snagged Sam back to the present as their horses splashed clear of the water.

"What?" He scanned the woods at the edge of the parade grounds outlying the fort. He, not the adjutant, was supposed to be the scout.

"Not there. There." Ross pointed. "On the rampart."

Sam's stomach knotted. "A woman in a dress."

Susanna gaped as the clearing outside the fort filled with men and horses and—

"What are you doing up here? I thought you were going to the privy." Polly seized her elbow. "Get back in the cabin before your father sees you."

The windowless cabin hardly eight paces wide? That stank of the lye soap they'd had to scrub it with as soon as Dr. Hawkins had moved the sick men out to make space for them? Dr. Hawkins had disappeared after that into the dispensary, thank heavens, but she couldn't linger another moment in the cramped, dark quarters. Not when the sentry had shouted that the army approached.

"Look! Are those women?" Susanna pointed to a huddled mass of individuals emerging from the trees, wrapped in blankets and head coverings, much like the deer hide scarf Nokassa had given her to wear, to keep off the November rains. "And children?"

"It is as Bold Hunter said." Polly's tone bottomed out. With pity? She tugged Susanna's arm. "Now come."

"Don't you want to try to pick out Father? I can almost see the faces of the officers. Oh …" Two horsemen broke away from the vanguard, trotting their mounts toward the fort. One looked so familiar. Her heart rate pattered. Could it be? "The one on the left. Is that Sam Hicks?"

"The one on the left is John Ross, son of white trader Daniel Ross and a part-Cherokee, part-Scotch woman. But the one on the right …"

At her stepmother's pause, Susanna's gaze switched to the taller man wearing white feathers on a band around his head, a hunting shirt, and buckskin leggings. A blanket crossed his left shoulder, secured beneath the right.

"Now that is Sam Hicks, son of quarter-Cherokee Chief Charles Hicks and full-blood Cherokee Nancy Broom of the Wolf Clan, which means Sam is Wolf Clan."

Susanna turned back to her, her jaw slack. "It cannot be. He is the translator and clerk for Colonel Meigs." *And he is white.*

"Was. He took the clerk position against the wishes of his father, who left the role himself because the colonel gave many bribes. No bribe too big or too small if he got Cherokee land. And now Sam Hicks is an officer of the Cherokee Regiment. Now do you see why I said it did not matter if he laughed at your jokes?" Sadness pooled in Polly's dark eyes.

Susanna laid a hand on the rough pike of the log before her. She couldn't believe it. The man who'd captured her imagination from a single day's meeting was a Cherokee.

White women did not marry Cherokee men.

Polly drew her away, rushing her down the steps and across the yard, but not before Susanna felt sure Sam Hicks had clamped eyes on her up on the rampart. And *that* clamped an invisible, squeezing hand over her heart.

Would he come see them? Her father would expect her to be polite to such a man, but no more. Never to encourage him.

Polly had left George watching the potato soup which simmered in her small Dutch oven from home. Now she bade him stand on the stoop to locate his father as the officers rode in. He sprang up faster than a fox released from a trap.

Susanna peeked out the crack in the door over his head. Where had Hicks and Ross gone?

Of course, she respected Polly's wisdom that her presence should not create a scene, but the rough and varied appearances of both militia and Indians fascinated her. Some of the Tennessee mountain men dressed like natives, and the Cherokees with their silver gorgets and tomahawks and white deer tails … they looked as fierce as their Creek captives, though they did wear more clothes, overall.

She spoke out loud, mostly to herself. "I wonder where the regulars are. I thought General Jackson might be here. Oh. Some of the men are bringing prisoners into the fort with them." There did not appear to be near enough tents to house that many people—certainly not if some of the army, elsewhere with Jackson, were still due to return.

"Susanna, strain the pleurisy root from your father's tea."

"Yes ma'am." Reluctantly, she left the door.

A moment later, she almost spilled the herbal decoction she poured into a tin mug when George yelled, "It's Father! I see him." He bolted into the crowd, which Susanna could hear and smell, surrounding the cabin.

She plopped the attached lid over the cup, set it in the warm ashes, and then scurried to peek out the door again. She needn't have, for plenty of cracks in the mud the soldiers must have hastily applied between the logs offered glimpses of the yard. When a tall figure turned into the doorway, she jerked the portal open.

And stared into the unfathomable, dark eyes of Sam Hicks.

The most startling thing happened. The customary guard he wore dropped from his face, and he smiled. He even released a little breath as if he was happy to see her. "Miss Moore." He offered a brief bow, making a smaller man following him bump into him.

She found her tongue. "Mr. Hicks. I thought you were Father."

"Lieutenant Hicks now, McNair's spy company. And he's right behind us. That is, behind John Ross, your father's adjutant."

Susanna opened the door wide enough to curtsy. "Honored to meet you, Adjutant Ross."

She'd barely gotten the words out when George darted around the men and whirled to face them under her arm, upsetting her balance. He gave a high-pitched parroting of Sam's phrase. "Spy company? Do you really spy on the enemy?"

Sam's hand darted out to steady Susanna, and the smile on his face widened into a heart-stopping grin. As he answered George, that grin disappeared almost as quickly as it had arrived. "I wish there were more spying and less of the rest."

"Susanna, get out of the doorway," Polly called from behind her.

The rest? What had Sam seen since early October that caused him to avert his gaze as he did now? Or maybe he was just moving aside for her father, for that familiar frame now filled her vision.

"Yes, out of the doorway." Father's voice rumbled even deeper with the congestion in his chest. "You're creating a spectacle for my men."

But he couldn't strain the affection from the reproof, and Susanna threw her arms around him. Relief flooded her. He was safe. He was alive. And he was well enough to scold her.

He hugged her back. Growled—"What are you doing here, my girl?" Then leaned away in a fit of coughing that raised all the alarm his appearance had initially squashed.

Susanna extended her hand to his shoulder as Polly appeared in the doorway, drawing her husband inside. Susanna angled her body to give them a moment of privacy. She offered the men a smile.

Ross tipped his head, topped with the Middle Eastern–style turban that was the height of fashion among wealthy Cherokees. "We can return later."

"No." Father projected his voice to reach them. "I want to dictate my reports now so that we can all rest tonight."

"Yes sir." Ross and then Sam joined them in the room.

Susanna left the door ajar for fresh air and light as Polly drew the bench and a stump close to the fire, fussing about the lack of places to sit.

"Let us fetch the colonel's folding chair and desk from his tent." Ross nudged Sam with his elbow. "We will get a table in here later."

Father shook his head. "I will go there with you to conduct our business."

Susanna stooped quickly to retrieve the tin mug, offering it to him. "But look, we made your special tea. You should drink it where you can get warm."

He accepted it with a grimace. "I don't need to be coddled in a cabin—with a fireplace, of all things—when General Jackson himself sleeps in a marquee. And his arm in a sling from the gunshot he took in Nashville." The fact that he'd collapsed on the stump and wheezed while he spoke stole some of the force from Father's protest, but he went on, wagging his finger at Polly. "And you should not be this close to the hospital."

"We should when you are a patient yourself!" A hand on her hip, Susanna blurted her thoughts without consideration. "And once you know more about the fireplace, you won't feel guilty. It smokes like an Indian chief."

"Susanna." Polly hissed her name, tipping her head to the two young men hovering sheepish-faced in the doorway.

She caught her fingers together in front of her, face flaming. "My apologies."

"We'll go get the furniture, along with the papers and quill the colonel will need. We will return shortly." Sam ducked his head toward her father, but she could've sworn he tossed a wink in her direction as he turned to leave. He must think her family was always in an uproar. His sudden, altered appearance put her head in an uproar too.

Her stepmother angled a frown at her but addressed her son. "Help your father with his boots, George." Taking her husband's overcoat, she continued in a gentler tone. "The officers were kind to let us stay here. Dr. Hawkins agreed that we use this cabin in exchange for our help in making broths, teas, and breads the *u-tlv-ga-ga-ni-si-ga-nv-ga* ... uh, sick people need. He will also come in here to make *nv-wa-ti*. Medicine."

"Well, that is something. Although you should not have come, Polly." Father tipped open the lid and sipped his tea. The strong medicinal brew invited a round of coughing and the appearance of his wadded handkerchief. When George stared up at him with his brows knit together, their father pulled out his pistol, removed the shot, and offered it to the boy to examine.

"I need one of these, Father." George ran his fingers over the carved ivory stock and pretended to take aim. "Much handier on horseback than a rifle."

Choosing to ignore him, Polly passed over an opportunity to disagree with her son to respond to her husband. "Who will make you take care of yourself?" She pressed the back of her hand to his forehead, frowning. His skin glistened in the muted light. "And how else will you get the *nv-wa-ti* you need?"

Susanna muttered as she hung the kettle hook over the fire near the Dutch oven. "If only Dr. Hawkins agreed." She skirted her parents before the full force of either's reproof could fall on her. Doubtless, the men would be wanting regular tea. She needed to locate the pressed block of dried leaves in their saddle packs.

Father grunted, replying over the sounds of Susanna's rummaging. "I am glad he came. He did what I asked and watched over you. And from what I hear, there were over two hundred sick and wounded here before Hillabee and before Jackson's men fought at Talladega. Hawkins is sorely needed. Now, that Ross—I will have something to say to him." He squinted an eye at his wife. "Is he the one who wrote to you?"

"Where *is* General Jackson?" Polly glanced back over her shoulder as she stirred the soup, releasing a mouth-watering aroma. Susanna scraped flakes of tea into the bottoms of two more cups and smothered a smile. "We thought to find the fort full when we came."

"Supplies are so low he took two thousand men to Fort Deposit."

George lowered the gun to look at his father. "Where is that?"

"Turkey Town is northeast of here, and Armstrong even more so, right?" He waited until George nodded. "Deposit is another supply fort even farther northwest, on the Tennessee River. I will show you a map later." He sat forward, peering at the Dutch oven. "Is that potato soup?"

Polly smiled. "It is. Almost ready. You want some?"

Voices sounded, along with a knock outside the door. "After I talk to the men. Come in." Father called out the summons before bending forward in another bout of coughing.

Susanna's unease blended into an odd mix with awareness and admiration as Sam Hicks hurried in, unfolded her father's wood-and-canvas camp chair, and helped him into it. Trying not to notice, everyone focused on other tasks, Susanna on snipping a bit of sugar cane into each cup. Once he settled, Father waved Sam off with impatience born, she knew, of embarrassment. Father never liked anyone to see him as weak, certainly not subordinate officers.

She slipped around to wrap a rag over the kettle's handle and pour the hot water, then stepped up behind Sam to offer him tea.

"Thank you." His eyes rounded, and he sounded as desperate and thankful as the indigent Indians who often begged at the back door of Big Springs Bluff. How often were these men getting decent food and drink?

Their fingers brushed as she passed him the tin cup. A spark of sensation jangled up Susanna's arm to her chest, where it fizzled out into a warm numbness. Their gazes melded. His reflected the same surprise she felt.

He'd stuffed the band with the feathers into his woven belt, and colorful garters knotted below the knees of his leggings. His hair had grown longer than at Hiwassee, curling over the collar of his hunting shirt. The firelight highlighted shadows under his cheekbones and in his eyes. She should find his frontier appearance repellent, the discovery of his mixed ancestry a deterrent, but she couldn't make herself step away from him.

John Ross cleared his throat. "Do I get a cup too?"

"Oh yes. I am sorry." Susanna blinked and hastened to the fireplace, bending to pour another serving. She handed the adjutant his tea, and her face heated as she encountered her father's glare.

He wheezed a command to Sam. "Now tell me of the scout your company took captive. Ross, ready to record this?" He flicked his hand at his adjutant, who had seated himself on the bench, secured Father's field desk upon its legs, and opened the front.

"Yes sir."

Sam remained standing next to the fire, one hand behind his back. "There is not much to tell. We captured him in a canebrake outside Hillabee. According to what I got from him, he was going to take news of the battle to his *tso-ga-li-i* … friends, comrades … gathering south along the Coosa. There are things I would discuss about the attack, sir, when …" His gaze trailed to Susanna, then dropped.

What didn't he want her to know?

She shouldn't care. She wasn't privy to the secrets of the military. Nor did she possess any right to expect Sam Hicks to include her. But the familiar indignation that her sex made her an inconvenience, an obstacle to honest conversation, made her limbs tingle, anyway. Stepping over and taking hold of Polly's arm, she said the first thing she thought of. "Dr. Hawkins will want to see you, Father. We will fetch him so that we do not disturb your council."

CHAPTER FIVE

The doctor was here too? A dreadful possibility took up squatting rights in Sam's head. If they had traveled here together, had the colonel already required Susanna to wed the man? Was that why Susanna seemed so discomfited in his presence? He knew how much she'd wanted to avoid attachment to Hawkins. She wasn't the kind to admit defeat with grace.

Or maybe his implied suggestion that she withdraw had offended her. But he couldn't tolerate her reaction if she learned he'd shot a man today who'd lifted an empty hand in supplication rather than the blade Sam had expected.

He took a seat and did his best to focus on Colonel Moore after the man's family left—although that soup Mrs. Moore had swung to the cooler side of the fireplace smelled awfully good. Hunger threatened to gnaw through what remained of his composure.

Why did the notion of Susanna being married make desperation run rampant inside? He was in no position to be thinking about women. He had one goal. One that he shared with his father—even though they sometimes disagreed on the best way to go about achieving it. Fight this war in such a way that would strengthen their relations with the white leaders to give them the best chance possible of keeping their land.

Sam cleared his throat and attempted to put his concern into words. "Sir, that morning, at daybreak, it was as though those in the village were not expecting us."

"Well, that means we did our job, does it not?" Moore stretched back in his chair, his breathing shallow. His tea wafted strongly of ginger, and something else.

"Not just not expecting us. Not expecting us to attack even when they saw us." Sam closed his eyes briefly, the startled faces flashing before him—men, women, and children frozen in apparent shock as they ran out of their cabins … only to be cut down like wheat before a scythe.

In a soft voice, John Ross expressed the fear crouching on Sam's shoulders. "Could they have thought we had made peace?"

Moore shifted. "I have heard that Jackson took his men to Lashley's Fort near Talladega. Chief Chinnabee's son escaped from there even though the fort had been surrounded. He wrapped himself in a hog skin and pretended to root with the swine."

"How clever," Ross murmured.

The colonel nodded and continued. "Jackson felt compelled to go to their aid, and I believe he expected our support. But we had our orders from Generals Cocke and White. What else were we to do but obey? Whatever the enemy thought, whether they fought back or not, you men did your jobs well. Especially Colonel Lowrey, who killed six with his sword, and your unit, Hicks. I plan to give appropriate public honor tomorrow."

The colonel's admission raised a half dozen more questions in Sam's mind. He sat forward. "But sir—"

"There is no need to discuss the expedition further, Lieutenant Hicks. My next order of business is for Adjutant Ross to send a dispatch to Jackson at Deposit. When he returns, everything will be sorted out." The tin cup hung from Moore's hand, and his skin looked gray in the fading light. The man needed rest.

Sam stood. "And the scout?"

"Tell your Cherokees they must be patient. I will hold him under guard until Jackson determines what to do with him."

"Very well, sir."

"You are dismissed, Hicks."

Sam saluted, then turned and headed for the door.

He swallowed back any sense of disappointment. He wouldn't tell Colonel Moore he hoped the scout would be transferred to Hiwassee with the other male prisoners of war rather than given to his fellow Cherokees for sport. Neither would he cast another glance at that pot of soup. Or at Moore's daughter, returning to the cabin on the arm of Dr. Hawkins as Sam strode across the yard. She looked just as fetching in her moccasins, leggings, and homespun dress as she had wearing a fancy gown and hairdo. In fact, more fetching, because her current costume reminded him of the heritage they shared. Never mind. Even if Susanna wasn't Dr. Hawkins' wife—yet—Sam doubted Moore would ever agree for her to be his.

Tossing and turning was a luxury that the cabin's hard-packed dirt floor denied Susanna. Her tick's narrow width prevented her even from rolling. Rather, she had to gently shift her weight, and in place, unless she wished to arise with bruises. At least, she envisioned them springing up all over her body as she lay there, listening to her father's raspy breathing, George's soft snoring, and the more distant movements of restless men and horses.

The tick didn't even rustle as she turned over. They'd removed most of the straw they'd stuffed them with at Turkey Town so they could fold them onto the pack mules. A time for requisitioning more had yet to present itself, if straw was even to be had in this hardship-plagued stockade.

She ought to be hankering for her feather mattress in her lovely private bedroom at home. But her thoughts skittered between Sam Hicks and the women and children prisoners. Sam because she couldn't reconcile the two different men she'd seen in the same body. Even more a feat, how did they share the same mind? One a scholar and one a warrior? So many questions materialized behind Susanna's closed eyes. Where did he come from? Why had he enlisted? And most of all, was anyone waiting at home for him?

A wife? It had never occurred to her that he might be married. But Polly wouldn't have said what she did about Father discouraging a connection, then, would she? She would if she didn't know. Men got married all the time and didn't go around announcing it.

Best to think about the women and children in the tents. Though the log walls surrounding Susanna broke most of the wind, cold seeped through the chinking and hardened the ground even inside the cabin, where the embers of the fire provided a faint measure of warmth. How chilled they must be, those huddled beneath mere flapping canvas. And how hungry.

Father had said the Cherokees had taken many as slaves in the tradition of tribal warfare and kept those captives in their camp outside the fort. But some of the officers, according to George, guarded their human acquisitions in several tents only feet away. George's fresh-hatched desire to spy could be used to her advantage. And to keep the energetic youth occupied.

When Polly rose, stirring up the embers, adding fat knots, and placing her coffee bean roaster over the flames, Susanna sat up and pulled on the wonderful deerskin moccasins Nokassa had lent her.

She crept over to her stepmother, whispering. "Let me help."

Polly glanced at her. "No need. I am going to make eggs for your father. For everyone."

Susanna nodded and held her hands out to the warmth of the fireplace. "May I make corn flapjacks?"

"We do not need both. Your father says we must not waste the supplies we brought."

"Not for us. For the Creek women and children." When her stepmother's lips parted, Susanna hurried on before she could protest. "I know we could never feed them all, but George said there are three tents packed with captives close to our cabin. He never saw anyone take them anything to eat yesterday—only buckets of water for drinking and washing. The flapjacks would be simple but filling. Easy for them to share. Please, Mama."

Where did that come from? She never called Polly "Mama" except to reference her to the children. A hot flush stole over Susanna's face. What if her stepmother thought she was merely wheedling her?

But Polly reached out and squeezed her wrist. "You are a good girl. Use my frying pan."

Susanna didn't miss the sheen of tears in the eyes of a woman who never cried. She tiptoed away to get the supplies she'd need, her heart warmed.

Father had always made sure Susanna stood on one side of an unspoken divide, separate from Polly and Susanna's half siblings—the side with his parents who lived in Tennessee and the memory of her mother, an English lady he told Susanna she should aspire to resemble. He'd sent her to finishing school in Kingston, Tennessee, to that end. From their fine brick home attached to the ordinary where they lodged travelers, her grandparents had arranged countless introductions to businessmen, clergymen, and soldiers. But to her father's veiled consternation, she'd returned unwed. And possibly unfinished. And now, she'd followed him to the wilderness, where somehow the divide disappeared.

When John Ross approached, Sam had just started a letter to the two of his brothers at the Springplace mission school. That wasn't exactly true. He'd settled by the campfire with his lap desk, quill, and paper, and he was still staring at an empty page twenty minutes later, while his comrades made conversation around shoveling in corn mush. As a weak, late-November sun warmed the horizon for the second day in a row, glinting on puddles of icy slush, the men rejoiced at the break in the weather. But Sam had no idea how to capture the clash of worlds—the old and the new—that he struggled with daily into a missive to his admiring younger kin. They had mostly seen the new. His greatest fear? That it would expire far quicker than the old.

Ross' arrival was almost a relief, except for his stern expression. Duty, not pleasure, then. Everyone stood when the slender officer in European clothing stopped at their campfire.

"Go about your business, men." Ross spoke in stilted Cherokee before extending his hand in Sam's direction. "Lieutenant, Colonel Moore requests your presence at his cabin."

He'd said the last in English, but a gray-haired sergeant in a battered felt hat lowered his pipe. "Has the enemy been sighted?"

Ross shot him a brief, brows-lowered glance. "Nothing like that. I believe this is a personal matter."

"Personal?" The man chortled as Sam secured his writing implements in his tent behind them, planting his hat on his head. "Hope you don't get beat with a pistol, loo-ten-ant."

"Why would I get beat with a pistol?" Sam's gaze shifted to Ross. He couldn't think what he might be in trouble for. And smiting a soldier with a firearm was hardly a standard punishment of this army.

Ross tugged his arm, but before he could lead him away, the sergeant called out an answer. "That is what the colonel did to the Tennessee private yesterday who dared to touch his daughter."

His daughter? Lurid images accompanied by something akin to panic rose up. His feet planted, but Ross gave him a little shove. Sam hissed out a question. "Something happened to Miss Moore?"

Ross grunted. "More to the militiaman than her, but yes."

Sam swallowed hard as dread and relief battled in his mind. His friend had not corrected the title, so she was still "Miss Moore." Ross would know. But if anyone had dared hurt her, assaulted her virtue …

The adjutant lowered his voice as they threaded their way past dirty ecru tents and flickering fires toward the separate camp of the Tennessee volunteers. "Miss Moore took food to the prisoners being held in the fort yesterday morning. One of the white guards kept asking why she was feeding the captives when the militia hadn't had anything to eat. She tried to ignore him, but when she drew nigh him at the final tent, he … grabbed her, uh … backside."

Sam stopped again, his eyes widening as fury fired his veins. "Where is the man?"

"Hiding somewhere in camp, but you are not to look for him. You are not even to know about him. I am simply telling you this so that you will understand what the colonel asks of you." Ross nodded toward the fort and waited until Sam started walking again.

"Tell me the rest. What happened?"

A chuckle. Ross actually chuckled. "I did not see it, but from what I heard later, Miss Moore walloped him in the face with her plate of flapjacks and took off running."

Sam chuckled, too, the tension draining from his shoulders. From Ross' grin, he shared Sam's admiration for the young lady's spunk. Thankfully, he also had a wife at home that from all accounts enjoyed his devotion—and with whom he was expecting his first child.

Ross went on, nodding at the sentry as they entered through the wide gate of the fort. "The colonel heard Miss Moore cry out. He burst from the cabin in a state of semi-dress and aimed his pistol at the militiaman. When the man's excuse was that he'd taken Miss Moore for a Cherokee, the colonel fell to beating him about the head and shoulders with his firearm and yelled out that he would shoot the next man who laid a hand on his daughter."

Sam froze. The busy fort yard receded in a haze as cold shock doused him head to toe.

"Hicks, we are never going to get there if you keep stopping. The colonel does not like to be kept waiting."

He stared straight ahead. His mouth went dry, making it hard to form a question. "Did you say … 'taken her for a Cherokee'?"

"Of course, that is what I said. Did you not know?" Ross touched his elbow, leaning close. His eyes narrowed. "Were you thinking …? You were not thinking of her, Hicks."

"I thought Polly Moore was her mother."

Ross shook his head so rapidly his turban wobbled. "Her mother was Elizabeth Smith Moore, a white woman of high standing who died in childbirth."

"Her stepmother." He breathed it out, along with his withered notion that he had anything in common with Susanna Moore. "I never heard talk of her having a white mother, and … I didn't see it."

And when he had been there, he'd worn his nicest frock and waistcoat, his breeches, Hessian boots. He'd boasted of his command of languages while in the library with her. Nothing had identified him as anything but a white military clerk, and he'd let it be so because he'd wanted to feel on the same par with Moore and Hawkins. To sit at their table and pretend he was one of them. He'd made Susanna think he was white. No wonder she'd looked as though she might faint when he'd appeared at the door of her cabin here in the fort dressed like a native. "God, forgive my pride."

Ross stared at him a moment. Ross, who had taken a full-blooded wife. Then he looked away as if giving quarter to Sam's humbling. Spoke low. "Colonel Moore has fine plans for his daughter. He will send her away as soon as he can. But until then, he needs your help. You should consider that refusing him could provoke not only his displeasure … but his suspicion."

Sam shot him a dagger of a look, but the adjutant's brown eyes revealed nothing.

He extended his arm to indicate the tiny cabin emitting a curl of gray smoke. "Go."

"You are asking me to serve as a guard to your daughter, and the first errand I am to escort her on is to gather *pine needles*?" Sam stood in front of the colonel, hand on his knife sheath, moccasins planted at shoulder width. Moore had not invited him to sit, even though the older man enjoyed a relaxed position … feet in an aromatic, steaming bath his wife had prepared before departing the cabin.

The man's bushy eyebrows flew up. "You think yourself too good for such a task?"

"No, indeed, sir." Sam licked his top lip. Ducked his head. "Quite the contrary. But … why choose me?"

"Why? Lots of reasons. My daughter is already acquainted with you, and I know you to be an honorable sort. You speak three languages. Or is it four? You saved the life of my adjutant at Tallushatchee. And you are the lieutenant of a spy and scout unit, for heaven's sake! What other reason do I need?" Cheeks flushed, Moore paused to catch his breath.

"What about … your adjutant? He shares some of those qualities."

"Ross? Ross is my adjutant. I want you to be hers. Be her adjutant."

Susanna Moore's adjutant, a fixture at her side, at her beck and call, every day watching the expressions slip across her face but never having the right to guess what caused them. One more name rasped past his lips, though it galled him to proffer it. "Hawkins? I know you … intend for them to wed." How would *he* feel about another man tailing his intended everywhere? If Sam were he, he'd never stand for it.

Moore waved his hand, then jerked it back down to catch the slipping cuff of his breeches. "Fires of hades, man! The doctor has his patients to tend to, and you think I want Susanna exposed to a bunch of naked ruffians? You act as though I burden you with an onerous task. I will compensate you and have your tent moved inside the fort. She will be gone before you are needed for active duty again."

Gone … just when the object of his admiration became a real person rather than a mere ideal. That could not happen. If he did this, he must consider it a military duty, not a personal one. It must be no different than if he was guarding a male prisoner of war. That brought another question to mind, if he dared ask it. "Miss Moore strikes me as the type who might, er ... resent being guarded. What says she about this?"

A sly grin slipped across Colonel Moore's face. "She did protest about her privacy."

Sam clasped his hands behind his back, focused on his leggings, and allowed a soft laugh.

"But then I told her it was my condition for her staying. I would send them back to Turkey Town except my wife wishes to remain until this ..."—he rolled his fingers in front of his chest—"this wheezing subsides. And since we expect no action for some time ..."

Sam nodded. "I am glad you are taking care of yourself."

"I also told her it was you." The colonel's statement caused Sam to jerk, booming out as it did over a restrained cough that then exploded.

"Me, sir?" He shifted, waiting.

Moore wiped his mouth with his handkerchief. "Yes, that you would look out for her." Now *that* hung a weight of responsibility around his neck. "And she relented. Said she felt comfortable with you."

She did? If only he shared the feeling.

"Something about your book learning and Bible reading. I know she's given you the impression she's uncontrollable, when in truth, she's a fairly biddable girl if you are firm with her. Firm, but respectful!" He stabbed the air under Sam's chin with his index finger. "You hear?"

"Yes sir. I regard your daughter as a lady of the highest order." As he had before he knew she possessed no Cherokee blood.

"Good. What I told that mountain coot I repeat to you. Any man attempting to take advantage of Miss Moore in any way will reckon with me." Splashing, Moore leaned for a small woven towel just out of reach on the table. Sam stepped forward and handed it to him. With a grumble, the colonel proceeded to dry his feet. "In order to observe propriety, my son, George, will join you any time you accompany Miss Moore on an errand. And I have told both of them they are never to leave the fort without you."

"Thus the pine needles." The sentence escaped under Sam's breath.

Moore's gaze flicked up to him. "That is correct. My family needs to refill their bedding. They have not been sleeping, and I cannot have them getting sick."

"I understand, sir."

"You understand, but do you accept?"

Did he have a choice? Ross' warning flashed to mind, and Sam tightened his balled fists until his nails dug into his palms. "I accept."

CHAPTER SIX

Her father's decree that Sam Hicks should serve as Susanna's bodyguard offered the perfect opportunity to satisfy her curiosity about the man. Maybe once she understood him, she'd cease to think about him. And today offered the perfect timing.

Susanna drank in the crisp, woodsmoke-scented air as they stepped from the fort compound. She blinked in the golden sunshine and hugged the ticking mattresses Polly had sewn together. Now was her chance to enjoy a couple hours of freedom and, hopefully, interesting companionship. If only scholar-Sam would show himself again. He seemed to have been swallowed up in warrior-Sam, fully armed and sporting a face to match his weapons. He'd scarcely spoken three words to her since presenting himself at their cabin door.

Maybe he disliked being ordered to trail a woman like an attentive puppy.

And if only her brother would cease his jabber. He darted in front of them, eyeing Sam with admiration. "I heard you killed that warrior with a single knife throw to the heart—from twenty paces." George mimicked tossing a blade. "*Swish*. Whap!" He acted out being stabbed in the chest, clutching the area, and pretending to stagger.

Susanna expected Sam to respond with amusement, but his face clouded. "That wasn't exactly how it happened."

"Then how *did* it happen?" George danced ahead of them on the path, pivoting to walk backward. The basket he carried for her swung wildly, and she reached out with a reminder for him to have a care.

Sam shook his head. "Battle is not all bravery and glory, George. It is not something you should wish for."

George's eager expression faded. "Mama says this war will be over before I am old enough to enlist. Instead, what do I get to do?" His mouth twisted. "Chop and carry firewood and empty chamber pots. Even gathering pine straw sounds good next to that!"

Susanna chuckled. "Be glad you are of use." She stayed close behind Sam as he led them between the camps of Tennessee militia and Cherokees, keeping her eyes looking forward even when conversations quieted as they passed. "Father won't let me help in the hospital, and while we make bread and broth for the patients, it seems so unimportant."

"It is not unimportant." Sam's gaze locked on her, his words firm.

"It's not enough. I plan to start taking in mending and washing."

He glanced at her hands clasping the ticking and frowned. Concerned the lye soap would roughen her soft palms? Appreciation warred with indignation. He was as bad as her father. She lifted her chin a mite. "I help with the laundry at home."

"Not in those quantities. And not with that much filth, I can guarantee."

"I don't suppose a little dirt will kill me."

One of Sam's dark brows lowered. "It could."

"Are you only going to speak to argue? This is a beautiful day. Let us not ruin it."

"Yes, Miss Moore." He ducked his chin.

Susanna drew in a breath and opened her mouth to reprove his false contrition, then decided against it. Another tactic might work better. "I packed us a lunch." She indicated the basket George carried. "Cornbread, apples, and *salted ham*." She whispered the last, leaning toward the lieutenant ever so slightly.

His gaze jerked to hers, and indeed, betrayed a spark of interest.

"I wager it has been a while since you had ham." She allowed a smile to tease the corners of her lips.

He blinked as though the sun rose right behind her, then glanced away just as quickly. "I did not think our errand would take half the day."

She refused to allow him to dampen her spirits. "I intend to stay outside that dreadful fort with its stinky privy pits and livestock pens as long as possible. Ah …" She sighed, breathed deep of late autumn's pungent decay, and turned in a circle as they entered the woods. "So much better. Fresh air and quiet. And look at that oak tree, how red its leaves remain."

"I believe it is a pine tree we seek."

"Lookee here!" George shouted and ran ahead to a white oak with a lower branch that bent at almost a ninety-degree angle before climbing parallel to the trunk. "A perfect seat for our picnic."

"So it is." She hurried over to her brother as he scooted onto the limb.

"It's a bent tree. A marker tree." Sam came up behind them.

"You mean, it's not natural? What does it mark?" After draping the ticking next to George, Susanna turned back to Sam.

He gestured. "See how it points toward the river? Native people shaped it that way years ago, I'd say, to indicate the shallow river crossing."

"Do the Cherokees do likewise?"

"There are many bent trees in our wilderness."

Susanna was gazing around for other such specimens when a distant flash of waving feathers snagged her eye. A bird? No, feathers in a man's hair. "Get down, George!" She grabbed Sam's arm hard as she lunged for the cover of the white oak's trunk, jerking him off-balance with her unexpected assault and causing him to topple almost on top of her and her brother. George squatted under her with an "Ow!" of protest.

Sam crouched, righting himself with the fingers of one hand

pressed to the earth. Rather than question her, he drew his rifle from over his shoulder. He sidled up to the tree, peering beyond.

"A man. An Indian." Susanna gasped her warning just above a whisper—and above the thundering of her heart. "Over there." She pointed in the direction she'd spied the movement. When Sam cocked his eyebrow at her, she added by way of explanation, and with as much humility as she could muster, "I possess very good eyesight."

Why did he lower his gun? "It is very impressive you spied Six Killer from this distance, Miss Moore."

"Six Killer? He's not a Red Stick?"

A smile played in laugh lines she hadn't even known Sam possessed. "I do not know the names of any Red Sticks." He stood and, slinging his rifle behind his back again, extended a hand to her. "Did you think I would bring you and your brother out here without a party of my scouts combing the area first?"

A Cherokee. Of course. They probably patrolled these woods regularly, regardless of a visit from the colonel's children. How foolish she must look to him. "I'm sorry." With a sigh, Susanna got her feet under her.

"Do not be sorry. A good eye and quick reflexes come highly prized in the wilderness."

When she slid her hand in his, Sam gave a good tug, bringing her upright with a little bounce on her toes. So close to him, she could smell the buckskin he wore and detect his pulse thumping in his neck. And discover that there weren't lighter flecks in his eyes. Just dark, fathomless depths … that seemed to harden as she looked into them. Susanna's cheeks heated, and she looked away.

"Well, *I'm* sorry." George blundered into her, bumping them apart as he sprang to his feet. "I wanted to see Sam shoot somebody from that distance."

Sam's eyes narrowed, and he shook his head. "We should never wish for bloodshed when it can be avoided."

"'Tis so." Susanna seized that moment to reach for the sleeping pallets. "It is Lieutenant Hicks to you, George. And we should stop wasting his time." It had been silly of her to think he might share her enthusiasm over an outing together.

The mystery-of-a-man accompanying them bent eye to eye with her younger brother, as natural as if he addressed one of his own. "You can call me Sam." When George grinned and took the ticking Susanna offered him without complaint, Sam straightened and focused on her. "And you are not wasting my time. My day is yours to command."

In that case, could she call him Sam? Susanna almost giggled at that first thought that popped into her mind but stifled both question and laughter. "Good. Then you can tell us about yourself as we stuff these pallets. If we are to spend time together, we ought to know a little about each other."

His mouth drew into a straight line, but he gave a single nod before leading them into the forest. "What do you want to know?"

"To begin with, where are you from?"

"Oothcaloga Creek."

"I have no idea where Oothcaloga Creek is."

"It is near the Cherokee meeting grounds at Oostanaula."

She nodded. Polly had referred to Oostanaula, where the Cherokee National Council met, a number of times. "About two days of hard riding down the federal road."

"From Hiwassee, yes. From here would be about the same due west with a good route. But obviously, there is no nice post road." Sam paused to catch the attention of George, who was launching pine cones at a squirrel's nest. He pointed at the tree. "That's a good one."

George punched his fist down to his side. "I *knew* I should have brought my gun."

"No, for pine needles." When George eyed the carpet around the trunk, Sam drew a thick long knife from a sheath at his waist and held down a low-hanging branch. "White pine. The needles hang in"—he appeared to search for the right word, curving his free hand—"cones rather than fans. Cut them off like this, in clumps, and the stuffing will be softer."

"Ah, yes. I can use your knife? Wait. Is this the knife you used to kill the Red Stick?" George's eyes widened as he gazed up into Sam's face, which drained of color.

He pulled the blade back. "Did you not bring your own? A boy should not be without his knife."

"I did, but it's not as big as yours. It will take me twice as long—"

"But half as long if you stop talking."

Susanna bit her own lip at Sam's terse reply. George's head wilted on his neck like a drying autumn leaf, making her heart ache. She stepped forward and twisted a bunch of needles until the stem weakened. "I will help you, George."

"No." Sam laid his hand on her arm. "I will. You hold the sacks open." When she hesitated, he added, "Please?"

At last, she nodded, picked up one of the ticks, and parted the top. But she stood closer to George than to Sam as both males sawed away with their knives. No doubt, with Sam's uncommon aim, having to toss the branches farther wouldn't trouble him. She couldn't stop looking at that shiny blade. Picturing him throwing it and hitting someone in the front, or back, or wherever it had hit, she shuddered. And needed to know more about Oothcaloga, where they might find some common ground.

"Tell us about your home. Does your father farm?"

Sam's arm stilled, then resumed its motion. He answered in a voice soft and raspy. "He does. The land was good when he and my mother moved there from Pine Log over ten years ago. Lots of little creeks and ponds. Beavers had been at work, building dams, so many of the trees were already felled. They built a house of the logs. Two-story. Called Fort Hill."

"Fort Hill." That sounded official, a large farm much like Big Springs Bluff. "Does your mother have a garden?"

There, his eyes brightened. "A huge garden with all kinds of vegetables and herbs as well. And there are apple orchards."

"It sounds wonderful. And you have brothers and sisters?"

"Many." He flashed her one of those rare grins that made her smile back and angle the bag for his contribution. "Two younger brothers are in school at Springplace."

"That is where you attended also, isn't it? I didn't put it together with what you said in the library until … after." After she'd realized the reason for his association with Moravians.

They moved to a nearby pine when Sam explained they should only take so much from a single tree. Then he continued, "Yes. I owe the missionaries more than I can ever repay. I purpose to visit when I can, to encourage the boys to value what they are taught. Soon there will be a place where older boys of mixed blood can continue their education, but—"

"There isn't such a place now?"

He shook his head. "Not yet. But that will change. Men like my father will see to it. Thankfully, he owns many books. I continued to teach myself, and he helped me. He has even studied law."

"But there are no books written in Cherokee, are there?" George rested his arm at his side. "Those are all the branches I can reach. Can I look on the ground now?"

"Yes." Susanna smiled at him, sliding a half-empty tick his way with the toe of her moccasin. "Just make sure the needles you find are dry. With no bugs!"

"Girls." George made a face at Sam. "About the books …"

"No books in Cherokee, George. Almost was." Sam's expression twisted with an emotion that resembled regret.

"'Not yet.' 'Soon.' 'Almost.'" George picked up a pine frond and examined it carefully. "Seems like a lot of things not happening."

"That is the way of it for our people, George." In an unguarded moment, Sam's lips tucked into a fleeting ghost of a smile. Then he cast Susanna a quick glance, and he whacked off a small bough.

"Well, what do you mean about the book?"

Sam heaved a sigh at her brother's persistent questioning but began his story. "When I was a little younger than you, a missionary couple came to Springplace. John and Clarissa Kliest. He was a surveyor. A builder. She was an artist and good with languages. Her job at the mission was not just to teach us but also to record our language in a syllabary. A symbol for each syllable. My friend Dawnee and I were helping her." He paused.

What was that faraway look in his eye? More than remembrance. Fondness. And not over Mrs. Kliest. Over Dawnee. Susanna frowned at the slight burn that started in her middle. She must be hungry.

"So did you get it done?" George cast the prickly cluster away, bending to examine another. This one met with his approval, but he twisted off a pinecone before bagging it.

"We'd almost completed it when word got out to Doublehead's friends about what we were doing." Sam glanced at her, brow furrowed. "Do you know who that was?"

George answered before she could draw a breath. "The old chief murdered by the young chiefs because he'd sold Cherokee land without permission." He grinned. "I had a tutor. Mr. Brumley."

Sam smiled at him. "You are fortunate. Then you know that Doublehead also took many, many bribes. But he wasn't murdered. He was executed by decree of our National Council. My father's friend The Ridge and some others were chosen to carry out the order. But during that time, back in 1806, he was very powerful. He and many Cherokees believed it was witchcraft, a crime punishable by death, for a Cherokee to record our language."

Susanna gasped. "Surely, that has changed now." She'd heard from Polly of the dark side of Cherokee magic, but this archaic belief represented another way to keep the people in bondage to ignorance.

Sam puffed a slight breath of a laugh from his nose. "The old ways are slow to change."

"Did you have to fend them off?" George brandished a branch like a sword, swinging it wildly as he scuffled around. "Is that where you learned your knife skills?"

"Unfortunately, no." He dropped his arms to his sides, briefly closing his eyes. "I have never forgotten how helpless I felt when Doublehead's warriors dragged Mrs. Kliest and Dawnee from our classroom. It was one of the old missionaries who came running with his rifle and bought them enough time to escape. I always felt I should have done more."

"You were a child, though." Susanna placed her hand on her chest in an attempt to quell the sympathetic ache there.

"Yes. Just before I turned twelve, over seven years ago." So he was only—what?—nineteen now. So young still to be fighting his first war. "But I guess the incident did push me to learn some fighting skills—something every boy should know. I saw boys at the Tallushatchee village ..." Again his voice trailed off. Then he gave a slight shake of his head and grabbed a branch high overhead, snapping the tip. "The Kliests had to leave Springplace for good, taking Dawnee with them. The syllabary was destroyed."

"How sad."

Sam approached her, stuffing a final cluster into her sack and taking it from her to tie off the drawstring. "The last thing Mrs. Kliest said to me was to remember what she had taught me and that if the work was of God, it would not end."

She stared at him, willing him to meet her eyes. "No wonder education and books mean so much to you."

Finally, his gaze locked with hers. "That is why I like to visit Springplace. I tell the boys what I remember, but I would not endanger them by encouraging them to write it down. Who knows?" He shrugged, seeming to discard the serious moment. "There is a man named George Guess in our regiment, a silversmith who is always trying to get my father to help him sign his work. Perhaps he will make up a Cherokee alphabet."

Susanna gave a light laugh. "Perhaps." She wanted to thank him for sharing but knew from his earlier stoicism that he wouldn't appreciate her drawing attention to his transparency. Transparency she had practically forced. "Why don't we be done with this? We can try out these ticks during lunch, see if they are soft enough."

"Why not try them right now?" George tossed his on the ground and fell back onto it, stiff like a domino, but when Susanna met Sam's eyes, heat as intense as a blacksmith's forge licked up her neck and face.

When would she ever think before speaking?

CHAPTER SEVEN

Sam had made a mistake bringing Susanna and her younger brother back to the fort by way of the Cherokee Regiment's practice range. He'd thought to avoid the staring eyes of the Tennessee militia—and maybe a pair of them belonging to the cur who had dared touch the colonel's daughter—but now it was the Moore offspring staring and exhibiting no inclination to proceed to their cabin. Mouths open and brows raised, they discarded the full pallets in a pile and watched a trio take turns throwing their tomahawks at a cross section of a large tree trunk.

When the group wrapped up their semi-friendly competition with thumps on the back and an exchange of tobacco, George's gaze transferred to the nineteen-inch weapon on Sam's belt. "Can you do that? Throw it end over end like that?"

"That is generally how it is done."

"Have you ever spun it twice in the air before hitting the target?"

"Only if the target was my mother's prized rosebush." His unconsidered admission earned a giggle from Susanna. What an unexpected sound, airy in the rough wilderness, soft as the call of the mourning dove. He turned to her with one corner of his mouth upturned. "I was George's age."

George waggled his eyebrows. "Bet I could do that too."

"The goal is a single revolution, five to six paces from the target."

"Oh, let me try." The boy ran toward the range, paced off half a dozen strides, then jumped up and down.

Sam cringed at the notion of placing such a deadly weapon

in the hands of one so lacking in maturity, yet George claimed he was a crack shot with his rifle. "No one has ever shown you how to throw a tomahawk?" The skill was practically the birthright of a Cherokee male.

"My father doesn't own one."

Well, that could have gone without stating.

As if picking up on Sam's judgment, George lifted his chin a notch. "But he can fence, and he can outshoot any man. He showed me how."

"A needful thing for a father to teach a son, it is true. But as for the handling of the tomahawk, that is the responsibility of your mother's male kin."

"They live far away. But you are here. And you did say every boy should know how to fight, didn't you?"

Sam sighed, and Susanna's attention shifted to him with an amused smile. She set her basket, now empty, at her feet. He'd blame the pleasing contents of that basket, mostly now in his stomach, for his capitulation. "It is true that all Cherokee boys should learn their way around a blade. Stand aside." He slid the hawk from its loop, weighting it in his hand. "Attend to me carefully."

Now, if he could do this without thoughts of Miss Susanna Moore intruding on his concentration. Sam attempted to block her out. "Dominant foot forward, weight resting on that leg. Turn the back foot a bit to the side. As if you're throwing a ball." He paused for a glance at George, who gave an eager nod.

Sam slid his grip down the carved hickory handle. "Hold it at the base as though you are shaking hands with it, with the blade at the top. Bring your arm straight up—no twisting the shoulder or wrist. Keep your arm extended, eye on the target, and … release." The pound-and-a-half tomahawk whirled on a horizontal trajectory, and the blade planted in the wood with a satisfying *thunk*.

George hooted and Susanna clapped. He didn't dare search for admiration on her face but instead directed the boy to fetch the weapon back and count off five, rather than six, paces. Sam stood behind him, positioning his grip.

"Tell me what your target is."

"Why, that piece of log, of course."

"If you want to hit the log, perhaps you will hit the log. But if you aim for a splinter or a groove on that log, perhaps you will hit the splinter or groove."

Susanna crept closer while he spoke, distracting him again.

George squinted one eye. "I've got it!"

Sam reached over and jiggled the weapon in his hand. "Too loose. Lock your wrist. When you release, it does not move. That way, you have the same control every time."

George nodded, respiration shallow with repressed excitement, solemn now.

That reminded Sam … "Breathe in as you raise your arm, out as you throw." He stepped back and fell silent, letting the boy find his timing. A second later, the tomahawk took flight—and chipped the edge off the log.

"I hit it!"

"Excellent. Lean forward a little less this time, and it should be dead center."

George retrieved the tomahawk from below the target and paused to peer back at him. "You said to aim for a splinter. I aimed for a splinter—the one hanging from the bottom. I got it!"

Sam swiveled to face Susanna. "Does he jest with me?"

She laughed. "I don't know. Surely. George, pick a spot in the middle this time."

"Yes ma'am." He saluted and paced back with the precision of a British regular. "Now watch. It's in the blood." Over his shoulder, he favored his sister with an exaggerated wink.

When the boy indeed landed the hawk near the center of the upended log on his next throw, Sam exchanged an amazed glance with Susanna.

She clasped her hands under her chin as she watched George fetch the weapon again. "I wish I had it in the blood." Her statement sounded strangely wistful.

Was she actually wishing Cherokee blood flowed in her veins? "You have no idea what you speak of." His response came out just above a whisper, like the scraping of a drawknife separating bark. Her eyes pierced him, hooking yet another admission. "Your kind does not have to rely on skill with the tomahawk to stay on this land."

"It isn't by fighting that the Cherokees will stay."

"But we *are* fighting. Fighting the white man's war against the Red Sticks and British."

"You are." The tendrils of dark hair that escaped Susanna's bun drifted over her shoulders as she nodded. "But it is the fact that, of all the tribes, they are becoming most like the white men, which will allow them—you—to remain."

"Do you think we are alike?"

George threw again, but they paid no attention. Susanna's gaze remained locked on his. "Yes, down where it counts, I do."

"And how do you know this?" He couldn't seem to stop questioning her—almost as if he wanted to push her until she betrayed secret prejudice. "You have not felt what we have felt as our lands have been gobbled up by greedy settlers. You have not had anyone's opinion of you change the instant they learned you had Cherokee blood."

Her face turned bright red. "I seem to remember being grappled by an uncouth backwoodsman just yesterday."

"One instance does not a lifetime make."

"Maybe not, but I have loved my stepmother and my half brother and half sisters as much as I ever would have if they had been white!"

The force of Susanna's declaration whipped out and curled around Sam like a whip, at once censuring and drawing him to her with its earnest emotion. He stepped closer and bowed his head. "Miss Moore, I—"

Before he could get out any form of apology, George strode up, butting against Sam's elbow and giving the tomahawk a little shake. "Is there a problem here, Susanna?"

Was the adolescent threatening him with his own weapon? Sam cracked a small grin.

"No, George." Susanna's lips twitched. "Lieutenant Hicks was just about to offer to let me throw his axe."

"Tomahawk." He tapped a finger against his prized family heirloom. "It is made differently and for combat, not chopping down trees. And no, you cannot throw it."

"Wha—" The berry-colored lips now rounded.

Sam lifted a sheath hanging by a leather cord around his neck. He showed her the top of the blade inside, smaller than the one her gaze had earlier followed with undeniable alarm. "This is a better-sized weapon for you to start with, but you have to be careful. It is sharpened on both sides."

George poked a finger at the colorful design on the leather. "What's that made with?"

"Dyed porcupine quills."

"It's beautiful," Susanna said on a soft breath. "So intricate."

As the boy backed off, apparently satisfied, and no doubt more than content to keep the manlier tomahawk, Sam addressed her again. "I will teach you how to use this, but first, answer two questions."

"Very well." But she crossed her arms in front of her chest. And tapped her toe. "What?"

"Did you really shove a plate of flapjacks into the face of that 'uncouth backwoodsman'?" He attempted to keep his expression impassive, but he had to bite the inside of his jaw. Just picturing the scene threatened to steal a laugh—and, he hoped, any remaining tension.

A grin crossed Susanna's face, and she dropped her arms. "When I looked back, I could see that he didn't know whether to splutter curses at me or stop and chew."

"Ha!" The laugh escaped despite his best effort.

Susanna froze, then her startled expression melted to pure sunshine. She planted a hand on her hip. "I hear they're calling me Flapjack Sue around the camp. It's a moniker I'm right proud of." She paused, cocking her head. "When you laugh, you look like you did when I first met you."

Now what did that mean? Soft like a white man? He needed to maintain his resolve—a military duty, not a personal one. But he admitted, "Not many people make me laugh."

"I can see that. Well, George and I are glad to oblige. Are we not, George?"

"Yep." As he positioned his feet and took aim, the youth probably didn't even know what he was agreeing to.

Sam really ought to be watching him. The colonel would skip military protocol and apply some downright biblical justice if he brought George back missing a finger. But he was finding it increasingly difficult to tear his attention away from the big sister, her dimple as she smiled, her mouth as she spoke.

"What is your other requirement?"

"What?" Sam snatched his gaze from Susanna's lips to her eyes.

Her cheeks, already rosy in the cold, darkened another shade. "For letting me throw your little bitty knife."

"My little bitty knife?" Indignation laced his repetition of her words. "Let there be no doubt, this *dagger* could gut a man."

"Very well. Your lethal weapon, although you seem to think I can't handle the larger one, much less the *tomahawk*."

"Why do you care about throwing a knife or a tomahawk or any weapon when your father would order his entire regiment to fight to protect you?"

Susanna released a gusty sigh. "Because as much as I would like to think he will always be there, he may not. What if I lose him in battle? What if this lung sickness returns when he goes out on the next campaign and Polly can't save him? Then what will I have left?"

For one, Dr. Hawkins would rush to the rescue, although Sam would be wiser to bite his tongue than suggest that when she was this betwattled.

Thankfully, she continued without pausing to solicit any answers. "I should at least be able to defend myself. The lessons at finishing school may have taught me how to speak French and snare a husband, but they are useless out here."

"You know he will send you home at the first opportunity." As much as the thought pained him. Fort Strother would seem a cheerless place without Susanna Moore.

"But that's just it. I shouldn't have to leave." She balled her hands into fists at her sides. "I want to show him I am as strong as Polly. That I can survive, and not only survive, but be helpful on the frontier. I don't have to have Cherokee blood to do that, do I?"

The yearning for acceptance in Susanna's words echoed a similar longing in Sam's heart. She searched his eyes as she had earlier, but this time, he didn't close his soul. If she needed strength, and he could help give it to her, what cause had he to deny her?

"No. You don't." Sam reached for her right fist, pried open her fingers, and laid the handle of the knife in her palm.

She blinked, transferring the sheen of moisture from her eyes to her long, dark lashes. "Thank you."

He jerked his chin toward the felled log. "Count off five paces. Same principles apply for throwing a knife as a tomahawk." And once she felt comfortable with the knife, he'd let her try the latter, whether George whined or not.

She did as he instructed, her long, gray wool coat stirring with her footsteps. George made room for her but continued his practice with single-minded intensity. The boy would beg to return to the practice range on a daily basis now. But would that be so objectionable if Susanna accompanied him?

Sam frowned, concentrating on Susanna's stance. And that made him frown more because now he had an excuse to look at her. But he purposed not to touch her as he had her brother. No sir. Spoken instruction would have to do. "You do not need to draw your arm that far back." He sighed as she attempted to correct her posture. "Or extend it that far out."

"Like this?" She flexed with a chopping motion.

"Only if you plan to smite a mole when he pops out of his hole."

She burst into that musical laughter again. "You *are* witty. I knew it." Why that seemed to delight her so much, Sam had no idea. But her joyful response twisted his insides into a knot he didn't want to try to understand. Then her mirth disappeared, and she waved him closer. "Well, don't just stand there. Show me what I'm doing wrong."

"You are thinking too much." He sidled up behind her. So much for his noble intentions. Covering her hand with his, he slid her fingers farther down the handle and slightly extended her thumb. "Picture a part of yourself sailing through the air to connect with the target—if you could only fly."

"If I could fly, I would head due west today." She turned her head so that their faces hovered inches apart, but that fringe of lashes swept down. That was a mercy. His heart might have come out of his chest otherwise. "And see that apple orchard. The one at Fort Hill. And then, I would visit the library." Her mouth turned up at the corners, and that blasted dimple dented the cheek next to him.

She wanted to see his home place. Why? The picture of her there swept all kinds of confusion over Sam. He stepped back and pointed forward with two fingers. "Draw your arm just over your head. Wrist firm, and throw."

Only a quick blink portrayed any disappointment in his lack of response. Susanna faced front and complied. Someone murmured behind Sam when the knife tipped the bottom third of the log. He shifted to assess the cluster of Indians who had accumulated on the periphery when he'd been too distracted by Susanna to notice. Careless of him.

The sight of two braves flanking none other than Standing Wolf stiffened Sam's posture. And for good reason. In the Muskogean tongue, the Natchez Creek muttered what he would have done with that hand on Susanna if he'd been Sam. The younger man to his right, who—unlike Standing Wolf, still bare-chested in the cold—sported a colorful matchcoat over his muslin shirt, frowned.

Sam breathed deep, quelling the urge to turn around and plant his fist in the man's nasty mouth. While Sam had the wiry strength of youth and quickness on his side, he wouldn't delude himself. A warrior in his prime like Standing Wolf would pin and pummel— or stab—him to death in a few quick moves. It would be foolish to challenge him now, especially when the man had backup and Sam didn't. Just because the one young warrior had protested an unseemly comment didn't mean he wouldn't defend Standing Wolf in a fight.

But neither should he appear to run. He weighed his options.

"Sam?"

His first name jarred him. Susanna was looking at him, not for praise of her aim, but for direction. Her gaze darted to the newcomers, her forehead puckered.

He nodded, planting himself between Standing Wolf and the Moore children. "Three throws each." He spoke loudly and, in the likely case that the Natchez Creek couldn't understand English, held up the accompanying number of fingers. "Then we must return to the fort. I don't want your father to come looking for us."

"Aw, do we have to?" George started with his complaints, but Susanna hushed him.

"Do as the lieutenant says, George. And make them good." After fetching the dagger, she edged close to Sam and whispered,

"The one in the middle makes my skin crawl."

"Like your keen sight in the woods, you show keen sight of the mind." Resting his fingers on his long knife in its sheath, Sam kept the trio in his peripheral vision. "That sixth sense will serve you better than any knife skills."

"But will you teach me what you can to help me?" Her wide, dark gaze bore into his, demanding his attention, his commitment. "Please."

The reminder of his failure at Tallushatchee stood behind him … and pressed Sam into offering the truth, however humbling. "I may have good aim with a blade, but I am not a strong warrior, Miss Moore. There are others who could teach you. I could find someone for you."

"I don't want you to find someone else. I want you."

She wanted him. And when she'd been afraid, she'd called him Sam.

He would face any foe to earn the trust in her eyes. But how could he do what she asked of him? He could not wrestle Miss Moore in mock combat the way he'd been taught as a boy—the way the warriors practiced in camp. The mere thought made a hot flush start to rise. And he could not take her to the camp to watch them. In her long skirts, with the lovely curves of her figure, she would be like a bright cardinal in the winter woods.

"We will see. For now, finish your throws."

Though her efforts fell short due to the tension in her body, Susanna completed her brief practice as though her life depended upon it—with nary another glance spared to the spectators. As George returned Sam's tomahawk, Standing Wolf and one of the men walked off, leaving only the one who had frowned. Sam blew out a breath as Susanna brought his knife back.

He lifted the cord from his neck and extended it toward her. "Keep it."

"Truly?" She turned the carved bone handle over in her palm.

"I have others. You have greater need of it than I."

"But the case—it's so beautiful, and it was probably made by someone in your family."

In response, Sam jiggled the leather holder and waited until she slid the blade inside. He met her appreciative gaze with a smile. "You can also tie this, well … elsewhere, if you don't wish to announce you're carrying it."

She gave a nod. "Thank you."

A movement behind him forced him to break eye contact—the young warrior in the matchcoat, his hair worn Mohawk-style, coming their way. "Gather your things." Sam directed the Moores with a nod. Before turning, he curled his fingers about the handle of his tomahawk.

Eyeing George and Susanna as they scurried to the forest edge, the Natchez Creek spoke in the Muskogean language. "It is good you teach the children of the colonel."

"There are those foolish enough to wish to hurt them." He tightened his hand on the weapon, even though this warrior's wide, boyish face softened into an amiable expression, almost a smile.

The man's gaze shifted to the curlicue designs etched into both handle and blade. "A beautiful weapon. I am no threat. But Standing Wolf, he does not like you. He says you make a better babysitter than warrior."

Sam gritted his teeth. If only he possessed the battle skill of The Ridge or even his father. Susanna and George watched from the fringe of the woods, the basket on Susanna's arm, the ticks held between them. He willed them to remain where they were as his companion spoke again.

"Save your anger. To show restraint is wiser than to engage a fool."

Sam searched his memory. Was that a proverb? Wise or not, there was a limit to how much he could overlook before being deemed a coward. "There is a time and place for everything. I will be watching Standing Wolf, and I have many friends. He should have a care with his tongue."

The Natchez Creek nodded. "I know who you are, son of Charles Hicks."

When the man turned to go, Sam called after him. "What is your name?"

"They call me Spring Frog. Standing Wolf is my brother-in-law, but he is not my friend."

CHAPTER EIGHT

Susanna dropped the linen bandage and scrub board into the wash bucket, but the remaining chunk of lye soap she placed on a flat rock. 'Twas only early December, but their supply ran dangerously low, so low she'd not conquered the stains on the hospital linens near to Mammy Kate's standards. Of course, she didn't possess near Mammy Kate's wash skills either. Despite her boasting about helping with wash day, all she'd done back at Big Springs Bluff was hang the sheets out to dry on sunny days.

She wiped her hands on her skirt as she straightened. "You can move those over now," she said to George. Thank heavens. The last load of the hospital's laundry.

He hopped up from a stump and, using the clean end of the stick with which he'd been writing in the dirt, hooked one piece of laundry at a time. The bandages and clothing created drip trails to the rinse bucket.

As Susanna pivoted at the waist in an attempt to unhinge the catches in her back, she scanned the fort yard. Busier than usual. Not only had the 2nd Regiment East Tennessee Volunteer Militia arrived from Kingston and Fort Armstrong, but yesterday General Jackson had returned with the men he'd taken to Fort Deposit. She'd had her first glimpse of him from the door of the cabin— the famous officer the soldiers had dubbed Old Hickory for his stiff manner when he'd marched his troops back to Nashville after refusing to surrender his command to another in New Orleans. While his blue uniform with gold epaulettes and fringe caught the eye, his lean form had scarce filled it out. Her father cut a much more commanding figure, if she did say so herself.

To be honest, it wasn't Jackson's spare frame and bushy gray head her eyes sought. But she probably wouldn't see Sam again today. He'd helped them carry water from the river at dawn, then disappeared. Probably relieved to have her occupied for the day.

Oh no. Not Sam, but here came another rugged militia officer—the third to approach her since morning—this one sporting a buckskin hunting shirt and a long, dark beard. Hoping he'd pass on, Susanna reached for a knotty chunk of wood to toss on the fire under the main cauldron.

"Miss." He stopped behind her, and when she turned, he removed his felt hat. "I will recompense you handsomely to warsh a load of my company's linens."

His and every other company at Strother. She could easily become a full-time laundress. She'd considered the idea—before she realized just how much work the dispensary linens required. "I am sorry, sir. I volunteer for the hospital in this capacity, but after I finish my family's wash, I will be done for the day."

"The thing is, we haven't done warsh since we got here." He shifted his weight onto one skinny leg like a banty rooster, rotating his hat by the brim.

Poor man. But she couldn't, just couldn't. Her hands were nigh to bleeding already. "If you bring it early next Monday's wash day, I will assist you then." Susanna balled her fingers over her palms, closing them against the chafing of the cold wind. Would she have to go into the house to get rid of the stranger?

"But you got the fire already—"

"You heard her." Sam's deep voice rumbled with a threat as he appeared around the side of her cabin. "The lady said no. Come back next week, Ensign."

The volunteer frowned, his gaze latching onto the white feathers that fluttered from Sam's hair—now long enough that he didn't need the band to hold them in place. But the man must have known he was looking at a higher rank, for he jammed his hat on and stomped away.

"You did enough for today." Before she could hide her hand in the fold of her skirt, Sam took it by the back and gently spread her fingers—not only chapped red from the water and lye but nicked in places by the scrub board. Her fingernails scraped and broken. His expression bore silent reproach. And a tinge of pity?

She wanted admiration, not pity.

George ceased his agitating the contents of the rinse pot and stared at them. "Why are you holding Susanna's hand?"

"Your sister has need of ointment. I would imagine your mother makes one for raw skin?" Sam's thumb brushed the joint of hers, sending pin-pricks up to her elbow.

Susanna pulled away, her cheeks burning. "My stepmother is in the hospital, as she is every day, assisting Dr. Hawkins. I know where she keeps her salve, but first, we have to wring and hang this final bucket of hospital laundry." Trying not to imagine the pain of twisting all those bandages and shirts—and after that, plunging her hands into warm lye water again later—she took a deep breath. "Then, may we impose upon you to return with us to the river for one more trip? I fear your prediction about the filthy linens proved as accurate as your assumption that I was not up to this task."

"You have done well." There was the flash of approval she craved in his eyes before he turned away, leaning his rifle against the cabin. "But I will help George with this load while you tend your hands. Fetch your cloak too. I have something to show you."

Susanna's heart pattered as she slipped into the cabin. What could he mean, something to show her? She located the extra, smaller pot of Polly's healing salve that her stepmother always left behind when she went to the hospital and applied a minimal amount to her cracked skin. Others would have much greater need of the topical solution than she did.

When she returned to the yard with her hands encased in leather gloves and her cloak about her shoulders, Sam and George had draped the last of the bandages over the rope that ran between the cabin and the fort wall.

"It won't take long, will it? We can't let the fire die if I'm to finish our own wash." And likely, she'd have to hang it inside, cold as it would get once the sun set.

Sam retrieved his rifle, then hefted the yoke with two empty buckets over one shoulder. George grabbed a second yoke, yet when Susanna reached for the spare bucket, Sam shook his head. "We can manage without that. And I will stoke the fire when we return."

Susanna twisted her lips to one side but held in protest. He was coddling her. But walking unencumbered sounded too appealing.

As they passed through the gate, something else sounded appealing—the lilting notes of a fiddle wafting from the militia camp.

She clamped her hand over her chest as her heart swelled in response. "'Speed the Plow.'"

Sam nodded. "The musician's name is David Crockett. He plays to keep up the spirits of the men. Many of them are starting to grumble now that their enlistments are running out, and they want to go home."

"Is this what you wanted to show me? How did you know? I didn't even know I missed such music so much until I heard it." The aches in Susanna's back fell away as she swayed in rhythm to the familiar tune—one she had danced to with a not-too-objectionable suitor at her grandfather's house in Kingston.

"Well ... I didn't either." Sam glanced at her, his straight, dark brows lowering. "The man I want you to meet is by the river. I would say we can stay and listen, but your presence so nigh the camp ..."

His tone was so apologetic that Susanna clasped his arm, firm and warm under his hunting shirt. His muscles flexed before he drew away. She smiled. "I understand. It was an unexpected treat, nonetheless."

And she tried to hide her disappointment as the roaring of the shoals drowned out "Haste to the Wedding." But when the warrior in the colorful matchcoat from the practice range rose from a fallen log as they approached, Susanna could not conceal her dismay. Her steps faltered.

Sam appealed to her above the running water. "There is no need to be wary of Spring Frog. His sister is married to the man who frightened you—Standing Wolf—but he treats her poorly. He is here to help fulfill what you asked of me."

"What did I ask of you?" Susanna stared at him with wide eyes.

"He, too, believes you and your brother should be safe in this camp. As safe as you can be. He has agreed to help me demonstrate ways to defend yourself."

"But … why did you need him?" The man seemed very … native. And the complete language barrier made her uneasy.

"It is not something I can show you by myself."

Was she wrong, or did he go a bit rosy about the gills?

"He's going to fight you? Yes! Give 'im a good basting." George clunked down the buckets and hurried toward the man called Spring Frog.

Susanna had little choice but to follow. When she drew close, however, the Natchez Creek broke out in a smile and made an elaborate bow that melted her defenses.

"How do, Miss Moore?" He posed the question in halting English. Up close, he had a youthful, even a childlike, look.

"Very well … Spring Frog." She gave a little curtsy.

The men had selected a flat, sandy semicircle for their demonstration. Spring Frog divested of his coat, his common shirt rippling in the damp breeze off the river. Sam unburdened his accoutrements against a large boulder where he indicated she and George should sit. Susanna folded her hands in her lap, nervousness tightening her midriff, while George leaned forward with his elbows on his knees.

Sam drew the long knife from his belt, but Spring Frog countered by palming his tomahawk as he lowered into a crouch. Sam cocked his head, posing what must be the same question that erupted from Susanna's lips. "What are you doing?" She'd stood without even thinking.

The Natchez warrior replied in the language of the Creeks.

"He says he likes to get a sense of his opponent first." Sam sheathed his knife and tugged free the more lethal-looking weapon. "A demonstration of real fighting. No blades used." But his even tone and ready posture could not disguise the tension that had tightened every line of his body.

The men circled. Feinted. Spring Frog said something. Directions, Susanna hoped.

Sam went at him with the hawk raised in his right hand. With his left, the Natchez grabbed and hyper-extended Sam's arm, forcing his grip open while Spring Frog swung his weapon underneath, over Sam's shoulder, and into a hooking position around his neck. A spot of blood appeared against the tip of the blade. Susanna gasped, seizing George's hand. A sharp tug to Sam's arm and he hit the dirt.

When Sam planted his palms on the ground to rise, George shook off her grip. "Don't get your nose out of joint. They're just pretending, Susanna."

She kept telling herself that when Spring Frog went on the offensive. It did not look like he was playacting. He moved in on Sam with an aggressive speed that lit alarm in Sam's eyes. Sam leapt up, but his tomahawk slid across the clearing. He scuttled away, circled toward it, but Spring Frog charged again. When his weapon swiped forward, Sam blocked with his left and struck his opponent across the face with his right. Spring Frog's head snapped to the side. In that split second, Sam grabbed his forehead and crown and spun him around. A double knee-kick to the spine, so quick that George gave a yell, and the air huffed out of Spring Frog. He hardly needed Sam's shove to plant his face on the ground.

Sam lunged for his weapon, just the same.

At Susanna's feet—she had jumped up again, she didn't know when—Spring Frog raised his chin. His brows drew down as his fingers curled in the sand. Her heart pounded. He hadn't seen that coming. And he didn't like it. She backed away, edging past the boulder, fully expecting the man to jump up and plow into Sam's middle like an enraged bull.

But he spat a mouthful of grit and blood, and a grin wreathed his face. He drew himself to one knee and spoke again to Sam. His tone betrayed grudging respect.

Susanna let out her breath.

Sam glanced at her stance—frozen, yet tensed to flee. He nodded in her direction and answered. Both men broke into laughter, clasping hands in the middle of the circle.

George danced around them. "That was amazing!" He executed an awkward imitation of Sam's move. "Teach me how to do that."

"Later." Sam belted his tomahawk and reached for his long knife again. "Now, lest we scare your sister away, we should show her ways she can defend herself. We will show the steps slowly." Watching her closely, he raised his brows, as if seeking her permission to continue.

Her hand extended behind her, Susanna backed up and perched on the rock. Wetting her lips, she nodded.

"Lacking a man's strength, height, and length of arms and legs, a woman—or a boy—"—Sam tipped his head toward George—"will need to use other means. Surprise. Throwing your foe off-balance. Or whatever will inflict pain. For instance …"

Sam consulted with Spring Frog, and the man brandished his knife.

Sam narrated their actions step-by-step this time, often glancing over his shoulder to make sure she and George followed. "Use your left hand to grab his knife arm. With your own weapon, cut that arm as quickly as you can. More than once, if possible, while you extend and twist his arm. Don't stop. You have to make it hurt. Use that leverage to slip behind and place your weapon at his neck."

Susanna nodded again. She fought to keep her face impassive, to not show the unease the much more realistic images in her mind generated. Could she ever do as Sam suggested? If her life depended on it? She glanced at her half brother, who attended to the demonstration with none of her reservations. If George's life depended on it? Was this foolishness, when Father would send them home as soon as he recovered?

But home to what? To a house where Sam Hicks might never again walk through the door? To a marriage she did not want? No. If she could stay, she could show her father he did not need to secure a fine position for her in Tennessee. She was capable of choosing her own path—and her own match.

So she listened and watched with a raptness to match her half brother's, even when the frank descriptions and lurid movements caused her to shudder … or blush. She must not let modesty or squeamishness cause a hesitation that could cost her future.

Finally, Sam glanced at the horizon. The weakened, early December sun seemed ready to surrender its own fight for the day. "We better return. Your father will look for you when he leaves the tent of General Jackson."

"Yes." Susanna stood and brushed off the back of her skirt. "And my mother will wonder why I have not started dinner, much less finished the laundry."

How could she have failed to consider the potential trouble that could result from this detour? Her father had designated Sam as their guard, not their defense instructor. He would have an apoplexy if he knew his children had passed the latter part of the afternoon viewing a fight demonstration out by the river.

"Can we do this again?" George begged. "I want to practice all you showed me." No doubt, in his mind, the entire scenario had been created to train him as a Cherokee warrior.

Sam reassured him as he filled the water buckets and attached the yokes. "We will practice again, just as we will at the range. But now, we must help your sister with the chores, or we will all be in trouble."

Did he just wink at her? Susanna stifled a giggle when Spring Frog froze, gazing back toward camp. "What that?" He phrased the truncated question in Cherokee, which they could all understand.

They all straightened and stilled, attempting to listen over the gurgle of water as it rushed past multiple rocks and islands. Sure enough, a din rose from the Cherokee Regiment. Voices shouting, whooping, and shrieking.

"An invasion?" Scanning the tree line, Susanna grabbed her skirts. Her heart thundered like a war drum. There was but one way into the fort. Right past the disturbance.

Sam lifted his rifle over his shoulder but said, "No. No one stirs in the militia camp."

Spring Frog asked him a question, and he nodded, face grim.

"What is it, then?" George dragged his still-empty buckets by the yoke, but Sam motioned for him to leave them.

"We will come back for those. Let's just get you inside the fort." Sam pressed his hand on the back of Susanna's shoulder, urging her forward at his side. The rare touch testified of his concern. But why?

Locking his jaw, he didn't answer her questions all the way to the gate, and he attempted to hurry them inside. But George dragged his feet, looking back. Pots and kettles hung deserted over crackling fires in the Cherokee camp while the majority of the regiment gathered on the parade ground. Spectators from the Tennessee militia began to trickle over also.

"What are they doing?" her brother asked.

"Nothing that you need be part of."

Now that she knew an attack was not imminent, Susanna had her own questions. She placed her hands on her hips and faced

Sam, ready to order him back to the river. How did he expect her to get her laundry done without fresh water? And what if someone stole their buckets?

George strained on his tiptoes. "Is it a fighting match like you were just showing us?"

"No." Sam's voice turned raspy. "It's the scout we captured after Hillabee. General Jackson must have returned him to the Cherokee Regiment for justice. George, Susanna, please go inside." His eyes pleaded with them. He'd called her Susanna and didn't even seem to realize it.

A blood-curdling cry drew her attention to the parade ground.

The crowds parted, and one of the Cherokee warriors half led, half dragged a man into the opening by a rope around his neck. He was naked. And already scalped. The captor drew a knife, and the warriors did likewise, falling in on the prisoner, screaming and stabbing. Susanna turned her face away and shielded her brother's eyes as a heart-rending wailing erupted—the Creek women and children prisoners, forced to watch the execution.

This was not justice. This was not a pretend fight or even a fair fight. Here were the brutal struggles of the frontier that she wanted nothing of.

Taking George by the collar, she shoved him ahead of her into the fort. She didn't look back to see if the men followed. She ran to the cabin, dragged her brother inside, and bolted the latch.

"Susanna—"

With a chop of her hand, she cut off George's protest. "Hush. Just hush."

No words could do justice to what she had seen and what she now felt. Shaking, she collapsed on the bench and sat there with her head in her hands, waiting until full water buckets thudded on the ground outside. And then, she waited to open the door until she knew Sam was gone.

CHAPTER NINE

S am had never awaited a Monday *tsu-na-gi-lo-s-di i-ga*—wash day—with such impatience. How had Susanna avoided him for a whole week? She'd gone to volunteer in the hospital despite her father's protests—that was how. He knew because George had told him one of the two times he'd taken the boy to the practice range—without Susanna, of course.

His breath puffed on the cold, damp air—an empty sack symbolic of all the things he wanted to say but couldn't—as he knocked on the Moores' cabin door before dawn. He rubbed his gloved hands together until someone cracked the portal open. Mrs. Moore, her normally bright eyes shadowed in the sliver of light. Too many hours in the infirmary, and scant nutrition, same as them all.

"Good morning, Lieutenant Hicks. Susanna is making ready. Can you wait?"

Gladly, if he could only get in that walk to and from the river with her. Witness in her voice and gaze that she didn't find him disgusting. He wanted to explain … but how did one put such things into words? Any words—English? Cherokee?

The information Ross had recently shared with him—that the reason the Creek Indians at Hillabee had not fought back had been because those villages had reached a peace agreement with General Jackson—added to Sam's self-loathing. True, he hadn't known that then. Colonel Moore and General White hadn't known that. Whether General Cocke had or not was currently in debate—and might result in his court-martial. He'd used the Cherokee Regiment for his own intentions, ignoring Jackson's demand for reinforcements at Talladega. But in doing so, he'd made the Cherokees aggressors in a dishonorable action against the Creeks. Perhaps Susanna had even heard this truth from her father and it had strengthened her determination to avoid him.

"Yes ma'am. I'll be gathering the wood."

"Good, good. George can light the fire when he gets back. My husband sent him with a message to General Jackson."

Sam's heart leapt as Mrs. Moore shut the door. George would not walk with them to the river? This would be the first time he'd been alone with Susanna. Could he express how much he needed her understanding, her friendship, despite the savagery of their surroundings? He hadn't even known how much until she'd disappeared and he'd been left to a week of monotony. A week with his own thoughts, many of which he'd rather deny.

He pulled down the wide-brimmed, felt hat he preferred outdoors, especially in cold weather, and sought the woodshed, retrieving an armload of knotty fodder for a hot laundry fire. Sam stacked it where they boiled water in the main cauldron and returned for two more loads before the cabin door opened again and Susanna came out.

She wore her fitted, gray wool coat and the deer hide wrap over her head, a funny combination, but no different from the mishmash of Indian and European styles that everyone else favored on the frontier. Whatever best kept the weather off. And right now, a slight mist fell from the still-dark sky.

"I have a lantern." She held out the item. "Would you like to carry it?"

"Yes, I will." Gloved hands brushed, and he wanted to grab hold but never would dare. Lifting the light a smidge, Sam eyed her face. Paler than usual. "How are you?"

Her gaze skittered away from his. "Tolerable. Let's fetch the buckets and get this done."

So she could be rid of him faster? Little did she know, he planned to hang around and stoke that fire. He'd even scrub laundry if it offered a chance to restore their connection. She was looking at one desperate Cherokee. He'd like to blame the enlistment-up fever that had run rampant through the camps for the past couple weeks, but he knew it was more than that.

They fetched the buckets and yokes and set out. Susanna eyed the almost-empty enclosure, then the paltry campfires sprinkling the clearing around the fort. "Lots of men have left."

"Guess you've been so busy in the infirmary this past week you did not notice."

She shot Sam a brief sideways glance, as if she realized sarcasm came rare with him. He blamed his white roots when it did pop out. "Well, I noticed the day General Jackson had the cannon turned on a group of men trying to leave. Such a row, it was safer to be in the infirmary!"

"How did you get your father to agree?"

"My mother only lets me in one ward, which, shall we say, is more … modest?"

"I see." Did Dr. Hawkins frequent that ward? Bet he did now. Did he admire and laud Susanna for her services?

"So he had to let them go?"

"What?" Sam turned from his thoughts.

Susanna tripped on a small rock, but before he could catch her, she righted herself. "General Jackson. Did he let those men in the Tennessee militia leave?"

Holding the lantern higher, Sam nodded. "Had to. Three-month term was up. Same for the Cherokees. Many have already left, those who had new slaves to take home. It would have been safe at the practice range, Miss Moore. In truth." He walked a little closer to her, lowering his voice. "They would never hurt you."

He couldn't miss the shudder, though slight, that passed through her. She kept her focus on the ground as they picked their way toward the river—a faintly glimmering ribbon as the horizon lit behind it. "My father says he will dismiss the rest of the regiment this week. He says a few Cherokee volunteers will stay in the area, based at Fort Armstrong, while a skeleton force of Tennessee militia will remain here at Strother until Jackson can muster more troops to fight again early next year."

Sam agreed, nodding. "Most of the men are going home for needed food and rest."

"Will you?"

That was the question that had been plaguing him. "I don't know." He couldn't seem to decide until he knew what the Moore family would do. What did he want? To invite them to Fort Hill for Christmas. But never had a more ridiculous thought entered his mind. It was not on their way home, and he couldn't frame it as an alternative for provisioning when it was no closer than Hiwassee. "Is your father well enough to travel?"

"Polly thinks so. She's given him plasters and teas every night, and he's coughing considerably less." Susanna shivered and drew the collar of her coat up around her neck.

"Where will you go?"

She glanced at him, and her response twisted his heart. "There is no reason for us not to go home."

"You wanted so badly to stay."

"I did ..."

"But you no longer do?"

"I—I don't know." She tottered, as though the weight of the empty buckets became too heavy for her to bear.

Sam stopped, reached out to take her load before relieving his own. They were close enough to the river now. He'd do the rest. But first ... "Susanna, what you saw ... you know we are not all like that."

She shifted her shoulders, then gave them a light roll. "Of course not. Polly is not like that. George is not like that."

A woman and a child. "*I* am not like that."

Finally, she met his eyes. "You are a warrior in the Cherokee Regiment. Whatever happened at Hillabee, whatever happened with the Red Stick prisoner ..."

He drew a sharp breath. So she *had* heard about the massacre in which he'd unintentionally participated.

"I understand that means something different, and it is not for me to judge."

"No, it is for God to judge." Sam stepped closer, trying to control the intensity of his voice, his expression, but he wanted her to understand this so badly. "Some traditions are good. Some are not good. I ask God to help me choose."

As Susanna studied him, sweetness and sadness flooded her face with the gentle light from the east. He flinched in surprise when she reached for his hand. "That is not a job I would want. You are a very special person, Sam Hicks. If anyone can hear God on this subject, it would be you."

"Thank you ... Miss Moore."

"I liked it better when you called me Susanna." The murmured words fell away with her hand, almost lost in her turning. And something about her manner stole the awe that would have filled Sam had she said it differently. Because it was the type of admission one made in parting.

"Perhaps I could sit a moment before we go back." Hand extended, she eased onto a large rock. "The walk left me a bit winded."

He wanted to join her—sit next to her as the sun rose—and speak words that would ease this painful thudding of his heart, but she didn't invite him. Was it really going to end this way?

"You have worked too hard." Sam swooped up the first bucket and headed for the river.

"It's this damp and cold. Makes it hard to rest well. I don't know how you soldiers manage in your tents." As he returned for the next bucket, Susanna huddled into her coat. "I don't relish the idea of traveling home in this."

"You could stay a while at Turkey Town." Maybe he could accept a post at Armstrong, roughly half a day's ride from the village.

"I am sure we'll stop off there, but Polly has been talking about getting home to the little girls for Christmas. Father will want that even if he must remain at Armstrong. It's what he was discussing with General Jackson this morning." Susanna sighed, rising slowly. "Jackson is quite concerned about blankets."

"Ah, yes. For the remaining men. Ross says some may be available at his trading post."

"I suppose we will have to see what the next few days bring."

"I suppose so."

In a battle, one didn't have to wonder when to fight. Even surrender eventually became an obvious course of action. The war in Sam's heart was far more confusing.

He finished filling the buckets and hooked his up while Susanna knelt under her yoke. Took her a minute, but she soon established a steady if slow pace. Maybe it would be best for her to return to Big Springs Bluff. Selfish of him to want her to brighten this dismal winter of waiting when she could be not only safe but thriving at home. There was always the chance that if he resumed his position with Colonel Meigs after the war …

What was he thinking? This month, this moment, was all there would ever be. He would never be able to call on Susanna at Big Springs Bluff, and he could no more stand to watch Dr. Hawkins court her than—

Susanna gave a little cry, and the water buckets wobbled and splashed as her hand darted from the yoke to her side.

He hurried up next to her. "What is it?"

"Just a pulled muscle, I expect." But when she inhaled, she folded like a card table in a two-bit tavern. The buckets crashed to the ground.

Sam couldn't discard the weight he carried fast enough. "Susanna!" He pulled her upper body from the ground and encircled her with his arms.

She rested on her knees, her head lolling back against his shoulder. She tried dragging air in but stopped when her breath caught. "Hurts."

"Oh, dear God ..." That fragment was the only prayer he could compose as he cradled her sweet-smelling head against his cheek, his lips. Then he scooped her up and ran with her into the fort.

Sunlight slanting through the cracks in the chinking hurt her eyes. Everything hurt—arms, legs, head. Every breath. Susanna couldn't suck enough air in. When she tried, it never seemed to make it all the way to her lungs, and she coughed, which also hurt. Was this how her father had felt? How had he ever left his bed?

A long, square face with glowing green eyes bent over her. Dr. Hawkins. When he placed his hand to her forehead, she tried to turn away from his cold fingers. He spoke to someone behind him. "She's on fire." Then he patted her cheek to get her attention. Supposed to be a pat, but was more of a caress. "Susanna, how did this start?"

The mist, the breeze off the river, came back to her—and Sam's face, the agony of internal conflict he tried to hide. "I was so cold when I went to fetch ... the water." Getting her words out on tiny puffs of air felt like straining a gnat through cheesecloth. "And tired. Had to ... sit down. Rest." She'd wanted Sam to wrap his arms around her, hold her up and warm her, but what kind of scandalous desire was that? "The buckets felt so heavy. My side hurt."

She reached toward her ribcage, but her hand fell away. Exhausted.

"Don't try to speak. May I listen to your heart, your breathing?" Dr. Hawkins' face twisted with concern. And discomfort.

He mustn't be so afraid of offending her modesty that he failed to do his job. She gave a single nod, and he moved aside. Polly knelt in his place. Susanna closed her eyes as her stepmother gently unfastened her dress bodice and tugged apart her short, corded stays. Air permeated her thin chemise, and she shivered.

"Everything will be all right, *a-que-tsi a-ge-yu-tsa*." *My daughter.* Polly's murmur soothed her. "Dr. Hawkins and I together—God will help us make you well."

Her eyes were closed when a man's head rested on her chest. They flew open. Dr. Hawkins, listening. Smelling of oil and medicine, his hair tickling her chin. The intimate gesture felt odd but not as unsettling as she'd expected. She needed him. Needed his help.

Frowning, he sat back and quickly covered her with a blanket. Rummaging noises followed. "Ten grains Dover's powder. Linseed poultice ..."

Darkness tried to suck Susanna down. Sleep. She needed—

"This is my fault." Her father's voice rumbled, gravelly with guilt. "Letting her stay here when I was sick. Letting her help in that infirmary. Who will be next—my wife? My son?"

"No, Gideon," Polly protested, but Susanna couldn't rest until Father knew he mustn't blame himself.

She held her hand out, flexed it. "Father ..."

His rough fingers curled around hers. "Susanna. I knew you should not have come here."

She whispered through dry lips. "If we hadn't come, would you be this improved?" And would she ever have gotten to know Sam, the most complex and intriguing man she'd ever met?

"At your expense?"

"I will be fine." Susanna squeezed his hand. She had to be. Otherwise, he'd never relent until he'd installed her in a fine home somewhere far above the Indian boundary.

Nudging her father out of the way, Hawkins bent over her,

holding a small glass cup to her lips. "Drink this."

She raised her head enough to sip, then cough and choke on the bitter brew.

"Good girl." Dr. Hawkins gently wiped her chin with a handkerchief.

"Thank you." Too weak to be humiliated by her weakness, she rasped out her appreciation, and he answered with a soft smile.

"Now, go." Polly shooed the men from the cabin. "Both of you, so I can tend her."

Father pressed back into view, tucking something soft under her arm. "Sally's doll. I think you may have more need of her than I." He offered a wink and tried to look stoic with his low-hovering brows, but his chin wobbled.

"Lulu. Thank you." Susanna managed a reassuring smile before he edged from her side.

"I will return to check on her tonight." Dr. Hawkins' firm promise preceded the latching of the door.

Susanna allowed herself to drift as her stepmother scurried about the room. Polly whispered and murmured. Not incantations, but prayers passed her lips. Psalms that comforted Susanna.

She only woke when Polly applied a slick cloth to her left side. She tried to wiggle away from the wet, cool dressing, but her stepmother laid a hand on her shoulder.

"Lie still, *a-que-tsi a-ge-yu-tsa*." And she pressed a kiss onto her forehead.

Susanna's lips fluttered in a smile. "He did that too."

"What?"

"He was so tender with me ..." She would have sighed if she could have drawn in enough air. Her eyelids dropped down. So heavy.

"Dr. Hawkins? Yes, despite his shortcomings, he cares for you very much."

"Not Dr. Hawkins. Sam." She spoke his name as she fell asleep.

⁓

As Dr. Hawkins exited the Moores' cabin, Sam paused in tossing kindling atop the crackling fire while George stirred the pot of dirty linens with a big stick. The physician's frown deepened upon sight of them.

At the perusal, George turned away, muttering. "Might as well put me in a petticoat and tie ribbons in my hair."

But Sam knew Hawkins' disapproval focused on him, not the boy. He straightened and brushed off his hands. "Right now, this is as helpful as the role of any soldier."

"Because most of them have left."

Sam ignored George's plucky retort as he strode over to catch the doctor. "How is she?" When he attempted to touch his arm, Hawkins jerked back.

"Gravely ill with lung fever."

"Not the same thing her father had?"

George sidled closer, his ear turned toward the reply.

Hawkins shook his head. The deep lines appeared etched in his broad forehead. "Similar, but more acute. A cold on the chest such as Colonel Moore had can become serious, even life-threatening, but in Miss Moore's case, not only the mucous membrane but the lung itself—" He stopped, shifting his lanky weight away from Sam. "I fail to see how this is your concern. All you need to know is that Miss Moore will not be making any more *excursions* with you, now or in the foreseeable future."

Sam stiffened at the emphasis placed on "excursions," as though he and Susanna had been up to something disreputable. "My colonel will tell me what is and is not my concern."

"You should go home, like the rest of your people."

He shouldn't let Hawkins' attitude affect him. Only Susanna's health mattered. But the prejudice that slithered just below the surface, like the venomous cottonmouth in murky water, had always been the breed Sam most burned to seize and behead.

George intervened in what could have become a very unpleasant exchange. "Will she be all right, Dr. Hawkins?" His unguarded fear diffused Sam's ire in an instant.

The doctor, too, seemed to relax, his shoulders slumping. "The next few days will tell, George. If the fever breaks …" His voice caught, another reminder that the man set his affections on Susanna.

Would the increased time at her bedside, his tender medical care, worm a way into her heart?

Was Sam still here? Or had he and the rest of the fort's occupants left them alone in this wilderness?

Susanna sat up against a rolled blanket on the hospital cot Dr. Hawkins had procured for her the first evening of her sickness. How long ago? A week? She wanted to ask her stepmother about these things as Polly wrapped Susanna's fingers around a cup of her wild cherry and white pine tea, but she daren't. She had already given away enough of her feelings to the wise woman. And no doubt those revelations winged their way straight into her father's ear.

The hot liquid made her cough, and she held her handkerchief to her mouth, then peeked at it. Thank goodness, not the red-brown stuff she'd been expectorating during the first few days of her illness. Had anyone tended her but the best with English and Cherokee medicine combined, she'd not likely have lived to see today.

If nothing else, her admiration for the doctor's professional aptitude had risen.

The door opened, and George's hopeful face peered inside. "Is she well enough for me to come in?" Father had banished him to a nearby tent for the duration of her illness, but judging from the healthy glow on his cheeks and the sparkle in his eyes, he counted it quite the adventure. Susanna's heart surged at the prospect of hearing all about it.

Leaning the hearth broom against the wall, Polly propped a hand on her hip. "I suppose. I need to see Dr. Hawkins for one more dose of Dover's powder. You can sit with her while I go to the infirmary." She frowned as George entered bearing several branches of scraggly, yellow blooms drooping from crimson central buds. "Witch hazel? I don't need witch hazel. Susanna has no more fever and no sore throat."

"But are they not pretty?" George held up the tin cup that supported the branches.

Polly grunted, then pointed to the table. "You can set them over there."

"Yes, Mama."

After Polly left, George grinned and dragged the stump seat over next to Susanna's cot. "I just let her think those were for her. They're really for you."

"Oh, George, that was so sweet of you."

"Not from me." Leaning back in faint offense, he frowned. "From Sam."

"He's still here?" Her hand snaked out of its own accord and hooked around her half brother's skinny wrist.

He shook her off. "Of course, he's still here. Who do you think I've been staying with all this time, freezing out in the cold with no fire at night?" He assumed a tragic expression.

"Oh, George." A glance at the witch hazel, the only thing blooming this time of year, filled her with a tenderness that she didn't mind if her brother mistook for pity over his martyrdom. She knew better, anyway.

"Haven't you heard him pacing outside the cabin? Pleading for updates every hour?" When Susanna opened her mouth in astonishment, George wobbled his wind-tousled head from side to side. "Well, maybe not that often because I keep him pretty busy. Throwing knives and tomahawks. Target shooting our rifles. Wrestling. He even showed me some tracking skills." His dark eyes brightened.

"Father let him stay for you?" That was good. Perhaps he didn't suspect after all about the slow but undeniable connection growing between his daughter and his first lieutenant.

George nodded, trying to balance while tipping the stump on edge. She feared he'd topple backward and take her cot with him. "Father gave a rousing speech a couple days ago when he disbanded the regiment. He said, 'Not fifty days will pass before your swords, lances, and knives drink the blood of your enemy.' Was that not inspiring?"

"Disturbing, more like, but about Lieutenant Hicks …" Susanna sat forward, tucking her blanket around her chest.

"After the speech, Sam asked permission to stay and escort us back to Turkey Town when you get strong enough. Some of the men are remaining at Fort Armstrong, so I guess he'll go there after that."

Not too far from the village. And Polly had said she'd sent a message ahead to Walani to expect them within the fortnight. Susanna had turned the corner, but she would need to gather her strength at Turkey Town for some time before completing the journey home. In Turkey Town, Polly said, she would have the milk and eggs needful to fortify her constitution.

Susanna's toes tingled, hankering to touch the floor, to dance. Silly, when she could hardly stand.

"Please thank Sam—Lieutenant Hicks—for me. For everything."

George shrugged. "I told him how you kept grumbling about being cooped up inside. He said you might not could come out, but he could send some outside in. Oh, and here." He dug in his pocket and extended a rumpled scrap of paper. "This was from him too."

Her chest ached, protesting the increased rhythm of her heart. "Thank you." Breathless, she took the note and stared at him.

George stared back. "Do you want me to leave or something?"

Yes. No. She wanted to ask him everything about what he and Sam had been doing and what Sam said about her, but she wanted to read that note even more. At the same time, she feared it. Would its contents disappoint her—or plunge them into so fierce a wilderness that even a seasoned scout like Sam would be ill-equipped to help her navigate?

George tilted on his stump again, folding his fingers over his flat belly. "I already know what it says."

"What?" Susanna gasped, her mouth falling open.

"Had to sit and wait while he wrote it out. Some poet he'd memorized from home. Doesn't make a lick of sense to me."

She flipped the page open and scanned Sam's cramped script with eyes so eager they hurt. Or maybe that was just one of the lingering effects of her illness.

> For thou art with me here upon the banks
> Of this fair river; thou my dearest Friend,
> My dear, dear Friend; and in thy voice I catch
> The language of my former heart, and read
> My former pleasures in the shooting lights
> Of thy wild eyes. Oh! Yet a little while
> May I behold in thee what I was once,
> My dear, dear Sister! And this prayer I make,
> Knowing that Nature never did betray
> The heart that loved her.

Scholar Sam. He'd chosen the lines of William Wordsworth to show her he was stronger than the warrior.

Susanna clasped the page against her chest and closed her eyes. "Tell him it makes perfect sense to me."

CHAPTER TEN

Sam shifted on his stallion alongside the other three Cherokees who'd ride with them to Turkey Town—men he trusted and whom he'd asked to delay departure to Fort Armstrong for this purpose. Colonel Moore had waited for the weather to clear—several days now since George told Sam that Susanna had been happy about "that silly poem" he'd sent—before loading his family and their supplies on a caravan of horses and mules. The route was not conducive to a wagon. They'd debated long and hard about the use of a litter for Susanna. Eventually, they'd decided the bouncing entailed in that mode of conveyance would be worse than sitting astride a horse.

Finally, the cabin door opened, and Dr. Hawkins supported Susanna to the mount she would share with her stepmother. Even the coat and blanket wrapping her did not add much bulk to her spare frame. Could she withstand travel at all?

Crossing the parade ground once they'd ridden from the fort, Sam edged his stallion close to the mare bearing Mrs. Moore and Susanna. George trailed them on his gelding, slender form erect, his rifle slung around the back of his woven coat.

"Good morning." Susanna's dark eyes shone from beneath her head wrap … a much warmer greeting than the last time he'd seen her. George must've spoken the truth.

That gave him courage now, but had she thought the poetry that spoke of a dear friend, a sister, assuming? Such addresses had been far safer than romantic ones, the warmest ones allowed. Warm enough that he hoped she hadn't shown the poem to anyone. But he had wanted her to know, in case anything happened …

Sam swallowed past the lump in his throat. "It is good to see you out, Miss Moore."

Good to see her at all. Concentrating on anything had proven almost impossible until George had brought news that Susanna's fever had broken. After that, not only relief that she would recover had flooded him, but relief that the recovery itself would keep her near longer. Then came the guilt for desiring such a thing.

How could one girl plunge him into this unwelcome muddle?

"It is good to be out. I am ready for an adventure today." With a cheery smile, she attempted to sit up straight in the saddle, but her stepmother's stiffened arms clearly braced Susanna more than they guided the horse.

Sam's heart lurched with concern for her. It was warmer today, but still … "I hope not too much of an adventure."

"Me as well, Lieutenant Hicks." Mrs. Moore's concern showed as she pressed her lips together. George had told Sam it would have been her choice to remain at Strother for several more days, but dwindling supplies had swayed her in favor of making the day's ride sooner.

"If you ladies don't mind, I'll take point now. The colonel and doctor have agreed to ride in the rear." Sam nudged his stallion around them so he could lead on the trail. "Please call out if you need me."

George rose up in his stirrups. "I'll go with you."

"I would feel better if you stayed close to your mother and sister." Maybe the boy could catch Susanna if she started to fall off her horse.

George took the request as a rejection, of course. He poked out his lips and tugged down the brim of his hat.

Gesturing for one of his comrades to join him, Sam encouraged his mount to gallop. He wanted to reconnoiter the forest ahead of the party. The small mountain to their right descended into rolling terrain thick with hardwoods, pines, and craggy boulders, plenty of good places for enemies to hide, though he didn't expect it. This area was held firmly by the American forces and their allies.

They scouted to Canoe Creek before doubling back.

"Any ambushes ahead, Lieutenant?" Susanna attempted to joke with him as he approached, but her spine no longer held straight. Already, she became tired? And Mrs. Moore strained to see around her stepdaughter, for the women were roughly the same size.

"All clear." Sam gestured to George, who'd refused to look at him when he'd ridden up. "Join me now?"

A flash of interest was quickly concealed, and the boy tapped his heels into his gelding's sides. A few minutes later, he interrupted Sam's attempt to identify birdcalls with a sullen statement. "You know, I'm not a child."

"I do know that, but you are the colonel's only son. His heir. He would give anything to protect you and your sister, and that job falls to me right now." When George sat up straighter in the saddle, Sam smiled. "And I cannot be there all the time for your sister like you can. I rely on you to help me keep an eye on her."

"I know." A smug smile tugged at George's thin lips. "You're sweet on her."

The observation smote Sam's chest with a thud as pronounced as if George had thrown his boot. A hasty protest would only make him appear the fool. Best to stick to the friend-sister stance. "Miss Moore is a special person. She laughs when others complain. I have grown fond of her, as I have of you. But the only connection I hope for from both of you is your friendship."

George shifted in his saddle, one eyebrow arching as that bedeviling grin teased his mouth. "Uh-huh. Whatever you say."

The little stinker. Sam just shook his head.

Minutes later, the knowing look cemented on the boy's face when Sam offered to take Susanna onto his stallion. She swayed so at the creek crossing that he feared she'd slide off into the water.

At his request, Mrs. Moore's eyes widened, then her shoulders dropped. Sam's heartbeat hitched while he awaited her answer.

"I admit, I struggle to support her. But …" She glanced behind at the men catching up.

"Your husband is a large man, and the doctor's mount is laden with medical supplies. I can keep Miss Moore secure." Question was, could he keep his own emotions secure? And how did she feel about riding with him? Sam swung his gaze to Susanna, who watched him, unblinking, her cheeks the color of a holly berry. "Will you ride with me, Miss Moore?"

A nod was all she gave him, but it was all he needed. He edged his mount close to theirs, twisted his reins under his saddle, and held out his arms. Susanna leaned toward him. He caught her under the arms, and she gave a cry of fright as he pulled until she landed sidesaddle on his stallion. He didn't miss Mrs. Moore's frown when he wrapped his arms around her stepdaughter. And no wonder. The curves of her womanly figure, her fast-beating heart, smote him with far more awareness than he'd anticipated. He'd never held a woman this close. He hadn't wanted to until he'd met one he'd consider taking to wife.

"Good?" he murmured against the back of her head. When she nodded, he pinched up a bit of fabric on the left side of her skirt. "See if you can swing this leg over now."

She gave a muffled laugh. "Well, at least you'll have less view of my ankles from up here than from the side."

Sam rumbled a chuckle. "I wasn't looking at your ankles." He might have. Once. Not much to see but striped wool stockings, though.

"Oh, brother." George rolled his eyes. "Are you going to lead us across the creek, or should I?"

"We're going." Especially since Colonel Moore and Dr. Hawkins both pulled up on their stallions, their scowls fierce enough to scald the hair from Sam's head.

Mrs. Moore straightened in her saddle, securing her reins as she pivoted to face the colonel. "I needed help, husband. I was not strong enough to hold onto our daughter in her weak state. She will rest better against Lieutenant Hicks."

He gave a brief nod, but Dr. Hawkins looked as if he might come off his horse. Or throw his medical chest in Canoe Creek and seize Susanna from Sam's clutches and gallop away. It would seem that the diminished restraints of the frontier and his lack of progress with Susanna were evoking some deeper emotions in the poor man.

He'd hoped the physician might remain at Strother, but Hawkins seemed to have pledged his services to Colonel Moore and his regiment.

As for Mrs. Moore, Sam had no idea why she took up for him—except for the fact that she shared his native blood—but she deserved the status of a Cherokee Blessed Woman. He waited only for a terse nod from Colonel Moore before he set out, splashing across the creek. Was he mistaken, or was Susanna chuckling?

"Are you all right?" he asked when they cleared the other side.

Rather than addressing the men's ire, she allowed her shoulders to relax. "Yes. You do provide a more solid frame than Polly. I was afraid I would squash her."

"You won't squash me. You can lean into me." Sam's heart pounded as Susanna's back contacted his chest. The exhilaration of having her close topped racing across the darkened land on an errand with the Lighthorse. He slid a forearm around her waist. "Is this all right?"

Again, she nodded, the sweetest permission he could hope for. Well, not quite.

"Are you glad to leave Strother for Turkey Town?"

"Polly thinks I will be much more comfortable there. Her sister has a two-room cabin and will be much better supplied. I am fond of my cousin, Nokassa." Susanna darted a smile over her shoulder, making Sam's breath hitch. "'Tis her clothes I'm wearing.

We swapped dresses for the time I'd be away. Of course, I brought another old dress with me, too, but she looked so pretty in my royal blue gown."

Not near as pretty as Susanna had, he'd reckon.

"I'm sorry. I'm chattering."

"You can chatter all you want." Her airy voice wafted among the pines, instilling a warmth that felt like hope in Sam's chest and leaving him free to enjoy her closeness. He wanted to tighten his arm around her but had no call to.

"What will you do once we get there?"

"I will ride with my men to Fort Armstrong. Then I will see what your father requires of me. I may make a brief trip to my parents' home if I am free."

"For Christmas? Oh, I had thought you might come have a meal with us that day." Unmistakable disappointment laced Susanna's statement.

Sam drew in a quick breath at the wonder of it. "I would be delighted—if I am able."

"Of course, you must do whatever Father requires." Susanna adjusted her skirt to better cover her leg, her tone now almost apologetic. Embarrassed. "And of course, you would like to see your family if possible. And so you should."

"I wish that you could meet them." The admission tumbled out of Sam of its own accord.

She turned her cheek toward him a fraction. "So do I. In all the time at Strother, there was never an occasion for introduction to your father, though I understand he was there for a while. He sounds like a fascinating man. So he has gone to Fort Hill?"

"For now. He will return." Father would love Susanna, but he would be the first to warn his son not to misplace his affections. To do nothing to incur the wrath of the white colonel.

"'Tis a peaceful day, not overly windy." Susanna folded down her deerskin wrap. "I want to feel the sun on my head and see the forest around us. I feel starved for the sight of it."

Sam grunted a laugh—more than anything, an attempt to ignore the scent of her dark hair, wound into a braid at the back of her neck that made her seem far too like a Cherokee maiden. "I fear winter is upon us. You may find there is not much to admire."

"Oh, but there is. I love autumn's beautiful colors, but when the foliage falls away, you can see everything. Nature gives away her secrets."

He quickened with surprise and the excitement of shared understanding. "Yes. Every swell of the land, every rock and boulder. The ferns and winter berries. The nests in the trees." Sam pointed out a squirrel's brushy home in a branch high above them.

Susanna twisted to look at him. He discovered tiny hazel flecks near her pupils. How had he not seen those before? "Did you know you were just speaking in Cherokee?"

"I was? I suppose I was." Sam laughed. "Did you understand me?"

She nodded, smiling. "Most of it. I knew from your poem we shared a love of nature." Before he could defend or explain that, she stretched an arm toward the forest, wiggling her fingers. "I love the way the light hits the bare branches. The moss and the different shades of bark. Isn't it beautiful?"

"I think so. I am glad you do too. Most people do not find beauty in simplicity."

"The winter forest has always seemed magical to me, like an elven wood."

"Elven?" Sam tried out the unfamiliar English word.

"Elves. Magical beings from … mythology. Kind of like your Little People."

"*Yv-wi-tsu-na-s-ti-ga.*"

Susanna repeated the Cherokee name. He corrected her slight lapse, offering the term more slowly, and then she got it right. She fell silent, the squeak of leather and the snorting and plodding of horses the only sounds. Finally, she spoke again. "The poem …"

"Yes?"

"You truly had that memorized?"

"I told you my father owned many books."

"But poetry. Wordsworth." Wonder suffused her musing.

"I like a good rhyme. My mind is such that it sticks in my head. Scripture requires me to labor a bit harder, but I try to commit a verse to memory each week." Sam tapped his bandolier bag where he kept his Testament. Susanna glanced back with such a flash of joy on her face that he hurried on. "I thought of that particular poem because we had been at the river together, and I could tell how much joy nature brought you."

Another nod of her dark head. "I never wish to be closed up in a house in town somewhere. But I wondered … did you intend some personal meaning from that one part—'I behold in thee what I was once'?"

Sam drew in then released a deep breath. It would be easiest to let her think the lines had meant nothing to him other than a nice poem to cheer her up. But if she was really his friend, he owed her honesty. "The way you look at the land, at life, reminds me of the way I once did."

"Once?" She quirked her chin.

"When I was a boy. When I believed education would enlighten my people and diplomacy would let us keep our home."

"You don't believe that anymore? You think you have to fight this war to keep it?"

"I only hope fighting it will be enough." And that was all Sam wanted to say on the subject. He had no wish to spoil this bright day with the memories and fears that woke him from sleep most nights. But he did tighten his arm around her now. "Do not lose your hope, Miss Moore. It is a priceless thing."

"Susanna … when we are alone." On her waist, she placed her hand over his, and the sweetest ache exploded in his chest.

He must not entertain this feeling. Mind over emotion. Military duty over personal desire. Feelings weren't important. Only actions, decisions. His choices led in one direction—away from Susanna Moore.

Then she relaxed against him, her head under his chin, and all logic fled. What took over was the sixth sense he'd admired in her. And the sense was telling him of rightness and completion.

Just as dusk-time welcome lights shone from the cabins of the Cherokee village ahead and the tang of cook fires fragranced the air, Colonel Moore and Dr. Hawkins blocked Sam's path. Susanna's father dismounted, handing his reins to George, then approaching Sam.

He narrowed his eyes as he looked up. "Before joining my family at Turkey Town, I will ride with you and your men on to Fort Armstrong. We will lay plans with Adjutant Ross and the officers there for the furlough time."

Sam's heart sank. He'd anticipated that they'd all stay the night in the village and continue to the fort in the morning. He wasn't ready for this parting. Somewhere along the way, he seemed to have absorbed Susanna's sweet warmth into his own. "Yes sir." He shifted her weight against him.

"I will take my daughter now and hand her up with the doctor. He will help my family settle before joining us at the fort."

A sigh escaped Susanna, and she nestled her cheek into Sam's shoulder, effectively ripping out his heart. "She has fallen asleep."

Rather than soliciting tenderness, Susanna's vulnerability—as displayed to a Cherokee lieutenant—evoked a brusque response from her father. "Well, wake her." The colonel stepped forward and shook his daughter's moccasined ankle.

Susanna jerked, giving a little gasp.

Sam had wrapped both of her arms under his own to keep them

from dangling at her sides. He spoke to her in a murmur, as gentle as he could make it without incurring the wrath of her parent. "We are here." He waited until she looked around, blinking sleepily. "Your father wishes you to cross the river with Dr. Hawkins while he and I continue to the fort."

"Oh. Very well." Her voice sounded thick. With sleep or emotion?

Sam dared not hope for the latter. He cupped his hand over hers. "Can you swing your leg over the side? I will lower you to him."

"Yes." She struggled against her binding skirts to comply, then swiveled in the saddle to regard him, meeting his eyes squarely. "I thank you."

Would she have said more if she could have?

Expressing even a portion of his pleasure at having aided her in such a wondrous way might result in Colonel Moore tearing him down from his stallion and planting a fist in his face. So Sam merely gave a nod. He didn't trust himself to speak. And he didn't trust himself, after he eased Susanna to the ground, to watch her father hand her up to that grim-faced doctor who looked as though he'd just gotten his prized laying hen back from a thief. No, not for a second.

With a wave to George and Mrs. Moore, Sam wheeled his stallion away and headed up the path to the fort.

CHAPTER ELEVEN

Three days after their arrival at Turkey Town, Christmas Day, in fact, the flame of the fat-pine-knot lamp didn't even flicker as the wind gusted outside Walani's cabin. The sleeping chamber remained toasty with its dyed cane wall hangings and floor coverings under the deerskin rug. Yet Susanna felt far from comfortable— because she sat perched on the edge of her bunk, alone with Dr. Hawkins, who leaned forward on his stool. Too far forward and close to her, rummaging in his medicinal chest. Even though Polly and Walani prepared dinner in the next room and the door was open, Susanna shifted away.

"I want to leave some syrup of ipecac with you. Take a quarter teaspoon if coughing delays you falling asleep at night."

She nodded. Anything to curtail the private conference the doctor had requested when he'd arrived at Turkey Town today ahead of her father. She strained inside—and barely refrained her muscles from straining—to return to the main room. He proclaimed concern over her health, of course, but the way he'd been looking at her ever since he got here …

Polly appeared in the doorway, a rag in her hand and a frown on her face. "My wild cherry tea is working just fine."

Susanna stifled a smile. Bless her sharp ears and her defense of her herbal cures. "I suppose we can keep the ipecac for now, just in case." Having offered that compromise for Dr. Hawkins' placation, she gave her stepmother a wink before he straightened enough to notice. "Do you need help with the stew?" And that she said although she knew very well that Nokassa had already prepared the venison hindquarter her newly declared suitor, Culsowee, had left outside the door that morning.

Susanna scooted forward to stand. The straw they'd garnered at the village to refresh their ticks—so much superior to pine needles—rustled under her.

Polly hesitated, picking up on Susanna's unspoken plea. "Stew and cornbread are ready, but you could parch the chestnuts for coffee. We will have some with my special treat tonight. A Christmas surprise." Her rounded face brightened with the joy of a secret.

A secret that was beginning to give itself away in a delicious aroma. Susanna's eyebrows shot up. "Did you make a cake from the dried apples?"

Polly clasped her hands together. "You must wait and see."

"Speaking of Christmas ..." Dr. Hawkins touched the folds of Susanna's skirt, then aimed an apologetic glance at Polly. "May I have one more moment with Miss Moore?"

Polly's brows drew down, but she turned from the doorframe.

Dr. Hawkins placed the vial of ipecac in Susanna's hand, then, still clasping her fingers, reached into his coat and withdrew a small deerskin pouch. She tried to tug away, but he held on, his green eyes bright.

"Miss Moore, at Fort Strother, tending to the sick and wounded naturally monopolized my time—time I wished to have divided more evenly. Had I been more attentive, you might not have—"

"Please, Dr. Hawkins." Susanna succeeded in freeing her hand. "My illness can hardly be laid at your feet."

"Nevertheless, both your father and I feel responsible. We should not have allowed you to come to Indian Territory, much less abandoned you to uncivilized company and pursuits at the fort."

Uncivilized? Surely, he did not speak of Sam Hicks, a man probably more widely read and traveled than he. Susanna's spine stiffened. "What did you expect me to do while in residence, Dr. Hawkins? Labor only in that tiny cabin as the camp cook, shut away from daylight?"

"Of course not. But I should not have allowed you to assist in the dispensary."

"It was not up to you to allow or refuse." She planted her moccasins on the ground and rose, chin lifted.

He stood, too, angling his body across her route of escape. "Miss Moore—Susanna, I realize you remain under your father's care and that he has given permission for me to court you, but I hope you will allow it. I would like to continue to call on you, not only as your physician but as your … friend." He hung his hatless, sandy head. "I realize, I must not seem much of a prize to you. I am not deserving of your attention or affection, but I hope you might consider the future. We will only remain here for a short time. After that, things will go back to normal."

Susanna gazed past him. "Will they?" How could they, when the past three nights since her abrupt parting from Sam, she'd dreamed she still rode in front of him on his stallion, the smooth, loping gait melding her body into his? Felt the strength of his arms around her and heard again the soft Cherokee words he'd surely spoken in reality as she'd dozed? What had those words meant? She'd already wondered a hundred times.

"A new normal, I pray. A better one. Susanna, I am very fond of you. Please accept this gift as a token of my admiration." He extended the pouch.

She shook her head. "I require no gift, Dr. Hawkins." She placed a bit of emphasis on his name. Perhaps he would get the hint that he'd taken a liberty with hers.

"Please. Let us remind ourselves tonight that even in this foreign and hostile land, we celebrate Christmas."

"I have nothing in return."

"I require nothing in return." He took her hand again and pressed the small, soft bag onto her upturned palm. His eyes locked on hers. "No promise. No understanding. Not even a hope. Just the acceptance of a Christmas gift, to honor our Savior's birth."

Susanna released the breath she'd been holding and tugged open the drawstring. She turned the pouch and drew out the item inside—a sparkling, long necklace of multicolored glass beads strung together with silk thread. "Oh my."

"I saw you admiring your cousin's the day of our arrival, so I commissioned Walani to make this for you. It will look lovely with your dress."

Her chest squeezed, and not from shortness of breath this time. She couldn't accept this. She couldn't. It would only encourage the doctor, no matter what he said. But if her own stepaunt had made it for her, how could she refuse? And she did so want this beautiful token of her stepmother's people to keep with her always.

Susanna strung the beads around her neck and positioned the end to hang just below the curve of her breast, a stunning juxtaposition to the solid blue material of the gown Nokassa had returned for the holiday dinner with her family.

The broad smile of Dr. Hawkins belonged to a man with a fresh joy in life. "Thank you," he whispered.

"No, thank you. But please know, I still think this is too lavish a gift. I accept it because Walani made it." As he'd no doubt known she would.

Dr. Hawkins bowed his head in humble acknowledgment, then closed and hefted his medical chest. He followed her to the door. "I am pleased with the progress of your recovery, but I cannot state strongly enough how vital it is that you rest and partake of as much dairy as your stepmother can procure." He raised his voice to carry to the women at the hearth. "And a little brandy every now and then would not hurt either."

Polly straightened, placing a fist on her hip. "And you are always scolding my husband for the same."

Dr. Hawkins grinned, lightly touching Susanna's back. "Yes, but the two conditions differ. And I doubt Miss Moore will become a tippler. Oh, I think I made a rhyme."

Indeed, levity from this unexpected source took Susanna off guard, and she giggled.

They were all still laughing when Nokassa burst through the door, eyes bright and cheeks flushed, followed by two tall forms. "Look who I find at the square."

Susanna's heart stuttered. "Father!" Him, she'd expected. He'd assured them he'd come from Fort Armstrong for Christmas dinner. But for the presence of Sam Hicks, she'd only hoped. His eyes met hers as he ducked through the door, removing his felt hat and holding it against his chest. The chest she'd leaned into for precious hours she couldn't forget.

She wanted to run to him but had to content herself with a smile—which he returned. So brightly that Nokassa's gaze swung between the two of them before fixing on the glittering beads at Susanna's neck.

Polly greeted Susanna's father, and Nokassa hurried over. "It looks beautiful," she said in English as she fingered the jewelry. Then in Cherokee, in a whisper, "I am not the only one with a suitor. And you have two."

Susanna's face flamed, her gaze skittering to Sam. Dr. Hawkins would probably not understand, but had Sam heard? He watched her intently, taking in the necklace and the man beside her still standing in the doorway of the inner room.

She sought to subvert the focus on herself by murmuring a question to Nokassa. "How was it?" Her cousin had met Culsowee for a walk around the meeting house after she'd offered him a bowl of stew, her official acceptance of his offer of courtship as expressed by the gift of venison. Of course, Bold Hunter had been on duty outside the meeting house, able to keep a watchful eye on his daughter.

Eyes rounded, Nokassa nodded and clasped Susanna's hand, but Dr. Hawkins responded aloud to her praise of the necklace. "I agree, it turned out beautifully. I thought it a perfect Christmas gift to help Miss Moore always recall her time here."

As the doctor's confident statement echoed off the walls, Susanna wished she could crawl under the rug. Her father beamed and came forward to hug her and clap Dr. Hawkins on the back as if he hadn't seen him earlier that same day. Nokassa stepped aside with a knowing glance. Polly covered a loaf pan she removed from the coals, her lips drawn tight. And Sam stared at the doctor. Unlike a white man who might glare, his expression gave nothing away. But when he divested himself of his accoutrements and took a seat at the table without another glance at Susanna, her heart shriveled inside.

Walani shook her head with a sigh and protested in her native language. "I still don't understand all the fuss over the birth of a baby a long time ago. But the stew is ready, and we are happy to help eat your cake."

Eager to have something to do, Susanna rushed to slice the bean bread while Nokassa gathered the wooden bowls.

Polly laughed, placing a finger over her lips and continuing the conversation in Cherokee. "Shhh! Do not ruin my surprise." She slanted a smile at her husband, whose broad shoulders took up most of the bench opposite Sam, before turning back to her sister. "Remember what I told you about Jesus being the son of God-the-Great-Spirit?"

Walani gave her head a firm shake. "Great Spirit has no son, only sun and moon."

Polly tapped her index finger on the table. "But sun and moon were created by God and do not deserve worship like He does."

Susanna hated to interrupt the most appropriate and important telling of the Christmas story she'd ever witnessed, but … "Where are George and Bold Hunter? We cannot serve the stew until they arrive." Swiveling toward her stepmother, she held an empty bowl in her hand.

Adjusting the roaster containing the chestnuts over the fire, Walani straightened as she again answered in Cherokee. "Bold Hunter should have returned from the council house by now. And George ..."

"We saw him playing *chung-ke* with a group of boys when we rode in." Susanna's father frowned. "We also bade him follow us. I will fetch him, and he will be sorry for dallying."

He made to rise, but Sam put his hand out and slid back his bench. "Allow me to go, Colonel. Please, remain with your family." And his gaze swept Polly, Susanna, and Dr. Hawkins with a cool reserve that chilled Susanna's bones.

Sam only masked the angry restlessness brewing inside by stalking from the cabin of Polly Moore's relatives. He'd been so eager to see Susanna again, and for what? To find her in private conference with the doctor—laughing—accepting personal gifts. And her cousin's comment had indicated that Hawkins had resumed his attentions to Susanna. Well, what had he expected when, after only joining the men at Armstrong for a day and a half, the man had insisted on riding ahead to pay a medical call to Miss Moore?

Medical call, indeed.

To contain the influx of National Creek refugees, Turkey Town swelled with the construction of new cabins. But Sam headed toward the central plaza, which contained a ball field and the seven-sided, raised winter council house built to accommodate representatives of the seven clans. Sure enough, a group of boys eked another few minutes of play from the dwindling light, throwing sticks to hit a five-inch, concave chung-ke stone they rolled down a makeshift ramp.

Pretending to watch, he paused to calm himself. What had he expected? That Susanna would run to him? Tell him she was so glad he'd accepted her family's invitation to Christmas dinner? There had been no opportunity for such an expression of pleasure. And indeed, any type of emotional display would have drawn comment if not censure.

But what his mind knew his heart struggled to accept. He *wanted* the right to claim an attachment to her, the attachment he already felt. And her father was not helping him put it aside by asking Sam to remain in the area. He'd agreed so long as Moore's family felt comfortable with the plan, although he'd been fairly confident Susanna would agree. How would the colonel react if Sam told him he'd decided to go home over the furlough instead?

"George." Slapping his hat against his thigh, Sam ground out the name with impatience directed more at himself than at the boy. "George Moore."

The scrawny youngster stopped and straightened. Sam expected his face to fall in protest, but instead, it lit up. "Lieutenant Hicks!"

"Your family expects you for dinner. Come."

With waves to his new friends, the colonel's son trotted over to Sam, much like an obedient puppy. "All right. We can go."

He didn't deserve the boy's devotion. "First, help me find your uncle."

"Bold Hunter? He's in the council house. Been there all afternoon."

Sam frowned at the trail of smoke coming from the single opening—besides the door—of the shake-roofed, log building. "Why?"

George shook his head. "Some kind of trouble. Some of the best warriors of the *a-ni-wa-ya* are meeting."

Well, Sam was Wolf Clan too. He set his hat on his head and strode forward. "Come on."

"Into the council house?" George's voice cracked with awe.

"Yes, but be silent." Likely, whatever concerned the Turkey Town warriors concerned him and the Cherokee Regiment as well.

He slid sideways through the narrow opening and was

immediately plunged into darkness. He moved slowly, drawing George behind him by the arm until their eyes could adjust. Horizontal logs provided graduated seating against the seven walls with tapestries hung for each clan. Uncertain of what type of welcome they would receive, he focused on the buckskin- and woolen-clad warriors clustered in the heavy smoke. The group faced the fire of seven woods burning in the central clay altar.

A tall man stood and lowered his pipe. "From the way my nephew hangs on you, you must be Sam Hicks, the lieutenant to Moore. Come. We have need to speak with you."

"An intruder? Are you certain?" Colonel Moore's bristly brows descended as he frowned over the table at Sam and Bold Hunter.

Sam's host paused with his spoon held over his bowl, chunks of venison steaming in the firelight. Bold Hunter was a massive warrior in the style of the previous century who made Sam feel like a mission school student again. Good thing they were on the same side. "The guard saw a form in the shadows of the woods nearest Path Killer's lodge. He lost him when he gave chase, but we later followed tracks to the river."

"Could have been anyone." Colonel Moore grunted.

"Not in those wee hours."

Sam looked up from crumbling bean bread over his stew. "The warriors guarding the principal chief believe someone was spying out his residence with plans to return."

He sensed Susanna's gaze on him but tucked into his dinner rather than acknowledging her. He also did his best to ignore the doctor, which wasn't hard since the conversation in Cherokee prevented most of the physician's understanding. However, the man seemed content to merely sit beside Susanna, occasionally gracing her with a tender smile and bending to pick up her handkerchief when she dropped it.

George piped up at his elbow. "I told them no one could track or use a blade better'n Lieutenant Hicks."

Polly Moore's eyes widened. "I hope you did not speak out of turn in the council house."

"No ma'am. I waited until we were outside."

A little snort came from Susanna, spearing Sam with a responding spark of mirth. His gaze dragged to her, but he quickly returned it to his bowl. He nudged George. "Thank you for the vote of confidence, but from what I saw and heard today at the council house, your uncle and his friends have the matter in hand." Even though they'd asked him for advice and support, he'd referred the matter to his superior officer.

"On the contrary." Colonel Moore rubbed his jaw, creating a rasping sound. He studied Sam through narrowed eyes before sweeping his focus over all those gathered at the table. "I had already asked Lieutenant Hicks if he would remain here in my absence. Now I am certain 'tis the best course of action. Not only him but also several of his men. And not just at Armstrong, but here, in the village. Not that I do not have faith in your abilities, Bold Hunter." As the unfolding plan made Sam's stomach churn, Moore extended his hand to his Cherokee brother-in-law.

The warrior straightened. "With all the people coming and going now, we could use extra eyes and ears to protect our village, our chief. I said as much to your lieutenant, Moore." He nodded at Sam. "We would be honored to have the son of Charles Hicks among us."

Agreement between the Turkey Town warriors and Colonel Moore left him no room for refusal. Retreating to center himself in his own private barricade of Fort Hill would have to wait. Sam touched the side of his thumb to his chest. "I would be honored to work with you to protect Path Killer ... and the family of Colonel Moore." He allowed a glance in Susanna's direction.

Little ringlets of hair framed her flushed face. Her fingers twined nervously in that hated, glittering necklace as her attention swung from him to the colonel. "What does this mean, Father? Where are you going?"

Colonel Moore cleared his throat and answered her English query in kind. "I'd planned to tell you later tonight, but I will be riding to my adjutant's trading post in an attempt to procure blankets and supplies for the regiment. As you know, some men remain at Armstrong. Others will return within a month. We must be adequately provisioned."

Polly's fingers brushed the sleeve of her husband's coat. "Of course."

Susanna caught her lower lip between her small, white teeth and lowered her lashes. "And Dr. Hawkins?"

Fire shot through Sam. Why would she inquire about the physician if she cared nothing about him?

Hawkins rested his hand briefly on her forearm. "I will accompany your father to Armstrong in the morning, but there I will stay. Rest assured, I will return frequently to monitor your health." He shot a slit of a look toward Sam's end of the table. A threat?

Sam could have choked on his venison, but he chewed evenly, tightening his fingers around his spoon. He glanced up to find Nokassa watching him.

"Are the Cornsilks not leaving in a couple of days for Oostanaula?" Susanna's cousin angled her head toward her father, speaking in Cherokee. "Perhaps the lieutenant and his men could stay there in their absence."

"That is a good idea." Bold Hunter nodded. "I will inquire with them."

"It is settled, then." Colonel Moore laid his palm on the table.

With a mysterious smile, Polly stood up and began to gather empty bowls. "Time for my surprise. But first, my husband will read the story of baby Jesus from the Gospel of Luke." As the colonel reached for a black leather Bible he'd laid on a side table, his wife gestured to her stepdaughter. "Come, Susanna, help me serve our cake and coffee."

She rose to assist Polly while George bounced up and down beside Sam, shaking the bench. "I knew it! Cake!"

Sam put an elbow in his rib. "Settle down and attend to your father." From the startled and somewhat guarded expressions of Bold Hunter and his family, this reading needed as much focus as possible. That Polly Moore was a sly one, an ally he wanted, for sure. Admiration—and eventually, peace—nudged aside his envy and frustration as Colonel Moore opened the Bible, asked George to translate, and began to rumble out the Christmas story.

"'And it came to pass in those days, that there went out a decree from Caesar Augustus that all the world should be taxed.'"

As the colonel continued, Sam stared into the fire. If the all-powerful God had sent His son in human form to die for mankind and then raised Him from the dead, was He not in control of all that happened?

"'And she brought forth her firstborn son, and wrapped him in swaddling clothes, and laid him in a manger; because there was no room for them in the inn.'" A reverent silence enrobed the room as Colonel Moore closed the Good Book.

If God made a place for His son on this lonely earth, would He not do the same for Sam's people? He would provide strength for that task too. For fighting this war. For keeping his heart from demanding the impossible.

As Nokassa questioned Polly about the importance of the baby Jesus, Susanna leaned over Sam's shoulder, the fragrance of dried sweetshrub coming with her. She spoke in a low voice. "Merry Christmas, Lieutenant." A plate of apple cake slid onto the table in front of him, and she met his eyes, sending a bolt of awareness to his gut.

"Thank you, I don't care for any." That apple cake spoke of a home he couldn't reach, and her smile spoke of a wife that would haunt his dreams. Suddenly desperate for air, he escaped by way of the end of the bench and jammed his hat on. Curious eyes turned toward him, and he mumbled an explanation. "Going to take a walk."

Before he could close the door behind him, Susanna hurried forward and placed her hand on it. In her other, she held a tin cup. "Don't you at least want your coffee?"

She was going to follow him out. His insides clenched with longing—the insane urge to pull her into the cold, dark night and fold his arms around her, but the vision perished the instant her father spoke her name on a note of warning. Eyes regretful, she drew back into the cabin.

Instead, Colonel Moore followed Sam outside, shutting the door behind him and offering him the coffee he'd taken from Susanna. He spoke in his customary low rumble that brooked no argument. "Hicks, because of your reputation as both a gentleman and a warrior, I am trusting my most prized possessions into your care. I do not need to remind you of the consequences of betraying my trust."

"No sir, you do not." Sam saluted, then, waving the same hand to decline the coffee, strode away. Over his shoulder, he glimpsed the colonel taking a leisurely sip. Watching him. Grimly confident Sam would remember his duty.

CHAPTER TWELVE

Polly slid a bowl of grits with a chunk of butter floating on top and a cup of thick milk in front of Susanna when she sat down at the table two mornings later. Truly, the woman spoiled her.

Lifting her head from a prayer of thanks, she dug her spoon into the rich, white mush. "I don't know how I slept through everyone getting up and eating."

"I do. You worked too hard yesterday."

"I only helped with the weaving." A bite of the grits traveled down to warm her empty stomach, chased by a swallow of foamy milk.

"All day long."

Which might have been an attempt to distract herself from thoughts of Sam Hicks. The abrupt manner of his departure and the way her father had barred her from ascertaining Sam's well-being the night before last had nagged her ever since.

As Polly bustled back to finish putting clean dishes on the shelf, Susanna glanced around the otherwise-empty cabin. "Are Walani and Nokassa already busy at the wash?" Somehow, the dreaded day seemed to roll around faster than any other. "I dressed to help them." She smoothed the old skirt of Nokassa's she wore, the hem a bit short, but all the better for avoiding sparks and spills.

"They are, and you will not." Polly angled her body to glare at Susanna. "No more wash day for you."

"I can't stay here and not help."

"You can help later with dinner. This morning, rest."

If Polly acted this firm, she'd already enlisted the support of her sister and niece. Susanna might as well betake herself to plan number two. "Where is George?"

Polly's hand holding the drying rag stilled. "Lieutenant Hicks fetched him this morning to practice his knife fighting."

Susanna let her mouth drop open. "And no one told me?"

"Why should you be told? You do not need to learn to fight with a knife."

Oh dear. For a moment, she'd forgotten that she'd kept Polly as well as her father in the dark about her training request of Sam. Now, her stepmother fixed her with such a demanding stare, she'd have to reveal at least a morsel of the truth. "Back at Fort Strother, Lieutenant Hicks sometimes showed us things about defending ourselves. He allowed us to practice at the range."

Polly came and sat down across from her, folding her hands on the table as she leaned forward. "Susanna, your father would think that very bad."

Susanna swirled her spoon in her bowl. "Why? Does he not want us to be protected? Sam couldn't be at our side every moment."

"Well, now you are safe, and soon we will go home." Polly nodded and stood up, as if that settled the matter. "And today your brother can learn to be a man, and *you* will rest." Not *can rest*. *Will rest*. And that emphasis on *you* left no doubt as to her wishes.

"I can finish up here." Susanna made the offer before her stepmother could continue her work.

Polly nodded. "I do need to go help them." She hurried into her coat and out the door.

An empty cabin wasn't the blessing Susanna had anticipated. She'd grown accustomed to company. As she scrubbed the pot with a corncob, washed her dishes, and banked the fire, the silence gave rise to memories of Sam's distant demeanor when last she'd seen him. The contrast to his gentle manner with her on the ride to Turkey Town wouldn't let her rest. She had to set things right between them. A simple explanation about the necklace should suffice.

Swinging on her coat, Susanna let herself out into the cold but clear morning. She set out on a path that should take her away from the washerwomen and toward the town square. Sure enough, a group of boys and men had gathered on the ball ground. She paused on the periphery. She'd found Sam—and Spring Frog as well. He must be among those now assigned to Turkey Town. In a scene reminiscent of the staged fight by the Coosa, they seemed to be showing a knot of gangly adolescents how to ward off a frontal knife attack.

Spring Frog grabbed Sam's knife hand by the thumb joint. The man's right took hold underneath and twisted Sam's arm upward. Weight thrown back on his left leg, he turned the blade away.

Susanna had just caught sight of George and called his name when Spring Frog stepped back. His gaze flashed to her, but Sam didn't seem to notice. He'd motioned George forward to take his opponent's place. Unfortunately, she'd also drawn the attention of a group of men. She recognized one of them, and he recognized her. Standing Wolf leered at her.

She should leave. Only a couple other women attended to the practice, and they stood together outside a cabin some distance away. She took a step back. But Spring Frog hurried her direction with a smile of welcome.

"Miss Moore. Come. Watch." He managed enough words in Cherokee and animated gestures to lure her toward a horizontal log placed across the stumps of what had been two large trees.

Tucking her skirt around her, Susanna settled next to him. In the manner she'd seen some of the Indians favor, Spring Frog pulled his colorful matchcoat over his head, making him look more like a turtle than a warrior. She giggled and he grinned.

His breath came out in a puff. "Watch. Brother good."

She turned her attention to the ball ground, where George

attempted to wrest the knife from Sam using the same tactics Spring Frog had just demonstrated. She gasped, then relaxed when she realized the blade had been blunted by a woven wrap. Everyone cheered when George forced it from Sam's hand. Had Sam let him do that?

Whether he had or not, he retrieved his weapon and straightened with a grin. "You remember how I showed you the other day? To escape when your opponent comes from behind?"

"I do."

George presented his back to Sam, and Sam moved lightning quick, sliding the covered blade next to his throat. George threw his head back and used a backward thrust of his hips and forward bend at his waist to simultaneously tug down Sam's arm. Susanna felt certain then that Sam refrained from using his full strength against her scrawny brother, and her heart swelled.

A few more moves and George was free. She clapped and cheered.

The men in Standing Wolf's group, whom she'd forgotten about during the match, said something and laughed. Sam turned their way, frowning. Not at Standing Wolf. At her. He strode over, snapped something in Muskogean to Spring Frog, and tugged Susanna up by the elbow. Hoots and hollers issued from the cluster of Natchez Creeks. Before she knew it, Spring Frog was instructing her brother and his friends, and Sam was leading her away from the square.

Cheeks burning, she jerked her arm free. "What are you doing?"

"I am taking you home. Or rather, to your temporary home."

Susanna planted her feet in the middle of the swept-dirt row. "But why? You promised I could learn the same things my brother did, yet you came and got him this morning and said nothing to me."

"Things are not as they were at Strother." When a young woman with an infant on her hip came to the door of her cabin and stood observing them, Sam drew Susanna under a cluster of thin pines. "You are going home soon and have no need to learn to defend yourself."

"So everyone keeps telling me."

"Because it is true. No matter how much you try to look like a Cherokee,"—his gaze swept from her long braid to the short hem of her skirt with burning disdain—"you do not belong here, and you draw the wrong kind of attention going about alone dressed in this manner."

Frustration and hurt mushroomed in Susanna's chest. Why was he acting this way, filling her with the need to shake him when she'd only wanted to embrace him? "I would not have had to go about alone if you had escorted me as you are supposed to. And are you saying my attempt to honor my stepmother's family by dressing as they do is somehow degrading me?"

Sam gave an impatient shake of his head, the white feathers blowing in his collar-length dark hair. "I am saying that appearing as one of them, you give some men ideas you do not want them to have. Trust me."

"Why are they here, anyway? The Natchez Creek?"

"They were at the fort, idle. Your father decided they should be part of the detail to help guard the chief."

"But why, when you had your own men you knew you could trust?"

He clamped his lips shut a moment before answering, jaw stiff. "I do not question your father. And neither should you. And what he—and the doctor—wants is for you to be safe. Warm. Inside."

"What does it matter what the doctor wants?"

"Were you not just sick?"

He took her arm again and tried to urge her forward, but Susanna pulled back. "Stop. Please just stop. And listen." She waited until he dropped his hand to his side. "I don't know why you are so out of temper, but I think it might have to do with the necklace

Dr. Hawkins gave me. I only accepted it because Walani made it."
When his face went blank, Susanna lowered her voice. "It did not
mean anything. Not like ... not like our ride did." The last came out
on a whisper, but a whisper that contained her heart.

Sam turned away from her. His shoulders rose and fell. "It was
an honor to escort you from Fort Strother, Miss Moore, and it is an
honor to be trusted with your safety while you are here. Nothing
else concerns me. Now ... will you allow me to take you back to
your cabin?" He angled his face toward her and crooked his arm,
like a gentleman offering to squire her into a ball.

Susanna's face heated again, and tears sprang to her eyes. "Thank
you. I can find my own way." She darted past him back onto the
path and ran the rest of the way to the cabin.

By the time Nokassa, Walani, and Polly returned home, Susanna
thought she'd adequately concealed evidence of her breakdown
earlier in the day. Tears had overwhelmed her at first. She'd
sobbed loud and heart-sore into her shaking hands. Then she'd
sat there holding Sam's poem and a witch hazel blossom she'd
pressed. She knew what she'd felt from him at Strother, although
she didn't know what had changed him. More than the necklace,
apparently.

She hadn't been able to discard the tokens of his affection,
though, so she'd stowed them away, stripped off Nokassa's work
clothes, and put on her second-best dress, a light wool in a color of
gray that matched her mood. She'd run impatient fingers through
her braid, loosening it, then brushed her hair with a small, painted
wooden comb before twisting it into a bun and securing it with the
tines.

Her eyes were dry, and *ga-na-tsi*—corn, bean, and hickory
nut soup—simmered in the Dutch oven when the other women
returned to the cabin. Yet Nokassa immediately drew her aside, her

hand chapped and cold on Susanna's.

"What happen?"

"Nothing. Everything is fine." Susanna attempted a smile.

"You lie. You tell me." Nokassa gestured her into the back room and closed the door as Walani rolled her eyes. "Let her think we girl talk. Something bad happen. I know."

A real smile lifted the corners of Susanna's lips this time. "Your English, it is getting so much better."

Nokassa rolled her hand in an impatient gesture. "Talk."

"You will think it foolish." When her cousin shook her head and sat on the mattress, waiting, Susanna sank down beside her and searched for simple words to frame her complicated emotions. What came out was the admission that had been working its way to the surface since her storm of tears. "Sam Hicks. I love him." The tears came back, too, rolling down her face in silent waves.

Nokassa's lips rounded, and she seized Susanna's hands. "You tell him. You no want doctor."

"I did—I tried. I told him about the *a-de-la di-ya-tso-di* … beads." She circled her hand around her bare neck. "It did not matter. He did not want me."

Nokassa shook her head again, this time with such vehemence that her braids slid over her shoulders. "Not true."

"I thought so. I told you about the ride, the things he said when he thought I slept. *A-qua-da-nv-do*." Susanna stumbled over the unfamiliar nasal syllable near the end, so she added the translation. "*My heart*. I know I heard that. But now, he wants me to leave."

"Not true."

"Repeating that doesn't make it so."

Nokassa squeezed her fingers, hard. "I see how he look at you."

A little laugh barked out of her. "Straight-faced? As he looks all the time? As all Cherokee men look all the time?" Now she was being mean, but she couldn't help herself.

"Like you are …" Nokassa snapped her fingers. "*A-de-la di-ya-*

tso-di. Bright beads. Like *a-qua-da-nv-do.* He looks when you not look."

Susanna sighed, her shoulders sinking. "Even if it were true, he must be afraid of my father. Of the doctor. Of their power over me."

"Cherokee women choose."

"I am not a Cherokee woman."

"Maybe. But why make it easy to let you go?" After lapsing into Cherokee for the last sentence, Nokassa shrugged, holding the pose for a moment while drawing her bottom lip upward. "He know you choose him, he fight for you."

Susanna stared at her, frozen by the tantalizing possibility. Could she be right?

Walani's call broke the silence. "Susanna. Nokassa. Come help."

They stood, but Nokassa nodded with confidence. "You show him. You see."

When they returned to the main chamber, Walani retrieved bowls while Polly sliced cornbread. Susanna's stepmother glanced at her. "I hope you made enough to share with the men of your father's regiment."

Her feet slid to a halt. In truth, she'd completely forgotten that the women of their family had assumed responsibility for providing supper to the soldiers. Thankfully, the trance of grief that had seized her earlier had been so strong she'd chopped and added far more ingredients than she'd intended. "There should be enough."

Polly gave a satisfied nod. "Go let them know it is ready, Nokassa."

"Susanna will go." Nokassa shoved her forward.

She swiveled, about to protest when her cousin raised an eyebrow. "She need air. But put hair down. Cold." Faking a shiver, Nokassa let a little giggle slip out. Then she reached up to jerk the comb from Susanna's hair.

Long tresses bounced down around her waist. Susanna's eyes

popped open wide. "Give me my comb back."

"What ... *comb*?" Rounding her mouth over the new word, the girl held said object behind her, face now straight. She backed toward the sleeping chamber with exaggerated, shuffling steps.

When Susanna attempted to grab her arm, Nokassa twisted out of reach. In an oddly graceful dance, she snatched Susanna's coat off the peg, placed it over her shoulders with another little push to her back, and spun into the vicinity of their mothers where Susanna was unlikely to follow.

Susanna let her breath out in a half sigh, half growl before turning toward the door. How in the world would she face Sam Hicks now, after running away earlier? With her emotions still a-jumble? And what in the world would she say to him, besides "Dinner is ready"?

CHAPTER THIRTEEN

The last person Sam expected to see when he answered the knock at his door was Susanna. Yet there she stood, looking in the soft light of the lantern she held quite unlike he'd ever seen her. She'd changed to an English-styled dress, yet over the shoulders of her coat, over the curves of her chest and waist, flowed her long, dark hair. Not straight like that of a Cherokee girl, but in soft waves, curled at the tips. He swallowed as if he'd tried to eat a chunk of the cold corn mush he'd just put over the fire.

The powerful combination of attraction and compassion prevented his reply from being anything but tender. "Hello." He only said one word, soft and astonished, but that was enough to round her eyes and flush her cheeks in startled embarrassment. What grit she had, showing up after the tears he'd provoked.

Yes, he'd heard her sobs earlier, having followed her at a distance to make sure she returned safely to the cabin. They'd carried to his ears and rent his heart.

She started stammering. "My—my mother—my aunt bid me come and tell you we ... I ... have prepared *ga-na-tsi*." When he just stared at her, she hastened to tack on an addition. "We promised Father we would share our dinners with you and your men, remember?"

He hadn't. Obviously. "Oh. Thank you."

"How many ... are there?" She craned her neck in an attempt to peek inside the cabin, which might not have been wise depending on what the men were doing. Thankfully, they lounged around, puffing so much tobacco smoke from their pipes she probably couldn't see them, anyway.

"My three Cherokees from McNair's are here with me. The Natchez Creeks occupy a cabin farther down the street. Can you ... stay right there just a moment?" Sam held out his hand. "I had already put a pot on to heat. Let me take it off and tell the men to go on to your cabin."

"I can walk back now if you will tell the others to come." She attempted to sidle off.

"Please." Already halfway into the cabin, he extended his whole arm this time. He didn't want her walking back alone—or with his men—without him. Not looking as alluring as she did at this moment, though he wouldn't dare tell her that after his comments about her appearance earlier. "Let me walk with you. I mean, walk with me."

His pleading tone finally seemed to arrest her, for she stilled and folded her hands over the lantern handle in front of her.

Sam grabbed a rag and swung the pot from over the fire. Shoving the front ashes toward the biggest flames, he explained the change of plans to the men. They wasted no time in bolting upright, gathering coats and hats and rifles, and tromping outside. Sam collected his own things quickly enough to keep an eye on them and shut the door behind them. As he'd expected, the most they offered Susanna Moore was a grim nod.

She kept her lashes lowered even as she raised the lantern for them to proceed in the opposite direction. Her voice came softly when she spoke. "I'd rather not see Standing Wolf, if the truth be told."

Of course. "You won't have to see him. I will go inside, then we will leave before they come out. I didn't want you walking alone at night."

"You didn't want me walking alone in the day either."

Argumentative girl. Yet Sam couldn't rally the strength to fight with her, not after those sobs he'd heard. The truth that had pierced him in that moment still hadn't found a place to settle anywhere inside him. "I thought you would only go about the village with one of your relatives."

"They were busy, and I wanted—I wanted fresh air."

Why did he doubt that had been what originally had come to her mind? Maybe the brief glance she tossed him, almost fearful. Sam cleared his throat. "I will try to do better, to be available."

"I cannot expect you to be at my beck and call. I know you take guard shifts outside Path Killer's residence."

"Those are mostly at night. You can send a message if you need me during the day."

"And I will try to be more circumspect." She ducked her head while Sam scrambled to recall the exact meaning of that word. She continued, choosing her steps and her words with obvious care. "I know I might have to leave soon, so what I need is not as important to you. But when we do meet, I would appreciate it if you will be … as you are tonight."

Sam's heartbeat hitched. Had she seen through his defenses so easily? "And how is that?"

"Not … rude."

A laugh snorted out of him before he could catch it. "Your honesty, Miss Moore …"

"Did you forget my name?" Her voice was such a low murmur, his heart didn't hitch this time—it stopped. As though he could ever forget that. Or the sweet weight of her in his arms. Or the lingering scent of sweetshrub in the hair that now curled over her shoulders, begging for his touch.

Sam stopped walking, angled toward her ever so slightly. He willed his voice to be … circumspect, but it came out raspy, nonetheless. "No. And it is not that I do not care what you need or that I mean to be rude. But—" There he'd almost lapsed and said her name. He bit his tongue, then allowed it to articulate the front edge of his fear, to rip the protective layer off his hidden agony. "I cannot be nice to you."

"Wha ..." She made a disbelieving sound that might have been the start of a question, but it never came to completion.

A scream sounded from the dwelling at the end of the row.

Sam slung his rifle strap over his head. "Stay here."

He bolted toward the cry, pausing only long enough to hammer the stock of his gun against the Natchez Creeks' door and call for Spring Frog. He didn't wait to see if the man responded or Susanna obeyed. He ran to the old woman tottering in his direction, flapping the folds of her shawl like the wings of a large goose.

He addressed her in rapid Cherokee but with a term of tribal respect. "What happened, grandmother?"

"A thief in my corncrib! Hurry. I have only a little corn left." She pointed to the outbuilding barely visible in the shadows—and beyond it, sure enough, a dark figure taking flight for the trees.

"Stop!" Sam yelled the command in Cherokee—to no effect. Not knowing who the intruder might be, he didn't want to shoot unless he had to. His weapon wasn't loaded, anyway. If he sprinted hard ...

A second later, he tossed his rifle to one side and launched into a tackle. His fingers wrapped around the handle of his long knife seconds after he knocked the slender form in a hunting shirt and breeches to the ground, the fugitive's felt hat flying off. Before the man could turn over, Sam shoved his shoulder forward and slid the blade against his throat.

"Hands in the air or I slit you open."

His captive rasped in English, "I don't speak Cherokee."

Sam nabbed a handful of buckskin and jerked the thief around. The light of December's Snow Moon shone on the gaunt face of a white man. "Tennessee militia?" He spat it out with the disgust he felt.

The man's hands came up then, and he gave a drooping nod. "I'm starvin', man."

"Then go home." An abrupt shake, and then he shoved the soldier's upper body backward so hard his head thudded against the dirt. "You don't steal from the very people who have fed you for the past three months—especially from old widow women."

"I'm tryin' to get home. But I been sick—"

"Get up." Coming to his knees, Sam gestured with his knife, only making the man cower further. Sam clenched his shirt again and gave him a helpful tug. He didn't want to listen to the man's sad story. Starvation he could sympathize with, but he'd heard too many tales of the Tennessee militia pillaging among his people, demonstrating wanton and wasteful disregard for property. Burning outbuildings and killing even the animals they didn't eat. Sam narrowed his eyes at the intruder as they both got to their feet, brushing off their clothing. "You alone?"

"Yeah. I'm alone." He stuffed his hat back on, then adjusted it to better assess Sam. "Hey, I recognize you. Ain't you in the Cherokee Regiment? You cain't kill me. We're allies. Supposed to help our friends out, right?"

"Spring Frog here, you think he looks friendly?" He tilted his head toward his comrade as he sidestepped into the periphery of Sam's vision, rifle aimed at the militiaman's chest. The weapon that had fallen from the man's grasp when Sam had tackled him lay on the ground a few feet away. "I'll take that musket." He toed it toward Spring Frog. As the Natchez swooped it up, Sam nodded to the sheath on the frontiersman's belt. "And that knife."

He cursed. "Aw, no, you can't take that. How'm I goin' to survive?"

Sam flexed his wrist, pointing his own knife. "Keep the hands up. Make a move, and Spring Frog shatters your head." He glided in to retrieve the blade and conduct a quick pat-down. Satisfied that the man concealed no other weapons, he stepped back and cast a glance behind him.

The Natchez men had closed around them, weapons drawn, two of them fanning out to check the field and woods for other possible intruders. Farther back at the cabins, the old lady and Susanna stood with the lantern glowing at their feet.

Sam returned his attention to the interloper. "Now listen carefully. Spring Frog is going to escort you to the river ferry. That is … unless you cross him or rub him wrong. Then I don't care what he does with you. Just make sure you never come back. If we see you in these parts again, we *will* kill you, no questions asked."

Spring Frog nodded at him, and Sam relieved him of the Tennessean's firearm as well as collecting his own. As the Natchez Creeks encircled their captive, Sam returned to the women.

Susanna stepped forward to meet him, an unexpected frown of concern creasing her forehead. "He said he was starving, Sam."

"And?" The question came out short. After disarming an intruder intent on stealing from a grandmother, he'd anticipated Susanna would admire him, not question him.

"And you have a pot of cold mush in your cabin."

"You want me to give him food my own men need to eat?" He did not even try to restrain his disbelief.

"Do you want him to leave? He must have strength to walk. Just a bowl, that's all I ask. You have your supper provided tonight." She prompted him with raised eyebrows and a gentler tone. "It is our Christian duty, is it not?"

Sam hissed out a sound between a sigh and a growl. Then he swung to face the Natchez men and issued the directions that might appease Susanna—and his own conscience—but that he fully expected to invite their ridicule. In fact, Spring Frog looked for a moment as if he might laugh. Probably because Sam had fallen so firmly under the thumb of the colonel's daughter. But Standing Wolf, who had returned from the field, merely stared at him, face expressionless. When he nodded, one of the men darted for their cabin to fetch the mush.

Sam bent toward the elderly lady and softened his voice. "Are you all right, grandmother? Will you feel safe in your cabin?"

She nodded, seized his arm, and chattered in indignant Cherokee all the way to her door. Susanna lit her way in and waited while Sam saw her settled. When he came back out, Susanna's gaze followed the party heading for the river. She let out a small puff on the frosty air. "Do you think he'll actually leave?"

"The lack of a weapon should speed him home. And of course, your bowl of mush." He secured both guns over one shoulder and indicated they should start walking. No doubt, Polly had already sent George after them, worried about Susanna's safety. Or worse, Bold Hunter.

Susanna did not respond directly to his rare jibe, but neither did her frown lift. "Did you mean what you said? That if he tries anything, you don't care if they kill him?"

"His enlistment ran out. There is no one to turn him in to. We are the law around here." He heaved a sigh that came up from the depths of his being. "I know you were right about the mush, but I am tired of being taken advantage of. Sometimes you have to say no … *no more.*"

Sam startled when Susanna leaned closer and wrapped her hand around his elbow. Even through the buckskin, her fingers tickled the flat part of the joint. "I agree, and I appreciate your evenhandedness tonight." The firmness of her voice surprised him too. "But sometimes … 'in truth the prison, unto which we doom ourselves, no prison is.'"

What did she mean, with her eyes so bright and intense? She remained silent the rest of the way to her cabin but left her hand on his arm. He savored it even though he shouldn't and finally remembered where he'd heard that verse before. Another poem by Wordsworth. And she wasn't talking about prisons for rogue Tennessee militia.

Susanna Moore cared for him. If it hadn't been obvious at Strother, her strong reaction to the emotional wall he'd tried to put up since coming to Turkey Town made it undeniable.

As Sam rode to Fort Armstrong several days later, leaving the Moore family enjoying some time with the colonel, amazement that Susanna could care for him still bounced about inside him like a loose cannonball, igniting all sorts of reactions. Disbelief. Amazement. Joy. And deep remorse. He should never have stirred her emotions with that poem and the flowers, courting her like a white man. Should never have whispered the secret that leaked out as his stallion bore them to Turkey Town ... that she held his heart. Her spirit must have heard him even if her ears hadn't. He had known Colonel Moore's vision for his daughter's future before the man had reminded him this past week. Reminded him to stay away.

But was there a way, one he did not see—as Susanna had hinted with the verse from Wordsworth?

Since then, he hadn't been alone with her. When they had encountered each other in company, he'd done his best to be polite and kind while avoiding any meaningful glances or touches. A fine line he walked—unable to push her away, yet painfully aware that as soon as her father returned from Rossville, Susanna would depart with her stepmother and brother. That left both of their hearts exposed, even if no declarations had been made.

Father, if it is Your will, show me the way.

Maybe his earthly father would have wisdom to share as well. Early this morning, a messenger from Armstrong had informed him that Charles Hicks had ridden into the fort with twenty-six warriors from their previous tour and thirty-nine new recruits. Most unmounted, but all willing to work alongside Colonel William Snodgrass' Second Regiment of East Tennessee Volunteer Militia to secure supply and communication lines during the next month between fall and spring campaigns.

He might hope to bring up Susanna Moore in some fashion, but the conversation with his father would center on the other person he was guarding, Path Killer—and the drama that had unfolded the day before.

Charles Hicks awaited him outside one of four lodges the men had constructed around a council house and a central square. Surrounded by their scalps and relics of war, chiefs occupied each dwelling according to rank.

Sam's father might be past forty-five and afflicted by a chronic hip condition, but Sam couldn't recall evidence of age or pain ever slowing his movements or marring his countenance. He greeted Sam today by clapping both hands on his back and inviting him through the front opening to smoke inside the lodge.

Sam took a few puffs for the sake of politeness but then leaned back in his rough-hewn chair. The fire crackled at their feet. "How is Mother?" He started the conversation in English to give them a little privacy from the men who wandered in and out of the lodge.

"Sad she could not see you for Christmas. She sends provisions for you. Some of the bread she made using the Moravian recipe."

"Lovefeast buns?" Sam sat upright and snatched the satchel his father indicated. Inside, wrapped in brown paper, he found the coveted bread made with cinnamon, mace, and citrus that he remembered from his days at Springplace. He tore off a chunk, popped it in his mouth, and closed his eyes. Dry from travel, but the flavor and memories remained. He was eleven again.

His father's chuckle brought him back to the moment. "She knew you would like that."

"Did she speak with you more about God?" He'd been praying his father's absence, followed by his furlough over the holiday, might make his mother more receptive to religious concepts. She'd cried all the way through her husband's baptism service last year but still wavered in her own commitment.

"She allowed me to read the Christmas story, and she asked a few questions. I believe she will get there. But right now, she is worried about you." Father fixed his dark gaze upon him.

Sam shrugged. "As you can see, I am in little danger."

"About what this war might do to you."

"I barely saw one battle, and Hillabee was not much of a battle." More of a massacre.

"But you did see the aftermath, the dark side of men it brings out. We hope this will not steal the joy you find in life. In God."

"I am strong in God, Father." Indeed, he read his Testament daily, and after his prayers ascended to the skies, he felt sure they'd been heard. Sometimes, he even received direction or confirmation in his spirit. It was the night he didn't wish to talk about. Not now. "But as for the dark side of men … since you left, I have not only been guarding Colonel Moore's family but Path Killer as well."

Father sat forward, lowering his pipe. "Have there been threats upon our principal chief?"

Sam told him how the intruder near Path Killer's residence had prompted the colonel to strengthen the guard of the Wolf Clan warriors at Turkey Town with Sam's Cherokees and Natchez Creeks, then how he'd caught the Tennessee militiaman pillaging.

"Could this intruder you tracked to Path Killer's lodge have been the same man? Or another white man who left the army?"

He rubbed the back of his neck. "I wondered that at first too. But last night, while Standing Wolf was on guard, the chief cried out. Standing Wolf had gone to the nearby tree line to relieve himself, turning his back only a moment. Someone in a dark cloak fled from the lodge. Standing Wolf's first thought was to check on the chief. He found the old man in a state. He had awakened to find someone standing over him and had wrestled this from the intruder." Sam pulled a wrapped knife from his beaded bandolier bag.

His father turned the weapon over in his hand. "Indian made."

"And this." He opened his palm to reveal a white feather. "Lying on the floor."

Charles Hicks' eyes snapped to him. "Is this from one in your company?"

Sam shook his head. "As expected, no one seemed to be missing any feathers today. I do not believe it. I know and trust my men."

"False evidence? But why would a Red Stick try to point the finger at one of the men guarding the chief? They don't think we would still assume it was them?" He gave a bark of a laugh.

"I don't know. But the person in question wants us to think a Cherokee soldier is responsible."

Leaning back and crossing one leg over the other, Father blew air through his lips. "Ridiculous. But what have you done to punish this Standing Wolf? Did the man drink too much *ah-me-ge-i* before reporting for duty?"

"I do not believe Standing Wolf would drink spirits before guarding the chief. He takes his skills as a warrior very seriously, as he is taking his failure." In fact, Sam had assigned Spring Frog to make sure the older man did not harm himself today. "But I did wonder ... Standing Wolf could have made up the story himself."

"Why would he bring down blame on his own head?"

"If he was the man in the cloak."

His father stiffened. "You have reason to believe this?"

"I have no reason to believe anything yet. In Colonel Moore's absence, I have doubled the guard on Path Killer—a Cherokee with a Natchez Creek every night. Tonight I will move the chief and ask Polly Moore's brother-in-law, Bold Hunter, to sleep in his place in his lodge from now on." He didn't want to ask his father's advice or approval, but he watched for it in the crinkles on the face of Charles Hicks, in the lines of his body.

At last, a nod. "It is as I would do." Father released a puff of smoke. Narrowing his eyes, he upheld his index finger. "Make the place Path Killer sleeps different every night. Not disclosed even to your men ahead of time."

"A wise idea."

"And have Bold Hunter's men, not your own or the Natchez Creeks, guard their chief."

"I will do as you suggest." Charles Hicks wasn't Sam's captain now, but his parental wisdom trumped even that.

"Moore will return within the week. Once he sends his family back to Hiwassee, you can fix your mind on this more important task. Pull the end of the ball of yarn."

"Yes, Father."

The older man lifted an eyebrow. "This does not give you relief?"

Hadn't he kept his reply agreeable? His posture relaxed? The way Charles Hicks saw through him always unnerved Sam. "It is true they have been a distraction." A blessed, life-giving distraction. "But it has been an honor to help protect them. They are good people. I would like you to come meet them before they go. Have dinner with us one night."

"Meet *them*? Or the girl?" When Sam failed to reply, Father shook his shaggy, dark head, the firelight glistening on the strands of silver. "Your mother, she did not worry without reason."

"What do you mean?" Sam took that moment to show interest in the kettle sitting in the ashes, lifting the lid and sniffing the contents.

"When I told her of the time you spent guarding Susanna Moore, she asked me of the young lady's manner, her appearance. Many questions to pester me with, I thought. But she has the wisdom of women about her."

Chicory coffee. Sam rummaged in his bandolier bag for his tin cup and helped himself to some. Should have done so sooner. He took a sip. "Mmm. I spend much more time with George Moore."

"But mention of him does not kindle the light in your eyes."

Sam's shoulders slumped. If his father had discerned that much, he might as well offer a nod toward the truth. "She is special."

"She is the white daughter of our colonel, promised to the man of medicine he brought with him."

"They are not betrothed."

"In the white man's world, she is as good as betrothed if her father says so. It is not like with our people. This you know. I raised you to know."

"You also raised me to recognize change when it is good. Headman John Walker, who operates the ferry on the Hiwassee—his son is married to the white daughter of Colonel Meigs." With a quick flick of his wrist, Sam drained the coffee in a hasty swallow and then flung the remaining droplets into the fire.

"I doubt Meigs opposed the union. Mayhap it served him well, but making Moore angry would not bring good change. It could go against all we try to achieve here, my son."

Sam couldn't look at him. His tongue tied in knots. This wasn't the wisdom he sought.

His father uncrossed his legs and sat forward. "Such matters will soon fall from your mind. Our men are rested. Many such as The Ridge, who is now a major, have achieved new rank. They are ready to fight. When the fresh soldiers from Tennessee arrive, General Jackson will lead us out to battle."

The dread the words evoked caused Sam's head to hang limp. "Pray for me, Father, that I can acquit myself well when that day comes."

"This I already do, my son. He will give you wisdom to only take lives with just cause."

At the touch of his father's hand on his shoulder, Sam lifted his face. "Is it ever a just cause to turn brothers against each other? Do we deceive ourselves that the English won't take the land of the Creeks if they win this war, then turn on us for ours?"

Charles Hicks hefted a sigh. "This, I ask many nights in my own prayers, Sam. All we can do is to take each step the Creator shows us." He sat back, seeming to release the burden that weighed on both of them with a puff of his pipe. "It is my prayer that our peace with the white men will be secured and that we can return to Fort Hill. And when the time is right, God will send a nice Cherokee girl to be your wife."

CHAPTER FOURTEEN

In the week since Sam accosted the militiaman, since Susanna had asked for his kindness, she had felt their tenuous connection strengthen again. Their moments together had been brief but fraught with awareness, with warm smiles and even moments of shared humor. And now, he was leaving.

She paced six steps from the target as Sam had taught her, whirled, and threw her dagger. The satisfaction of planting it squarely in the middle of the cross section of the tree only obliterated her pain for a millisecond. Then it rushed over her again—the ache of impending separation, the frustration of lack of choice. She could understand why Sam felt like a pawn in a game over which he had no control. As a woman, didn't she face the same? She could never compare herself to the poor Africans whom both whites and Cherokees held as slaves, but neither did having privilege equal having a choice.

She'd just let her shoulders droop, fingering the quillwork on the sheath above her breast, when his voice spoke softly behind her.

"Susanna?"

She jerked upright. Now that he was leaving, he could dispense with formalities? "Where did you come from?" Sam's silent approach always unsettled her. One would think she would've gotten used to it from Polly.

"From my shift guarding the chief … then from your cabin, where I did not find you." He glanced toward the edge of the throwing range where a group of adolescents had distracted George with a game of marbles. "At least, you allowed your brother to come with you."

"I am happy he still has moments where he feels he can be a boy. But you ..." Susanna went to fetch her blade. "You should find a place to rest. You will need sleep if you're to go on campaign tomorrow."

"You heard." Sam shifted his weight, resting his hand on the head of his tomahawk.

She returned to her throwing spot without making eye contact. "My father told us that the regiment will be leaving tomorrow to meet Jackson and his fresh troops at Talladega." He'd barely returned from Ross' trading post last night before breaking the news.

"The new recruits are only sixty-day volunteers. As frustrated as Jackson was by enlistments running out before he concluded things to his liking, no one is surprised that he's not waiting for spring to seek out his foe." He watched as she closed one eye and moved her upraised arm back and forth, preparing to throw her knife.

Instead, she stopped and looked at him. "No, the surprise was that you and your men posted at Turkey Town were going."

His face tightened. "This was not my choice."

"Seems to be our lot in life, does it not?" She took aim again.

"Susanna, would you please ... cease a minute?" He placed his hand on her elbow, but she jerked away. "Why are you displeased? Believe me, I protested being pulled from guard duty here. I fear for the chief's safety if we go. But Jackson expressed concern over taking green troops into battle and needs every experienced fighter he can get."

She pushed a strand of hair that the breeze had tugged from her bun behind her ear. "I am sure he does."

"I was told you are leaving the following day, regardless." Sam stepped closer and shook his head. "So what does this change?"

For a long moment, Susanna stared into his lash-studded dark eyes, searching for confirmation that she hadn't imagined that he shared her feelings. She had stupidly hoped that if they had a day or two together after her father left, something might merge their diverse paths. Something might be spoken. Something might be done. What wouldn't she give for just twenty-four more hours in his presence? Not someplace where they had to behave as everyone thought they should, but alone, when they could be real and honest.

Apparently, the desire for that had never crossed his mind, or he wouldn't ask what he did. And if it had, he had no business pressing her to vocalize her feelings. She'd done so already, more than she ought, and he had failed to respond. No, she must harden the shell around her heart.

"You are right. Thank you for all you have done for my family and me, but we … *I* … don't need you anymore." She turned from a flicker in his gaze, took aim, and released her knife. Dead on.

Jutting her chin up, Susanna stalked to the target and grabbed for the dagger's handle. But Sam on his silent feet reached it at the same time. They fumbled over the weapon—she cried out—and it fell into the dirt while a stripe of red appeared on both of their first fingers.

The cut stung like fire. With her left hand, Susanna searched her pocket for her handkerchief. Before she could get hold of it, Sam grabbed her right arm. He pressed his sliced finger over hers, holding the wounds firmly together as he stepped within inches. Breath coming fast, she released her bottom lip from between her teeth. His gaze followed her gesture, and her heart pounded.

"I do need *you*." His whisper both soothed and racked her soul. "But Susanna …" He tilted his head. Oh, he was going to kiss her. "I do not see the way."

With a final press of his hand that gave her Cherokee blood, Sam's square jaw firmed, and he walked away.

Susanna arranged her pallet on the floor while Polly rummaged through their belongings packed into saddlebags for the trip home in the morning. She sighed as she looked around the main room belonging to the family of Bold Hunter's brother. Of all nights, Bold Hunter had decided to secure Path Killer in his own cabin—meaning Polly, Susanna, George, Walani, and Nokassa must take shelter elsewhere. *Of all nights*, right before their journey home! But who was she to question the Wolf Clan guards and the security of the principal chief?

Polly sat back on her heels. "Oh, Susanna, my Dutch oven! I forgot it in the cabin." She swiveled to assess George, who wiggled into his blanket like a worm into a cocoon. She addressed him over the backs of Walani and Nokassa, snuggled under quilts by the fire. "I need you to get it. It must be packed first in the morning."

Susanna's offer subverted her brother's groan. "I will fetch it." She doubted she could settle down to sleep anytime soon, her thoughts and emotions jumbled together so, yet neither did she feel confident of crossing the packed room without tripping over something. Bracing herself against the table, she tiptoed toward the door.

Polly lowered her voice so as not to disturb those sleeping in the adjoining chamber. "I do not like you to go out alone at night."

"It is only two doors down, and the moon is full. Besides, I could use the air."

As she hoped, her stepmother's expression softened with compassion. Polly had bound up her cut finger yesterday when Susanna had been unable to stop the tears from running down her face. Today, Susanna had confided she now knew Sam shared her feelings, but it didn't matter. Their parting felt as final as death.

Polly nodded. "Come straight back. We must sleep."

Outside, silence hung heavy over the village, as if the residents mourned the loss of the regiment's protection. This perception, no doubt, reflected the abandoned state of Susanna's heart. Her father and Sam had ridden away today, though Father had denied his family coming to Armstrong to see them off. Even the doctor had left. After visiting last evening to remind Susanna that he would return to Hiwassee as soon as possible, he set out for Strother, where he would await the inevitable influx of wounded.

Susanna's stomach twisted. She drew her coat around her and looked up at the starry sky. "Please keep them safe." Her little prayer dissipated in a puff of frost.

As long as she knew Sam cared for her, she would not give up hope.

Nose tickling with woodsmoke and cold, she paused outside Walani's place. Shouldn't there be a guard at the door? Perhaps they weren't posting anyone outside so as not to draw attention to the importance of the individual within. Or perhaps the guard had just stepped into the cabin for a moment.

She knocked and received no answer. She knocked again. Called out in Cherokee, "It is Susanna Moore. We forgot something."

The door creaked open, and she blinked. Not one of Bold Hunter's brethren, but a familiar face peeked out.

"Spring Frog! I thought you left with the regiment today."

His posture tense, he managed to make himself clear with a few halting words. "You Father … say … stay."

It wouldn't be the first time her father had changed his mind at the last minute, but … "Did he tell anyone else to stay?" She held her breath as if to check the spiraling hope in her heart and attempted to peek past him into the cabin. Path Killer would be in the inner chamber, his guards in the outer. "Sam Hicks?"

"No." Spring Frog shook his head. "You need …" His fragment of a sentence lilted up in question.

She made a circle with her fingers. "Pot. My mother's Dutch oven." Before he could react, Susanna pushed the door open. Why was he barring her, anyway?

She took two steps into the room and knew. The door to the sleeping chamber was closed. Two men sat on the bench facing the fire, backs resting against the table, arms limp. The throats of both had been cut. A gurgling sound came from the nearest one. *Just* cut. The skin down her back chilled. *Spring Frog* had done this? Had he killed the chief as well?

She sucked in a breath, but long, strong fingers cut off her scream.

He'd moved lightning fast. Spring Frog held one hand over her mouth and wrapped the other across her arms and body. She kicked and struggled as he dragged her backward out of the cabin. Once they cleared the row, he paused only long enough to sling her over his shoulder. The wind whooshed from her body. She flailed, beating his running form and wheezing for enough air to scream again because in the village, voices raised, lights appeared, and men shouted.

A horse nickered from the trees. No! She must not let him take her out of here. If only she could reach the knife that she'd thought to secure with her garter. But he flung her stomach over the horse's back and mounted behind her before she could squirm upright.

She could at least find her voice now. "Help! Help!" Her cry sounded strangled.

A sharp command in the Muskogean tongue, and something smote her over the head. Hard. Susanna sagged across the saddle.

The crackling of the campfire offered a false sense of cheer. Sam extended his hands to the blaze. He sat near the old battleground outside the friendly Creek village of Talladega, where he should have fought with honor back in November. If, that was, General Cocke hadn't stolen their regiment to throw against the Hillabee villages that had already surrendered.

This wasn't the only former battleground they'd encountered today on their route from Armstrong. After fording the Coosa and riding overland for some time, they'd also passed near Tallushatchee. The images of the piles of bodies and burned women and children that haunted his dreams had flooded back in broad daylight. He'd fallen to quoting Scriptures in his head after that. By the time they crossed Chockelocko Creek, he'd restored some semblance of inner peace.

Would his regiment ever get the chance to fight with honor?

Would this next battle be the one where they would turn the tide? Secure their place in history? Secure their land?

A movement near the trees made Sam and several of his comrades in McNair's company leap up, drawing their weapons. A man wearing an open deerskin waistcoat over his tunic stepped forward, hands held up.

"Do-hi-yi, a-na-da-nv-tli." Peace, brothers.

When the firelight threw a shadow beneath Standing Wolf's scar, Sam wasn't so sure he wanted to put away his weapon. But he retired the tomahawk and sat back down. What was the man doing here, rather than remaining at the fire of the Natchez Creeks? Perhaps he had business with someone else.

But to his chagrin, Standing Wolf folded his legs and sat on the cold ground beside him. He addressed Sam in Muskogean. "I must speak with you."

"Speak."

"Spring Frog is missing."

Sam quirked his head. "Is this not the problem of the Natchez Creek Chief Sullockaw?" Perhaps the man had changed his mind about this fight and simply slunk off into the wilderness. It had been known to happen.

The older warrior gave a nod. "He knows. He sent me to you."

"Why?"

"Because I also told him that before we were assigned to Turkey Town, Spring Frog once snuck out of Fort Armstrong. This he did the night before Moore doubled the guard on Path Killer."

Sam's attention swung to Standing Wolf with hawk-like focus, and he rose slowly to his feet. "What are you saying?"

Standing Wolf stood beside him. "My brother-in-law held anger that we had to join another tribe. We shared that anger against the

French. When Tecumseh and the Prophet first came, Spring Frog grew wild-eyed with their words."

"He agreed with the Red Sticks?" Sam's heart raced, sending blood tingling into his hands. He flexed them.

"Only when everyone in our village chose the other path did he change his mind. I thought he had come to see that if we helped rid our new lands of Red Sticks allied with the British, we would gain favor with the Americans."

Exactly Sam's motivation. "You and I are not so different as I thought."

"There is a difference." Standing Wolf lowered his chin, and his eyes glinted. "When we give our word, we must fight. With our whole heart. Not a heart divided."

Sam tightened his fingers over his tomahawk's handle. For too long, he'd feared the old ways not only taking the ground he'd gained by embracing the new ways—but swallowing him whole. Standing Wolf's words invited a new possibility. Could he embrace the strength of the warrior without his brutality? "I was not raised to war like you, but in this next battle, I swear it."

"Sam Hicks, your battle will come. But now, the life of your chief is in danger."

His brows flew up. "You think Spring Frog did not desert to the enemy but returned to Turkey Town to ambush Path Killer?"

"His murder would divide your people, especially if some thought one of your own were careless … or responsible. You must go back and warn them … if it is not too late."

Light piercing her eyelids seared away fleeting impressions of an endless night of motion and pain, but cold, hard earth beneath her and a brisk breeze on her face testified that Susanna lay still, but yet outside. Some sort of lumpy object propped up her torso, though stiff joints hampered movement. Her tongue stuck to the roof of her mouth. But the ache in her pelvis protesting a full bladder demanded attention.

Susanna cracked her eyes open. The circle of weak sun haloing a dark head directly in front of her was still strong enough to make her groan. She tried to grab the sides of her splitting skull, but her hands were bound.

"Drink." The figure pressed a tin cup to her mouth.

She parted her lips and tilted her head. As the cool liquid doused her tongue, she became aware of the burble of a brook somewhere behind her.

The man shifted, his features coming into focus. Spring Frog.

The night before rushed into focus as well—the blank stares of the guards in the cabin, blood dripping on the floor, and the shocking betrayal of a man she'd thought a friend. She tried to scramble away but succeeded only in collapsing onto her side. Something lashed her ankles together as well.

When Spring Frog drew her up by the elbow and—shoving aside the bandolier bag on which her head had been pillowed—planted her back against a tree, she pulled away. "Why?"

"Why?" He spat out the word and laughed. Not the happy laugh he'd produced so well, but a manifestation of his true soul, cracked and frightening. He leaned forward, inches from her face. "French, now Americans, take land."

"Then join the Red Sticks."

His brows danced upward, then settled. "We go." His firm nod chilled her.

"Please, you go. Leave me here." Bold Hunter would send men after her. "If they catch you with me ..."

Spring Frog waved his hand toward the north. "Far. Ride ... all night. Ride more." He jerked his chin toward his stallion nibbling winter greens nearby.

"Please, I have to ..." Susanna tilted her head toward the bushes. If she could get over there and steal a few moments out from under his gaze, she could reach her knife.

"Go." He tugged her to her feet and gave her a slight shove.

She stumbled, catching herself by making several quick, small jumps. Whatever tied her feet only allowed her about an inch per step. She shuffled behind an evergreen. Breath coming in desperate little gasps, she scrabbled up the edge of her skirts and felt … only a garter.

A chuckle sounded from a few feet away. She peeked around the tree. Spring Frog stood there, holding her dagger. As Susanna's stomach plummeted, he grinned and slid the sharp blade into the familiar sheath now hung around his neck. Then he waved his hand. "Now go."

Tears filled her eyes as he stepped away to give her a minute of privacy. She had no choice. She had to relieve herself, or the pain of bouncing on a horse would become excruciating. As well as she could, she squatted and completed her business.

When Susanna returned to the clearing, Spring Frog held the head of his horse. She couldn't find it in her to take another step toward him. She would have done better to have placed her trust in Standing Wolf. She extended her bound hands. "Please, Spring Frog. I understand you took me so I wouldn't sound the alert, but you're away now. I will only slow you down." To wherever he was going. The notion made her dizzy with panic.

His smooth face hardened as he strode toward her, and he dragged her forward by the elbow. "You stop me kill chief. Life for life. You are mine."

With that statement, was it any wonder she did not take comfort in the fact that Spring Frog had failed to execute Path Killer?

CHAPTER FIFTEEN

Though the gray light of dawn made the trail the army had traversed from Fort Strother to Talladega easier to trace, Sam kept his stallion at a lope. Standing Wolf's revelation might have convinced Colonel Moore to send Sam back to Turkey Town to sound the warning, but he personally thought it more likely that Spring Frog had melted into the night with the intention of joining the Red Sticks.

How could a man he'd trusted as a brother-in-arms be capable of this type of betrayal? The man he'd allowed near Colonel Moore's children. He would accept any other explanation before he would admit such an error in his own judgment.

If, by some crazy chance, Spring Frog had indeed doubled back for another attempt on Path Killer's life, he'd claimed a bigger head start than Sam could hope to close. Standing Wolf hadn't been able to say when his brother-in-law had slipped away. He'd ridden at the tail of the column and could have parted from the regiment long before they'd joined Jackson's force at Talladega, which meant he could have reached Turkey Town around the same time Standing Wolf reported his absence.

The possibility didn't raise too much alarm, though, as Sam had indicated to Colonel Moore. Spring Frog was one man. After the two recent incidents, Bold Hunter and his men would be on the alert.

So where the trail forked—the left leading to the Coosa River and Fort Strother, and the right to Tallushatchee—Bold Hunter was the last person Sam expected to see. The man rode a massive stallion, and his thick frame bristled with weapons.

Sam's chest clenched as he reined his mount in. "Bold Hunter! Why so far from Turkey Town?" The Wolf Clan warrior had already traveled halfway to Talladega, which meant he'd departed during the night. His alarm rose further.

"Hicks." Bold Hunter drew his stallion alongside Sam's. "I ride in search of Colonel Moore."

"He will have moved out from Talladega this morning with Jackson's force. They cut across Hillabee country east to the Tallapoosa River."

"On the McIntosh Trail and Upper Creek Path?"

"Yes. They will make camp tonight at the Enitachopco village. Jackson left cabins standing there for that purpose. Why?" Sam's first thought was that more troops must have arrived at Armstrong or Turkey Town, but he wouldn't have expected Bold Hunter to act as courier for such news.

"There was another attempt on Path Killer last night."

"No! What happened?" So Standing Wolf had been right, only Sam was already too late.

"I had moved my family and housed him in my cabin. Someone killed both of his guards and was only prevented from entering the inner chamber by the niece of my wife."

Sam's mind scrambled to breach an inner wall that some part of his consciousness threw up, keeping him from landing on a painful truth. Then, there it was, with his stomach dropping away and coldness rushing over his entire body. "Susanna?"

He sucked in a shaky breath when Bold Hunter confirmed his worst fear with a nod. "She went back to the cabin for a cooking pot. Must have caught him in the deed. The family next door heard sounds of a struggle and raised the alarm."

"What happened to her?" Sam resisted the urge to close his eyes. Doing so would only magnify his mental image of the dark-haired girl lying in a pool of her own blood—and announce his love for the colonel's daughter to her stepuncle.

"He took her."

Sam's gaze snapped to Bold Hunter's. "She's alive?"

Another nod. "This is why I ride to tell her father."

All the air rushed out of him, and his heart started to beat an insane tempo. "The man's name is Spring Frog. He was of the Natchez Creeks. One of his relatives reported him missing and connected him to a previous attempt on Path Killer, which is why I was sent back to the village."

"This Spring Frog may alert the enemy that our men are coming." Bold Hunter's stallion tossed his head as if in response to his rider's urgency. "This makes it even more important that we find Moore right away."

"Susanna may also be running out of time." Sam could hardly argue the safety of one girl weighed heavier than that of an entire army, but neither could he deny that the need to find her overwhelmed all else for him. Walking his impatient stallion in a circle around Bold Hunter's, Sam, too, restrained the urge to fly—until he knew where to go. He must think. "He would take her to the Red Sticks on the Tallapoosa, wherever they have the women and children."

"There are many villages on the Tallapoosa. How will we know which one?"

"Our intelligence says the warriors gather near Emuckfaw Creek. The army plans to move down the river and cross the creek from the east. The warriors would not have their families in the war camp, but in the nearest village, Emuckfaw."

Bold Hunter nodded as if they'd reached an agreement. "You must return to Moore and Jackson near Enitachopco. I will cut through the Hillabee land to intersect the river farther down."

No. Oh no. Panic rose in Sam. He'd fight this massive warrior on the spot before he'd relinquish the opportunity to rescue Susanna himself. But he'd try words first. "Spying and stealth are my strengths. Battle is yours."

"Susanna Moore is daughter of my wife's sister. It falls to me to bring her home safe." Bold Hunter's jaw hardened to resemble granite after he made his pronouncement.

"Stepdaughter." Why did he say that? Bold Hunter probably didn't even acknowledge there was a difference, even though a lesser man would have used the lesser relation—and Susanna's lack of Cherokee blood—to abdicate responsibility.

He got a growl in response. "We are wasting time."

Sam didn't have to be told that, but under no circumstances would he skirt after the army like an errand boy when a traitor held the life of the woman he loved in his hands. "Bold Hunter, every one of my skills will be needful to sneak up to a village and locate Susanna." He swiped his hat from his head, and the feathers fluttered into his face. "But I will bring her home. I swear on my life."

The warrior considered him for a moment, his brows dark slashes across his broad forehead. "Because I see you vow this with your whole heart, I will allow you to go after the girl."

Firelight and wildly flickering shadows danced between the slender logs of the hut where Susanna had been held for the past three days. The drumming—that was what had startled her from fitful sleep. She jerked upright on the woven blanket Spring Frog had given her.

"What is happening?" she asked the other two young women lying beside the central fire, but they either didn't understand her Cherokee or pretended to sleep. Not that they had spoken to her before, except to issue brusque commands in the foreign Muskogean tongue. They were Red Stick women, wives of the warriors, not captives like her.

Susanna scooted over to the wall. Lack of chinking made it easy to glimpse outside—and for the cold to get in. The temperature dropped mere inches outside the circle surrounding the fire. In fact, she had to rotate regularly while lying down to keep one side of her body from frosting over. That had proven difficult for the first two days after their arrival when she'd been so sore from the saddle she could barely walk.

Not to worry about that, for she hadn't been allowed outside the hut, even to relieve herself. The women had brought her corn mush and water for drinking and washing. She'd spent her hours staring into the fire, praying someone sought her. Bold Hunter. Her father. Sam. And wondering what Spring Frog had meant by "You are mine." As a slave? Or a wife? He'd yet to make his intentions clear, a fact which both relieved and terrified her.

Now, she sucked in her breath. All of the encampment—for that was what Susanna had surmised it was, lacking any permanent dwellings or a square or council house—appeared to have gathered around a single, massive bonfire. Mostly naked warriors, painted in red, leapt and danced. Their shrieks and whoops rose in volume, snaking down her spine.

She gasped when the door jerked open. Spring Frog stood in the opening, his once-friendly features unrecognizable with war paint. He spoke with authority—not cruel but hurried. The two women immediately got up and rolled their sleeping mats.

"What is happening?" When Susanna repeated her question, Spring Frog strode over to her and seized her arm. He shoved her blanket at her and answered in his broken Cherokee.

"Come. Women to village." A smile cracked his face. There was the cruelty. "You not be here to see white father die."

Sam lay flat on his belly, not moving when some of the black paint he'd smeared over his face worked its way into the corner of his eye. He stared unblinking, not at the braves dancing around the fire, but at the activity outside the two huts. A couple of warriors had broken off from the gathering and gone to the doors of each. Now, figures in long dresses began to emerge.

His heart almost stopped when the firelight fell on a gray coat he recognized. Susanna's hair streamed down her back, as inky as any Indian's, and she clutched a blanket to her chest. A man whose build resembled Spring Frog's prodded her forward.

Fury almost choked him. If the man had harmed Susanna in any way, Sam would have no hesitation in tomahawking him to death.

Then fear settled over him with an icy current of night air. Some things, once taken, couldn't be retrieved. Or revenged.

He could not think about that now.

The bonfire and ruckus had led him right to the war camp. He'd managed to dodge their sentries, and now, these warriors must know what Sam knew, too, that the army encamped not three miles away. As he'd predicted, in anticipation of battle, they were removing any women still present to the village nearby. This camp appeared impenetrable. If Jackson assaulted it, he stood little chance of taking it, much less the village beyond.

He had to follow Susanna, find out where they secured her, and rescue her without hope of aid from any of his comrades. When the sounds of battle rose the next day, Sam would do his best to smuggle her out, but if he had to, he'd take his chances against whatever men remained.

Treading first on the balls of his feet, Sam only put his weight down once certain of a silent step. He glided through the woods, following the party on the narrow path, praying to be seen only by owls and God.

Sam watched the village before dawn, straining to detect any movement outside the rivercane-frame hut where Spring Frog had led Susanna the night before. Limb-numbing relief had weakened him when the Natchez had not accompanied her inside. Instead, he'd bolted the door of the clay-plastered, grass-thatched-roof hut from the outside before disappearing into an adjacent cabin in a cluster of four. So far as he could tell, no one had entered or departed Susanna's hut, and no smoke came from the top. She was being held as a prisoner until after the battle.

Thank You, God.

Had Susanna been housed with a family, or had Spring Frog bedded with her, it would have been almost impossible to get her away. The size of the village also played to his favor. As a subordinate settlement of the much larger Oakfuski farther west on the river, Emuckfaw was a small town of only about two dozen homes. And as such, it lacked the high, spiked-log stockade that often protected primary villages.

Now, before the residents stirred, was the perfect time to approach from where he lay prone on the slight creek embankment. With his long knife held at the ready, Sam crept toward the hut. No one. Nothing. He hadn't even encountered pickets in the nearby woods. The town must have truly drained of men for the coming battle.

He didn't dare whisper her name in case someone else *was* inside. Instead, he drew up the latch as slowly and noiselessly as he could, fixed it in place, and cracked the door open, also without a sound. In the pitch dark, he could see nothing inside.

Sam took one step in, and a rustle alerted him to movement on his right. A shadow fell fast toward his head. He shot out his open hand just in time to stave off a blow to his temple—from a woman's joined, bound fists. He grabbed the wrists and twisted. A gasp of pain sounded, and he tugged his assailant under his left arm.

"Susanna?" He didn't have to ask, not even if another woman had been in the hut, for her hair still smelled of sweetshrub blossoms … and *her*.

"Sam?" His name caught on a sob.

"Shh." He released her only to cover her mouth with his hand, sheath his knife with the other, and then wrap his arms around her. They couldn't afford to stay that way even for a moment, but from the way she sagged against him, he feared she might collapse. "Are you unharmed?"

A hundred more specific questions scrambled for release, but they must wait. Right now, he just needed to know she was of sufficiently sound mind and body to flee.

Her head nodded under his chin. "I prayed you would come for me."

"Hold out your hands so I can cut them free."

She did as he directed, but as he eased the point of his long knife inside the tight leather thongs, a din of musketry rattled in the distance. Susanna jumped, then whimpered. The blade must have contacted her flesh.

"The battle has begun. We must go now." In fact, it might already be too late. Securing the binding against his left thumb, Sam sliced through, then kept his blade in hand. "Stay behind me."

They'd made it halfway to the woods when a red-painted warrior—gray sprinkling his hair, but still tall and solid of build—skirted the far cabin and charged Sam with a drawn tomahawk. He barely had time to throw his weight to the left, an attempt to match the Red Stick's momentum. Sam raised his left forearm to deflect the cutting, crushing blow. Then stabbed for the neck. Missed as his opponent twisted away, then grabbed Sam's wrist. His grip failed. The knife flew through the air and skittered across the ground.

Sam scrambled for distance and the opportunity to draw his tomahawk.

Susanna edged toward the trees. So far, no one else approached, and the din of nearby battle had grown louder, but he had to finish this. Fast. Dying in the dirt in front of her, thus leaving her to the designs of Spring Frog, was not an option. That meant he needed the unexpected.

Weapons in hand, he and the painted warrior circled. The

man's gaze followed his slightest move. Searching for weakness? Sam would give him some. He feinted left as if he might flee with Susanna. When his opponent charged again, he reversed direction, sprinted with all his might and force, and grabbed the warrior's right hand while swinging his own tomahawk in an arch upward from the ground.

A grunt and the man froze.

As he withdrew his weapon, with a quick step forward, Sam wrapped his left leg around the man's right. The moment his weight toppled, Sam raised his tomahawk for the overhand, killing blow.

A blow which he prayed Susanna did not see, and a moment he already wanted to forget. But he could not leave the man to suffer and sound the alarm, and this time, Standing Wolf was not there to finish the job. It was on him alone to protect Susanna.

When he looked up, she stood frozen about ten feet away, her face as white as the moon in dawn's faint light. Sam didn't pause to wipe his blade, but the body in the open was a problem.

"Get my knife." Jerking his head toward where his smaller weapon had fallen, he grabbed the fallen warrior by the moccasins and dragged him under the low branches of a cedar tree.

He'd just released the man's feet when Susanna yelled his name. "Sam!"

He ducked a second before an airborne knife whistled by his head and lodged in the tree beside him. Spring Frog ran not far behind. Brandishing his tomahawk, he launched his weight at Sam. Sam grabbed Spring Frog's right arm with his left hand, but the blade caught his shoulder. Pain coursed through him, causing his tomahawk hook under his opponent's arm to go awry. The world tilted, and both careened down the slope toward the creek, tumbling and sliding.

Susanna stifled a cry as Sam and Spring Frog grappled in the mud and muck of the creek, each scrambling for higher ground. The men circled, engaged, and fended each other off. Then came together again, locked in a deadly dance. Seemingly one with his environment, Spring Frog used anything nature lent him—a rock, a root, a branch. A slippery patch.

Responding to the inner urging to get clear of view from the village, she eased down the embankment. She must stay away from the fight but find an open vantage point. In her fingers, Sam's long knife shook. What she wouldn't give for her familiar dagger, still secured around Spring Frog's neck. Could she use the larger, bulkier blade if she had to?

That she might became increasingly apparent. This ugly, desperate fight for life didn't resemble the mock combat staged at Fort Strother or Turkey Town. Spring Frog knew it too. He had the upper hand.

His teeth bared in an exultant grin, and he said something Susanna could not understand. Whatever it was, it enraged Sam. He let out a growl and threw himself at Spring Frog, water, sand, and pebbles spraying from his moccasins. The swing of his weapon missed the Natchez, who had levied his weight on a branch and sprung onto the bank. He descended like a panther.

"No!" Susanna edged toward the overlook and braced herself on a sapling.

Landing flat on his back, Sam blocked the man's tomahawk with the handle of his own. But Spring Frog bore down on him, pressing the blade toward Sam's throat.

Had she been on the practice range, she'd be roughly six paces from Spring Frog. She picked a small hole in the middle of his tunic, raised her arm, and threw. The blade lodged in his right lower back. The minute Spring Frog's body sagged, Sam vaulted up from under him.

Her middle clenching, Susanna turned away. She bent to vomit the only liquid that remained inside her onto the ground. Her arms shook so bad they scarcely held her up, and hot, uncontrollable tears ran down her face.

When she finally sat and attempted to pivot on the bank, Sam called out. "Do not look!"

She wiped her tears with both hands and remained facing the other direction, terrified that at any moment, warriors might come running from the village. But it was Sam who came, pulling her up by her elbow. He'd cleaned and stowed his weapons, but blood splattered his black-painted face. Her knees knocked together.

Nevertheless, when he asked if she could run, she nodded. He half supported, half dragged her down the middle of the creek. Her feet slipped on rocks and into deep pools, splashing frigid water up her legs, weighting the hem of her dress. Several times, she braced herself from a fall by grabbing hold of the man at her side.

Finally, the creek bed opened into a swampy area. Sam gave a soft whistle, and a nicker sounded from a thicket. "Thank God, no one found him."

Before Susanna could plunge into the shin-high, mucky waters, Sam lifted her with one arm beneath her back and the other beneath her legs. She clasped his neck as he waded toward his stallion. A few climbing steps gained them solid ground. He started to lift her onto the horse's back when he paused suddenly and muttered something in Cherokee.

"What?"

He cocked his head. "The battle. It seems to have ended."

Sure enough, the rattle of musketry had ceased. Susanna scrambled for the saddle and threw her leg over. "Does that mean we will try to find the army?" She wanted nothing more than the security of numbers right now.

"No. That was too quick. Hear that?"

A distant *pop-pop*. "Yes."

"Someone in pursuit." Sam untethered and led his stallion to a nearby log. With a quick, easy spring, he mounted behind her, drawing the reins on either side of her body. "The woods will be full of men, and I daresay the Red Sticks will make another stand. It is best to leave the area as fast as possible. I will take you to Fort Strother through Hillabee country."

If that was such a good solution, why was his voice full of dread?

CHAPTER SIXTEEN

They seemed to ride forever on a spider web of shadow-streaked paths. At first, they made their own, dismounting and Susanna leading the horse while Sam hacked passage through the brush with his tomahawk. Then they took a way no wider than a deer trace. Susanna constantly ducked branches. Sam had given her his woolen blanket to help protect her legs, but briars still snagged her stockings. She could stand it so long as they didn't encounter any more fleeing Red Sticks, as they almost had twice while leaving Emuckfaw Creek. Once, a patch of cane had sheltered them—the other time, a rocky glen. Not long after that, distant sounds of battle had resumed, confirming Sam's decision to flee the area.

Finally, when the winter sun began to wane, they came out on a wider Indian path. Susanna drew a deep breath but still couldn't relax.

Riding with him wasn't as it had been before. He spoke only to give her direction or inquire after her needs. What she wanted to tell him was that her need was for his comfort, but his stiff posture and granite jaw promised none of that. Was he angry that he'd missed another battle? That he'd needed her assistance to kill Spring Frog?

Hurt and confusion stirred the already volatile emotions swarming like a disturbed ant nest in her chest. So when he sagged, leaning on her for the briefest moment, she tensed, turning toward him. Maybe his stoicism had only come from the alertness of caution.

"Sam? Do you need to stop and rest?"

"We should ride through the night."

Susanna doubted she could continue through the hours of darkness without falling asleep, and Sam's weary voice indicated that he was just as drained. She tried skirting his pride by appealing to his common sense. "The horse seems tired. Perhaps we should let him drink in that pond ahead and eat the cane you brought from the creek."

His nod caught the corner of her eye. "You speak wisdom. My mount hasn't had more than a mouthful of grass here and there for a couple of days. But we will stop at the remains of a village ahead, by a small creek."

"Remains?"

"One of the Hillabee towns our regiment rode against last fall. If I remember correctly, one or two of the cabins may have been left standing."

The hard shudder that passed through him chilled Susanna too. Even more so did the sight of blackened ruins they soon came upon. In the twilight, an eerie silence hung over the place, and Sam's memory proved questionable. Only part of one American-style cabin remained, the chimney anchoring the unburned room.

He dismounted, then reached up to catch her. She slid into his arms, her hands landing against his shoulders. He grunted, and she drew back from an unexpected dampness, staring at her right hand. Blood glistened on her fingertips.

"Sam! You're hurt." How could she have forgotten Spring Frog's tomahawk slicing into his shoulder? Her legs trembled, but she forced herself to stand without his aid.

"A glancing blow. Nothing serious, and I padded it."

"Not very well. If you are bleeding that much, you need stitches." Susanna wiped her hand using the underside of her skirt hem. "But I have no supplies with me."

"I might." What did he mean, *might*? He either did or didn't, and he would surely know. Despite her questioning stare, Sam did not seem disposed to provide any details. His brow lowered as he gathered his stallion's reins. "I should take you straight to Strother. It is what your father would expect."

"He would also expect you to deliver me in one piece, which you won't be able to do if you bleed until you pass out. Please, let us rest here. Let me see to your wound. Do you have a needle and thread in that bag of yours or not?" She eyed the sack on his hip.

"I have a needle and sinew, and I will get it for you *if* I decide this place is safe. Hold my horse while I check the cabin. We would need a blaze for the needle, but we should not make a fire before dark."

"Very well." Susanna accepted the reins. She patted the stallion's head while Sam went into the cabin. Looking into the animal's eyes, she gave her thanks in Cherokee for his effort that day, only turning when his master emerged. "All clear?"

"No one has been here since the attack. There is a bed frame on the wall you can lie in while I water the horse and wash up."

She nodded but only took two steps before her knee buckled, and she stumbled.

Sam caught her by the waist, then retained a hold on her elbow, peering into her face with a frown. "I am sorry. I have pushed you too hard. You have been through much." His grip tightened on her arm. "Did Spring Frog—or anyone else—harm you?"

A random spark of humor made Susanna chuckle. "What are you going to do, go back and kill him again?"

His fingers bit into her flesh, and his blackened face loomed closer. If it had not been Sam, she would have been frightened. "I am not joking, Susanna. Did he lay hands on you?" The words ground out with such force she knew then that he'd been repressing the question all day.

"No, Sam. He told me that my fate would be decided after the battle. My virtue is intact."

He heaved a breath and moved his hand to cup her face. Then sorrow washed over his expression. "If we stay here tonight, that may matter little to your father."

"Let me deal with my father. I will wait inside."

Susanna held up her hand to show him she could make it without assistance, but as soon as she had passed through the outer shell of a room and into the one with the fireplace, she collapsed onto the bed frame. Once upon a time, she might have been worried about spiders or vermin. Now, her eyes closed the instant she pillowed her head on her arms.

When she awoke, firelight licked back the darkness of the room. A delicious scent tickled Susanna's nose—doubtless, the cause of her waking. A man sat before the hearth, bare back tapering to a waist wrapped with a blanket over leggings. He turned. With the paint gone, the youth of Sam's face tugged at her heart.

"Why didn't you wake me?"

"You needed sleep. Come. Eat."

Susanna scrambled from the bunk to sit beside him on the dirt-packed floor as he pulled two fish from a spit over the flames and laid them on a tin plate. Her thoughtless attempt to grab one resulted in her snatching back burned fingers.

"Wait." He laughed at her. "Let me cut it open."

"I don't recall the last time I ate. I am not even going to ask how you caught two fish in that little stream in the winter twilight."

"Some things I am good at." Regret tugged at his voice.

"Many things." Susanna met his dark eyes, but he shifted and pulled a knife from his pile of belongings. Thankfully, not the long knife she'd hurled at Spring Frog, but … "My dagger!"

"Did you think I would leave such a good blade on a dead man?"

"I will be glad to have it back."

As he filleted the small fish, her gaze drifted to the folded muslin—probably commandeered from the tail of a shirt—stuck to his shoulder with fresh blood.

He followed the path of her attention. "Eat first."

She nodded and did her level best not to stare at his lean but well-muscled torso. Her heart thudded. She didn't fear for her safety, only her own feelings. Father would be right to worry.

Sam slid the plate toward her, and she stuffed fingers full of smoked, white meat into her mouth. He nudged her. "Slow down. No need for me to rescue you only to have you choke on a fish bone."

Susanna spluttered, then broke into a laugh. Uncontrollable mirth rolled over her, a release for her tension. And uncontrollable affection, because even after all they'd been through, Sam showed her a glimpse of his softer side. They were indeed a perfect match. But while a faint smile twitched his lips, his polite tolerance seemed to fade as an almost visible weight again settled over him.

Of an instant, her laughter deteriorated into tears, and she clasped her hands over her face. "Please don't look at me like that. Like I've done something wrong." After not knowing if she would survive each day, she couldn't tolerate another moment of coldness. Not from him.

"You've done nothing wrong." Shoving the plate aside, Sam scooted next to her and wrapped his arms around her.

Oh, the haven she'd been longing for. She didn't need her father, or the army, or a fort. She needed only the security of Sam Hicks' embrace.

Face in his good shoulder, Susanna sobbed out the tension and terror of the past week. He rocked her as if she were a child. Finally, he smoothed her unbound hair with his hand, leaning his face in. Did he breathe in the scent of her hair? Kiss her forehead? Or did she only imagine it? A shudder ran through her, but as she turned her face up, Sam moved back, putting about a foot between them. He sat looking at her with a sobriety that belied his actions.

"What you must think of me." Susanna swiped at her face and hair, battling guilt over her emotional display. "I daresay Cherokee women don't cry like that. I know I have never seen Polly do so."

"She would if she had faced what you have. You have been very brave."

"As have you. Thank you for coming for me." On the way here, he'd told her how Standing Wolf, of all people, had revealed Spring Frog's desertion. And how Sam had met Bold Hunter on the path back to Turkey Town and sent her stepuncle on to warn her father. "I don't think my father could have done what you did."

His face hardened. So he *did* resent her part in her own rescue, feel his actions had not been adequate. Susanna bristled. Stupid male pride. Or worse—he found rescuing her a poor substitute for glory in battle.

She sucked in a breath and reached for the bandolier bag lying at Sam's side. "I should see to your wound."

He jerked the satchel away, nodding instead toward a muslin cloth in front of the fireplace, unfolded to display the items she had requested earlier. What did he not want her to see in that bag?

She narrowed her eyes and sidled up to him on her knees. Pulling back the sticky bandage, she used the edges to dab fresh blood from a two-inch gash under his collarbone. "You are fortunate this did not fall farther in any direction. But it is deep. I will need the thread."

"I laid the needle in the fire earlier." He handed it to her, then, sitting cross-legged, angled his shoulder toward her. Another trickle of crimson made its way down his chest.

Biting her lip, Susanna mopped the blood. She threaded the needle and, frowning in the firelight, made a knot. Then she knelt in front of him. Her hands shook. "I've plenty of experience with needles, but never through a man, so please sit still."

She didn't need to tell him. As she placed one hand on his shoulder and the other below his wound, he clenched his jaw and scarcely breathed. He didn't make a sound when the point pierced his flesh, although Susanna might have whimpered herself on a giant swallow. She closed her eyes for a moment, forcing her breathing and heart rate to slow. She must press ahead. In and out until the wound closed—and then tie it off.

Finally, when she snipped off the end of the thread with her dagger, Sam exhaled.

Susanna raised her hem and began to shred a long strip from her petticoat. "We should wrap this around your chest to keep some fresh padding in place." His silence galled her. Not even an expression of gratitude for stitching him up. Her heart burning, she paused and looked up. "Is that all right with you, or are you going to be nettled with me for bandaging you as well?"

His gaze snapped to hers. "*As well?* Why would I be angry with you?"

"You tell me! You haven't spoken since I thanked you for coming to my rescue, which I can only take to mean you regret the inconvenience. Or maybe you regret teaching me how to throw knives so I could cheat you out of besting Spring Frog, as I cheated you out of the battle."

"No." The answer cracked out like a whip. "You truly think that?"

"What else am I to think?"

He made a scoffing sound. "Without you, I would not have bested Spring Frog."

"And this angers you." Susanna put a fist on her hip, the strip of petticoat dangling from her fingers.

"This shames me. You think I wanted to fight in that battle?" Sam spat the question at her, his eyes gleaming slits. "Today showed how unprepared I was. Spring Frog anticipated my every move."

"Because he'd already gotten you to show him at Strother and Turkey Town."

Sam shook his head. "Because he was right when he said I was no warrior." So that was what the man had used to taunt Sam. "And yet, I took his scalp as though I was."

"What?" The air puffed out of her with that single word. Her gaze went to the bandolier bag as creeping horror took the place of breath. That was what Sam had done when her back had been turned? Her knees gave way, and she sank to the dirt floor.

Sam stared into the fire as if unable to look at her. "It is the only token Path Killer will accept as proof of his death. But I left part of my soul by that creek, as I did here last fall when I killed men who did not fight to defend themselves. This place … it still haunts me."

"The peace agreement." She found the strength to murmur a response. "You were only obeying orders. That was not your fault."

"But other things were." He sat forward, his gaze swinging back to her with the intensity of confession. "The day I saved John Ross, it was my fault he was in danger. I had spared a boy from Standing Wolf's knife. Despite his wound, the boy tried to kill your father's adjutant. Only then did I hurl my knife at him. Standing Wolf saw it all. He knew—Spring Frog knew—I am not worthy to be in your father's regiment, much less an officer."

Susanna shook her head. "Yet you came after me, and you killed that warrior in the camp. We would never have gotten out of there if you had not done what you did."

"I would do anything—" Sam's words cut off, and he dropped his chin. "It is right that you look at me with disgust."

Her heart clenched at this baring of his. How could he believe she saw him that way? She crept closer, nudging his leg until he sat up. Leaning in, Susanna twined a finger in the silky hair behind his ear, as she'd longed to do for months. "Sam Hicks, you are the noblest man I know."

She could think of only one way to convince him. She put her other hand around his neck and pressed her lips to his.

CHAPTER SEVENTEEN

She wanted him, even after he'd admitted his failures and showed her the dark spots on his soul. The first pressure of her soft lips drove all other thoughts from Sam's mind. A short, surprised exhalation, and he slid a hand around the base of her head, sealing her mouth with his. Driving the kiss deeper, kissing her over and over like a man without reason.

It was her sigh, a soft sound of surrender as she melted into his arms, which stopped him.

He froze, heart thudding, desire turning to guilt. He was taking what he had no right to take ... nor ever would. "Susanna." Sam whispered her name against lips that still pulled in every ounce of his being. "We cannot."

Releasing her, he stood abruptly. As he grabbed his tunic and tugged it down over his torso and hips, she turned away, seeming to sink into a puddle by the hearth. She covered her face with her hand. Sam didn't trust himself to speak, and if he stayed another minute ...

Hefting his belt with his long knife, he strode through the door, past the ruins of the next room where he'd stabled his stallion, and into the cold night air. It rushed against him, into him, like the return of sanity.

Oh God, what was I thinking?

She'd attempted to assure him she did not find him loathsome, and he'd taken what had been meant as a simple kiss—offered at a time when he knew Susanna's internal walls had crumbled—and almost turned it into exactly what her father had feared. Not only that, he'd also disclosed every emotion in his heart.

How could he go back on a revelation like that? Pretend it had never happened? Just deliver her to the colonel and walk away? Sam groaned and tugged his hand through his hair. But how could he go back on his promise to her father? Even his own father had advised him to walk away from the white girl.

Susanna Moore was never meant to be his.

For the better part of an hour, he paced the property, telling himself he scouted for signs of danger, but always keeping an eye on the cabin. Finally, when the fear he'd hurt her became too much to bear and the cold had surely frozen every spark of passion out of him, he trudged back inside. At his entrance, she grabbed for her dagger, then sank back down when she saw him. Sam knelt by the hearth and added a couple sticks of wood to the fire.

The golden light revealed the reddened rims of her eyes and the tracks dried tears had left through the smudges on her face. Sam dug for his canteen and wet a cotton kerchief, but when he tried to wipe her face, she shoved his hand away.

He deserved that. He hung his head, remorse clenching his chest. "I am sorry."

"I don't want to hear you apologize. I want to hear you say you don't love me." Her eyes challenged him, a quick follow-up to her shocking words.

To claim such a thing now would be a pointless lie. "A stronger man would make you believe so."

"Then you do."

Some greater force stealing control over his voice, the truth wrenched out of him. "I do."

Her spine stiffened, and she lifted her chin. "Nokassa said when you knew I chose you, you would fight for me."

Sam scooted closer to her, reaching for her hand. He searched her face. "Even if you choose me and I choose you, do you think your father would ever allow us to be together?"

"Maybe if he thought no one else would want me."

Her reply came so softly that Sam almost missed it. He straightened and jerked his gaze to her. "What are you suggesting?"

Yet her face shone with sweet, hopeful innocence. Thank God. He didn't think he could withstand yet another level of temptation.

"You said that from my time in captivity and from being alone with you, he would consider me damaged."

"That is likely, but, Susanna, even though your father married a Cherokee, this would not be the same." Stroking the tops of her fingers, Sam shook his head. "The white blood you and your father share has set you apart. You have always lived in a world of privilege, privilege that money alone can never buy me. Protection and security which education and diplomacy may never afford. How can I ask you to give all that up for me?"

She closed her eyes. "By simply asking."

Sam's heart thudded as heavily as it had an hour before, but for an entirely different reason, as she offered herself in an entirely different way. He reached for her, almost drowning in amazement when she yielded to his embrace, tucking her head under his chin. He whispered against her hair, "First, I must ask your father." He dragged in a deep breath. "If God our Father wills this, the wishes of earthly fathers will not stand in the way."

That night and the next day were both wonderful and terrible— torture, in truth, giving Sam a glimpse of what life as the husband of Susanna Moore would be like.

His promise to speak to her father had contented Susanna, and soon, with her head pillowed on his shoulder, her eyelids had begun to sag. He'd spread his blanket for her and lain down behind her, blocking the drafts from the damaged wall. Only the intense cold had kept him from securing her alone in the bed frame.

Their shared warmth allowed Susanna to sleep even though it produced a less soothing effect on Sam. Her father would kill him if he knew they had bedded down together, even innocently. Yet if Susanna contracted lung fever again, it would kill *her*. He'd insisted she remain facing the fire, and thankfully, she hadn't stirred all night. He'd rested his hand on the curve of her waist and stroked her hair, listening to her gentle breathing and savoring every second. But the moment she'd awakened, he'd risen and prepared for their departure.

As they rode, Susanna had chattered with the euphoria of one recently spared from death. She'd asked many questions about life at Fort Hill. What was his mother like? Did she speak English? What were the ages of his siblings? What did his father grow on the farm? Did they often go to Oostanaula, the nearest town?

At first, Sam could picture her there. He could fix up a smaller cabin on his family's land, and they could fill it with children until he needed to build her a bigger house—a white frame house like her father's. These things he did not say but he thought. Until the realization of all she would be giving up began to settle in, tightening his chest with fear. The worst possible outcome would be for him to marry Susanna only to have her come to resent him and his people.

She turned her head, the western sunlight softening her cheek with a golden glow. "You are growing quiet. Is my endless curiosity making you weary?"

"No." He gave her waist a reassuring squeeze.

With the jerky, joyous enthusiasm of a child, she pointed to the woods on their left. "Look over there! The red cardinal on that silver-white branch of the birch tree. And the deep green of the holly behind. Does it not take your breath away?"

Normally, he would share her delight in their surroundings, but Sam surfaced from his inner turmoil belatedly, providing only a mumble.

Susanna angled toward him again. "What are you thinking?"

Must this woman always be delving into the places he needed to keep private? "About how different life would be for you on Oothcaloga Creek."

"You have told me many things, and they all sound similar to my life at Big Springs."

Navigating a washed-out place in the path, Sam nodded. "Good."

She fell silent, and for a few moments, he dared to hope she'd leave it at that. Then she drew a breath and asked, "What things are you not telling me?"

The tinge of fear in her voice made him chuckle. "Your life would not be in danger, if that is what you're thinking. Because of our shared beliefs and the fact that my father owns land, life on our farm might be similar to that which you know, but outside it ..."

When he didn't complete his sentence, Susanna nudged his ribs with her elbow. "Yes?"

"There are few whites around."

"I see few whites now. I mean, at Big Springs."

"But they are there. Nearby. You are barely inside the border of our territory in Big Springs. You may think you would not miss the company of others like yourself, but when you are surrounded by Cherokees, you may feel otherwise. There is much superstition. Many administer justice in ways you would find brutal." He'd caught her attention. She'd cocked her head and sat very still, probably thinking of the scout tortured at Strother. "These things cannot be changed overnight. Could you live with that?"

She squeezed his arm. "If you are with me, standing between me and the darkness, I can."

Not the reply he was expecting. Her faith in him clenched his heart, challenging him to deserve it. He would be a better man as her husband, but ... "You could give up your claim to Big Springs Bluff?"

She laughed. "George and his future bride would boot me out, eventually."

"No. They would have no right to." Her white blood would trump a male Cherokee heir in the eyes of those with true power.

"I would give it up. It's just land."

Her statement reverberated in his head. Land was everything, the reason his people were gripped in this mighty struggle. So if love was most important to her, he had to ask the next question, or rather, make the next statement. "In the ways of my people, children inherit the mother's ancestry, so ours ... they would have no clan." He couldn't keep the emotion from his voice.

"This bothers you."

"To be without a clan is to be without an identity." Sam drew a deep breath. "As a Christian, I know that our identity is found in God our Father, but for children living in a society where clans are everything ... it would be hard for them."

"For *you*."

"Some things are carved deep in one's mind."

"I had not considered that." For the first time, uncertainty clouded her tone.

"There is something worse."

She sighed. "What? What is worse?"

"In the eyes of your government, our children would be Cherokee. They would have security only so long as your government gave it to them."

"Stop. Please, stop."

Sam did, literally. He tugged the reins of his stallion because Susanna was swinging her leg over the side and pivoting to face him, wrapping her arms around his shoulders. She buried her face against his chest.

"Please, just hold me."

As the setting sun bled red through the barren trees ahead, he threaded the leather leads through his fingers and cradled her body. "I cannot pretend with you, Susanna." Sam ducked his head against hers. "This love, it is almost impossible."

"You said it yourself—with God, nothing is impossible. I am going to hold onto that." She raised her face and cupped his jaw with her delicate hand, her eyes glistening with unshed tears.

He couldn't push her away when she looked at him like that. "Then I will too."

"Do you promise? Promise not to give up on me. On us." Susanna searched his face, her own pleading.

"I promise."

Sam tipped her chin up and kissed her, doing his best to convey tenderness rather than the sadness that warned him this could be the last time. He wouldn't give up—not until every door closed against them. But as much as he wanted to share her faith in God willing their marriage, in love's ability to overcome every obstacle, he could not deny the powerful forces against them. Once they entered the gates of Fort Strother, the expectations of family and society could destroy the dreams they'd shared during these precious days alone.

Somewhere around midnight, Sam gave the two whoops required of the Indian allies to gain admission into army forts. Guards opened the gates, and the weary stallion plodded into the enclosure. The presence of a woman quickly created a stir. As the sentries murmured and men stood from campfires, craning their necks for a glimpse of her, Susanna folded her hand over his. The simple trust in the gesture stirred his every protective instinct.

"I will take you to the officer on duty."

"Oh." She sighed. "How foolish of me. I was imagining riding straight up to my family's old cabin. It feels as though they should come running out to greet me." Disappointment—and likely, exhaustion—thickened her voice.

Sam tightened his arm around her into a gentle squeeze. "Your father will be here soon. He will make arrangements to send you back to Turkey Town, but we will send a messenger right away to reassure your stepmother and brother of your safety."

"Thank you."

He didn't add that he did not expect to be honored with the responsibility of escorting her to the Cherokee village. Under the circumstances, he would be lucky if Colonel Moore did not strike his name from the muster roll.

"Look!" Susanna tilted her head, for the door of her old cabin was, in fact, opening.

Dr. Hawkins' spare frame loomed in the threshold. The man rushed out, astonishment slackening his features. "Miss Moore? I thought you were safely back in Big Springs Bluff now. Was there trouble in Turkey Town? What are you doing here? And … with *him*?" Hawkins' face crumpled as Sam handed Susanna down. At least, he had the sense to come and steady her, though Sam would rather he didn't. And the physician would not let go of her hand.

"Oh, that's right. You don't know." Tugging her fingers free, Susanna looked between Sam and Hawkins.

"Know what?"

Sam swung off his horse and drew her close to his side. "Who is in charge in the absence of the senior officers? Miss Moore needs food and rest. Immediately. I bring her not from Turkey Town but from a Red Stick village."

Hawkins' eyes widened and his lips curled. "What?"

Perversely, Susanna seemed to take pleasure in the doctor's horror. A tiny smirk lifted the corners of her mouth. "It's a long story, Dr. Hawkins, but the short of it is that one of the Natchez Creek warriors doubled back to try to execute Path Killer. I happened upon the scene, and he threw me over his shoulder so I could not sound the alarm. So in a sense, I saved Path Killer's life." Her smile widened.

"He abducted you?" Hawkins stared at her, unblinking. "How

can you make light of this frightful situation?"

"I suppose I am very tired. I do tend to become silly when I am very tired."

The doctor grabbed her arm, then released it as abruptly as if Susanna had refuse rubbed all over her sleeve. "You say you were taken captive by this warrior? For how long?"

She tilted her head, puckering her lips in brief consideration. "About a week. He took me to the enemy war camp, then a nearby village. I thank God Sam found me there, or I would probably be the traitor's wife by now."

Sam didn't know whether to laugh or moan, so he coughed. His intended was behaving badly, and quite on purpose.

"But—but how ..." Dr. Hawkins looked from Sam back to Susanna, then shook his head. "The important thing is, were you harmed?"

Same code language he'd used himself a couple of days ago. He spoke up. "Miss Moore was well treated. I brought her here through Hillabee country as quickly as I could. Now can we please get her settled somewhere secure before the army returns with their wounded? I doubt they will be too far behind us. We heard the sounds of fighting yesterday when we left."

A slow-blinking silence from the physician indicated that the implication of Sam's words settled fully. Perhaps Sam was behaving badly, too, but he already felt the need to stake his claim. Hawkins licked his lips. "Ah, yes. As you can see, I am occupying the Moores' old cabin while I tend to some of my more delicate cases. I will have them moved out."

"And you will move out as well."

The doctor stiffened. "So that you can move in?"

"Of course not." Sam stepped closer. "I will take a tent just outside to guard the spotless reputation of Miss Moore." Even though he had to look up to Hawkins, the man faltered, his gaze dropping to the weapons on Sam's belt.

Susanna placed a hand on his arm. "Really, gentlemen. No one, especially sick men, needs to move anywhere on my account." She shook her head, rolling her eyes. "My father was right. I am beginning to see why a woman at a fort is such an inconvenience. *I* will take a tent and spare everyone the trouble."

"No!" Sam and Hawkins barked the same answer at the same moment. Finally, they agreed on something.

With a slight bow, Sam turned to the doctor. "I will help you carry the men out. Show me what to do."

"Very well." Hawkins nodded, but first, he approached Susanna, taking her hand. He bent over to press a kiss on her knuckles, then stared into her eyes. "Under whatever circumstances, I am grateful to have you back, Miss Moore."

Sam's stomach sank. The man remained undeterred.

And her father would be worse.

CHAPTER EIGHTEEN

The next day, Sam offered to take Susanna foraging in the woods surrounding the fort. Dr. Hawkins' displeasure was such that Sam suggested one of the recovering patients in need of exercise accompany them. Susanna decided that wasn't so bad, as the soldier tired easily, making for enjoyable interaction while she and Sam harvested mushrooms, watercress, and dandelions as the private perched on a nearby log. They even sat together for a few moments on the bent tree George had discovered. When their chaperone stepped away to conduct private business, Sam warmed her cold lips with his, just enough that she wanted so much more. What a perfect day in her elven wood, pretending the war and the world could never separate them and that they might go on like this forever.

The following day, Dr. Hawkins put an end to that notion. He insisted if anyone should be foraging in the woods, it should be him. Miss Moore could assist him in gathering herbs useful for medicine and the preparation of such that afternoon. Weren't the skills of Lieutenant Hicks better employed hunting for their dinner?

She wanted Sam to argue that, but even she saw the sense in it. He went off alone with his rifle over his shoulder while she filled her basket with blackberry root, yarrow, and chickweed. Then she cut bandages, sorted supplies, and folded blankets, all the while struggling to attune her sympathy to the needs of Dr. Hawkins' children as related from his latest letter from home. His sister, he said, grew weary of bearing the burden of his brood in addition to her own. But he had promised Colonel Moore he would remain until the Creek rebellion be dealt with.

The day after that, her father returned. An outcry sounded from the guards, the gates opened, and Colonel Moore came riding in, flanked by John Ross and Bold Hunter at the head of the column of soldiers. When he spied Susanna in the door of the cabin, he dismounted as fast as a man of his age might and ran toward her. The uncharacteristic display of emotion snatched her breath, but she stumbled from the stoop and sprinted for his arms. He wrapped them around her and buried his face in her hair.

"Oh, Susanna. My Susanna. How I prayed you would be here waiting for me."

"It is good to see you, Father." She inhaled his scent of smoke, horse, and wool and dared to peek up at him. "You are well? Unhurt?" She hadn't allowed herself to think even for a moment that he might not return. One's mind could only sustain so much stress in a certain period. Instead, refusing to give death the power of naming it, she had prayed God would protect him from wounding or sickness.

His craggy face split in a brilliant smile, but then tears filled his eyes. "I am. But you do not know what torture it was to ride away from the Tallapoosa, even with them attacking us as we fled. I had no way of knowing if Lieutenant Hicks had been successful or if I was leaving my precious daughter in some unknown village, in the hands of the enemy." He caressed her wind-chapped cheeks with his equally rough thumbs.

Sam stepped forward, his expression somber. As usual, Susanna had not noticed his approach. "You fought a second day at Emuckfaw, sir?"

She drew back just a little, and Father released her face but wrapped an arm around her as if to assure himself of her presence. "Yes. They came at us again, right when we had the cannon in the middle of Enitchopco Creek. Jackson wanted us to take another route back since we had such difficulty crossing Emuckfaw Creek on the way."

"Another opportunity to slay more of our enemies." At the rumble of a Cherokee statement, Susanna turned. She hardly recognized the feral gleam in her stepuncle's eye, but she reached for his hand, nonetheless.

"Thank you for riding from Turkey Town for help."

He nodded. "It is good for young Hicks that he did as he swore."

"Did you doubt me—when I had both you and Colonel Moore to answer to?" Sam lifted a brow at him. "And it would seem your role suited you as well."

"It had been a long time since my tomahawk split more than the broad side of a tree." Bold Hunter rubbed his finger over the head of said weapon, teeth flashing like a panther with cornered prey.

Susanna shuddered and thanked the Almighty she had not seen him in action, especially when her father spoke up again.

"Bold Hunter and many in our regiment distinguished themselves, but we lost two dozen and bring back seventy-some wounded."

"Seventy?" Susanna gasped, glancing around the compound, which now swarmed with able men, horses, and injured moaning from makeshift litters. Dr. Hawkins and the other personnel directed the flow outside the medical cabins. "Now that you are here, Father, we can take some men in with us. Dr. Hawkins had cleared the cabin for me while I was alone, and Sam—Lieutenant Hicks, I mean—is staying in the tent right outside."

For the first time, the debt he owed his Cherokee lieutenant seemed to register on the colonel. He dropped his arm around her and stepped forward with his hand extended toward Sam. "Lieutenant, there are no words to express my gratitude. Before we take in wounded, before we do anything else, will you both come inside and tell me everything that has befallen you since we last met?"

Everything? Susanna's heart sank to her stomach. And so soon. She'd hoped to inveigle herself in hospital work or, at the very least, to tend to her father before this momentous accounting took place. She swallowed. Snuck a glance at Sam, who gave an almost imperceptible nod. "Of course. Sa—Lieutenant Hicks killed a deer this morning, so I've prepared venison stew and cornbread."

"Ah, it sounds like a dream after eating acorns for the past two days."

"Acorns? Truly?"

Father nodded. "General Jackson ate so many, the army could scarcely move forward for him stopping to cure his stomach complaint by leaning against a bent sapling." As Susanna murmured in dismay, he glanced behind him. "You are dismissed, Adjutant Ross."

"Yes sir. I will take care of the horses."

Susanna remembered the short-statured young man was a friend of Sam's when the two clasped arms. How Ross did so while holding the reins of three mounts, she wasn't quite sure, but she called after him as he led them away. "I will save some stew for you, Mr. Ross."

That earned her a smile of surprise and delight.

"I will help you. I do not like anyone else to care for my horse." Frowning, Bold Hunter followed him, reaching for the leads of his stallion.

"Come, Father." Hooking her arm through his, Susanna led him inside with Sam following. She settled him on the bench and knelt to help remove his boots. "Put your feet toward the fire, and I will pour you some chicory coffee."

He caught her elbow and drew her down onto his knee. "Here you are, bustling about, serving me, when I feared that even if we found you, you might be in such a state that ..." He swallowed, twirling a strand of her hair around his index finger and drawing it tight. "In a state from which you might never recover. Is it true? Are you well?"

"I was not treated badly, Father. Roughly, yes, and left hungry and cold and so afraid and desperate for someone to save me. But I was not assaulted. Through everything, I felt our heavenly Father helping me." Susanna's insides lurched when her father wiped a tear from his cheek. She'd always known he loved her, but more like one values a prized thoroughbred or a painting by a famous artist. Not in the way that could rend one's heart. Hope swelled in her chest. Perhaps he would understand about her and Sam, after all. She hugged his neck, smiling beyond him at Sam. "Before I tell you more, let me fetch your dinner. Please."

"Very well." Releasing her, Father gestured Sam to the other bench. "Sit. I will start with questions for you."

Susanna blew out a nervous breath as she ladled stew into wooden bowls. She paused to close her eyes—not in thanks for the meal, but in supplication for the Lord's favor. Perhaps the amount of time she'd spent alone with Sam would not come up.

Sam seemed to be taking that approach as well, detailing how he'd located the camp and followed Susanna when the women had been moved to the nearby village. Before hearing about her rescue, Father asked her to relate how she'd come upon Spring Frog in his murderous act and been abducted. She placed steaming cups of chicory coffee in front of the men and sat down next to Sam to fill in her side of the story, up to the morning he had burst into the hut. Then, together, they told of fighting off the two assailants.

"Your daughter drew the first blood of Spring Frog." Sam's gaze slid to hers, and he played with the handle of his tin cup.

"What do you mean?" Father cringed, his one brow nesting in the crevice above his smoky eye. "Susanna was in the midst of this brutality?" His hand snaked across the table to grasp hers.

"Believe me, I looked away when I could, Father." With an expressive shudder, she squeezed his fingers.

"But only after the knife she threw from the creek bank found its mark, buying me the opportunity to escape Spring Frog's war hatchet." Sam's lips lifted at the corners for a moment as he gazed at her. "Your daughter is very brave, Colonel Moore."

She knew what he was doing. She'd told him how she yearned for her father to realize she did not require a pampered life. But this was backfiring. She knew it the moment florid color crept up Father's neck.

He jerked his hand from beneath hers and bellowed his retort in Sam's face. "Bold Hunter and I did not entrust you with Susanna's care so she could save *you*. If you are that inept, it is nothing short of a miracle that you got out alive."

Susanna shot to her feet. "It was no miracle, Father. Well, it was, but because God guided Sam. But once he got there, we would have never gotten out if he had not taken down that first guard. He took a blow when Spring Frog charged him. And I would never have been able to help him if *he* hadn't instructed me in the Cherokee manner of throwing knives. I am grateful that he thought me capable of learning how to protect myself. I owe Sam my life!"

"Sit down!" Spit flew through the air and landed on her sleeve as her parent, minutes ago coddling, turned into the dragon she had always feared. "Do not address me again thus, as if *you* would instruct *me*. And if you refer to the lieutenant by his Christian name once more, I will forbid you ever to speak of him again."

Susanna quaked, and now it was her turn for tears to fill her eyes—and to give a slight shake of her head to Sam. Because, stiffening, he moved as if he would get up. Her lip wobbled, and she wilted back onto the bench, wrapping her arms around herself.

Almost instantly, Father softened. "I am sorry. Susanna, my dear, to think that I could have lost you—and now to berate you as if you did something wrong. Of course, I am grateful. I know you both did whatever you needed to survive." He reached out to pat her shoulder.

All she could muster in response was a tremulous nod, so entangled was her heart in vines of longing and fear. Longing to go bury her head in Sam's shoulder—her father certainly would not look kindly on that—and fear of losing him.

The crackling of the fire filled the silence. Sam's tension stretched as taut, as palpable, as it had before he'd rushed the warrior at Emuckfaw. She prayed him to silence and stillness. Finally, her father released a loud sigh, then bent down and started tugging his boots on.

"I would like to hear the rest of the story from Lieutenant Hicks. Will you accompany me for a brief walk, sir? In sight of the cabin, naturally. I know we both wish to keep Susanna safe."

"That is my utmost concern." Sam rose. For an instant, his dark eyes met hers. Then he followed her father out the door.

Susanna sank against the table, too weak to hold herself up another moment.

Walking proved an impossibility in the overcrowded enclosure. Instead, they sat on stumps in front of a campfire that had been deserted by soldiers busy tending to the wounded and horses. As Sam should be. But he'd known nothing concerned the colonel more than the welfare of his eldest daughter—a fact which did not bode well for him.

They'd scarcely settled when Moore ran a hand over his bearded jaw and spoke in a raspy voice. "I am no fool, Hicks. My daughter scarcely attempts to hide her preference for you. What passed between you these past few days?"

"Nothing dishonorable, sir." Sam raised up from leaning on his knees.

"How long were you alone with her?"

To hesitate or force the man to repeat his question would make it look as though he was hiding something. Sam met the colonel's eyes even though a pit gaped open in his middle. "Two days."

"Two days ... and a night." Moore leaned over and rubbed his eyes, as if he'd like to scrub away the sight of Sam sitting in front of him. He let out a groan. "God in heaven, help me."

"I took the fastest route to Strother. We sheltered in a partially burned-out cabin in Hillabee country. I saw no other recourse. The horse—and your daughter—were nigh to dropping."

Colonel Moore jerked his head up as though remembering something. "And you had sustained a wound."

Sam gave a single nod. "A flesh wound in the shoulder which Miss Moore sewed up."

He should have left off that second detail. Moore's bushy eyebrows flew to the middle of his forehead. "Saints preserve us."

Sam couldn't keep a tinge of pride from lacing his response. Whatever Moore thought he knew of his daughter, there were parts he was blind to. "I meant it when I said she is strong."

"She is also tainted. I could ask you to conceal the details of your journey, but it would do little good. Speculation and talk will arise merely from her time as a captive. The damage may have been done here, but I can hope it won't reach into Tennessee."

The colonel's outburst in the cabin had led him to expect a far more forceful expression outside, yet the man was not behaving as expected. More like a parent hurt for their child than a protector bent on revenge. "You are not … angry with me?" Venturing to voice his question, Sam tilted his chin, then held his breath.

"Angry? Yes, I am angry!" There was the spitting again, and the fire in Moore's eyes. "But not, as I said earlier, because you did what you had to in order to survive. Because you allowed an attachment to grow when I made clear there was to be none."

Sam sat up straighter. "I cannot apologize for the love I have for your daughter. I did not seek it or encourage it." Well, there had been that poem and those witch hazel branches, but that had been when he thought she might die. He pressed on despite Moore's slack jaw. "I would like to propose a solution to both problems. I would like to ask for your daughter's hand in marriage."

At first, Moore tensed as though to spring off the stump in his direction. Then relaxed, releasing his breath in an audible rush. "I see it is the honorable thing in the white man's world that you do, Hicks."

"I am serious. I would want to marry Susanna even if she had not been compromised in your eyes."

"Even if she is compromised, you think I cannot find a better match for her than you? Why, pray tell, should I for one minute consider the proposal of a Cherokee soldier?"

"Because I love Lieutenant Hicks, and he is the only man I ever wish to marry," came a voice from behind them.

Sam pivoted and rose to his feet after Susanna spoke, her hands on her hips and her face set in lines of determination. He smiled his admiration and received the same in return.

Moore stood, too, but he frowned. "This is a gentleman's conversation, daughter."

She lifted her chin a notch. "A conversation about me, about my future. I realized just now that a woman bred to the frontier wouldn't hide in a cabin while destiny unfolded around her. She would get up and address herself to that destiny. And you spoke rightly just now. Sam is a gentleman. He is everything you taught me to desire, Father—well-spoken, educated, courageous, honorable, faithful, and a man of faith. I would live with him in a hut, but he also happens to have a fine home on Oothcaloga Creek." Her dark eyes twinkled at Sam. "And now, I am going to help in the hospital." She held up a hand. "No, do not protest. I am a colonel's daughter. Would you have me serve my country to the best of my limited ability or not?"

Moore spluttered into silence at that.

Sam managed to keep a straight face. And restrain himself from sweeping Susanna into his arms. This woman who grew in stature daily before his eyes, who saw in him what he might yet be—there could be no other for him now.

She raised herself on her tiptoes and kissed her father's cheek, but Sam could hear her whisper, "I ask you to consider your daughter's happiness."

He stared at her for a long moment. "I will consider it."

CHAPTER NINETEEN

"You must be the colonel's daughter. I heard tell about you." The long-haired Tennessee private with a hole in the back of his leg lay on his stomach. That fact did not seem to deter his ability to speak.

Susanna paused in pulling up her stool and pressed her lips together. "I am Miss Moore. Now you must lie still so that I can apply this poultice, or the fact that the bullet passed through your leg will mean little."

"Yes ma'am. I mean, miss." He fell silent only a moment as she lifted a bandage soaked in yarrow ointment from her tray and laid it over the worst part of his wound. She jumped when he again spoke rather loudly. "But I would rather have a bullet blow through me than be captured by savages. Tell me true. Was it awful?" He turned his head to the side to fix the aim of his exposed eyeball on her.

Susanna sighed. "Awfully frightening, but I am not awfully damaged." Let him make of that what he would.

"Oh. That's good. You must be one strong woman to endure that and then come in here to help us wounded men."

"I am not strong yet." A smile played about her lips. "But I am working on it."

"Most men would hide their daughters away from such sights."

"Believe me, he tried." So had Dr. Hawkins … at first. But once she had announced two days ago that she wouldn't be leaving until after he put her to work, something flashed across his dour features. Admiration? She applied herself again to the conversation at hand

and to the man, gently wrapping the medicated bandage around his leg. "But the physicians have used discretion in the cases I tend, and the men have been respectful."

Except for the fact that almost every one of them had asked about her abduction. She didn't even cringe at the questions now. In fact, she'd considered making a stump speech in the middle of each ward to reassure the curious and concerned that both her virtue and sanity remained intact.

"Tell me how you came by this wound." She found that keeping the men talking about themselves deflected their interest in her. Most loved to brag of their bravery and were more than willing to receive her gratitude.

As she covered the poultice cloth with a dry strip of linen, he commenced his narrative. "Happened at Enitchopco when the enemy came down upon our rear guard. The right and left columns got into a panic, plungin' down in the creek. With their officers in the lead, no less! There will be some harsh discipline for that, I can assure you. Some may lose their commissions. But not Colonel Carroll. No, he should be honored for gallantry. We checked the savages all by ourselves until the others rallied."

"I am sure your family will be proud of your bravery." Susanna tied a knot at the end of the linen strip.

"Ma will, but I ain't married." The scruffy fellow grinned, then grimaced as he shifted in an attempt to move onto his side.

Setting aside her implements, she hurried to rise, assist him in a full turn, and slide his haversack under his knee.

He settled onto his back with a huff. "That sure feels good. Tired of starin' at the tickin'."

"Good. I can fetch you some broth now."

"That would be most welcome, miss. You know, I will be outta here just as soon as I can bear weight. Jackson ordered the sixty-day volunteers to march to Huntsville for honorable discharges."

"I heard that."

He winked. "Would love to take a bride back to Nashville."

A movement near the door caught Susanna's attention. Her heart surged, sending heat into her cheeks. Sam. She hadn't seen him since the conference with her father, after which he'd requested and received permission to ride to Turkey Town to present the scalp of Spring Frog to Path Killer. He'd made the trip in record time, but she'd still been thankful for the hospital work to keep her busy. His gaze searched the room until he found her.

She clasped her hands in front of her skirt and offered Sam a smile of greeting while answering the private. "Thank you, sir, but I am afraid I am already spoken for."

He let out a ragged sigh. "Ah yes, that lanky doctor from Hiwassee."

"What? No." She frowned at him and gave her head a brief shake. What would make him think that? "Please excuse me. I will return in a few minutes with your broth."

She hurried across the room to the man she loved—with whom she now had hope of spending the rest of her life. She'd hardly slept even during the few hours she'd returned to the cabin last night for thinking of it, for picturing things that filled her with joy, anticipation, and longing. Perhaps her father would even allow them to wed before she returned to Turkey Town and Big Springs. The probability of Sam participating in a decisive battle come spring roused her deepest fears, but she didn't want to wait. Oh, couldn't wait.

Susanna took hold of his hands and squeezed. "How did it go? Did Path Killer express eternal gratitude?"

A reluctant smile flitted over his features, endearing for its sheepishness. "He did give a feast in my honor."

"And ... the trophy of war?" She swallowed back bile even at her euphemism. "Did you make the right decision in taking it?"

His Adam's apple bobbed. "It was the first thing he requested, and he displayed it in his most prominent location."

She sighed and nodded. "Then it is done, Sam."

"Your family rejoices that you are well, but they were disappointed you did not accompany me. They are impatient to leave for Big Springs."

"Oh dear." Susanna glanced around, then caught his sleeve with her finger. She spoke just above a whisper. "But I am thankful that Father did not send me, to be shipped straight home. The fact that he didn't must mean he recognizes the need for me here—and that he is considering your proposal."

Alarm jangled through her when no agreement lit his features.

Instead, he leaned in and answered in a low, somber tone. "Susanna, our company moves out at dawn."

A giant hand squeezed her heart. "What?"

"McNair's warriors have been ordered south to scout the Coosa and rule out signs of Red Stick approach. And barring that, to ascertain where the enemy is regrouping on the Tallapoosa."

Her lips parted, but for a moment, she could force no sound out. "Th-there must be some mistake. Who gave such an order?"

"Your father, I assume."

"I can see why your unit might be called to such a task, especially when the sixty-day recruits are already leaving, but not you. He cannot mean for you to go. Not when nothing has been settled—"

"Maybe it has been."

"No. No!" Susanna smacked her fist into her other palm. "I do not believe it. I will go ask him right now."

"You cannot. He is at the tent of General Jackson."

She chewed her lower lip. "It is possible he intended for you to complete this task while he considered your proposal, knowing I am also needed here at the moment. I believe he is beginning to see I am not such a fragile flower, after all. Perhaps he is testing us. Perhaps … he might even allow me to remain here through the spring."

"Susanna … the way he looked at me …" Sam shook his head, eyes narrowed with something that resembled regret.

Apprehension stabbed her breastbone, and she moved closer, placing a finger over his lips. "Shh. Do not give it the strength of speaking it. We will trust. I will talk to him, and you will see. Every man in here has got wind of my little adventure. Father cannot fail to acknowledge that marrying you is now the best course for me."

Sam kissed her finger before she moved it away. Instinct raised her to her tiptoes, but he put out a hand, steadying her, denying her. "Not here, my love. I will meet you later. After dark."

She nodded. "After I have talked to my father."

Susanna stared at the colonel, reaching for the edge of the table to hold herself upright, since it seemed as though the earth moved and the corners of the cabin rushed away. Surely, she had heard him wrong.

She repeated his last words. "One week. To marry him."

Seated on the other side of the table, he puffed on his ever-present pipe, then blew out a small smoke ring. "After that, you may either remain here through the spring campaign or await his return at Big Springs. He is committed through the end of the war, so he will have to report back to Strother, but there will be time for him to escort you home if you wish. Naturally, I think the latter would be superior, but in view of your helpfulness here, I … *we* … will allow you to make that choice."

"You will … *allow* me …" Susanna's knees gave way along with her voice, and she sank onto the bench. She must stand now. Show strength. Fight. But she couldn't. The shock was too great. Father had secured her match. Not with Sam. But with Dr. Hawkins.

"You should be grateful. The man is besotted with you. He must be, or he would never overlook your escapade into hostile country and your obvious attachment to Lieutenant Hicks."

"Grateful?" Her chin snapping up, she spit out the word. "When you know I love Sam and swore I would marry no other?"

"The fact that a white man of standing will still have you is nothing short of a miracle. How can you fail to acknowledge that? Foolish, foolish girl!" Father jumped up and started pacing, all three steps to the fireplace, then back again. "Why would I give you to a Cherokee when there was any other option?"

Sarcasm bit through her answer. "I don't know, perhaps because you married a Cherokee yourself."

Father pointed his pipe at her, and his reply shook the rough-hewn log structure. "It is *not* the same!"

"How? How is it not the same?" Susanna splayed her hands. "Did you not love Polly?"

"Of course, I love your stepmother. But I can protect her and our children. The same could not be said of a Cherokee man married to a white woman."

"I think he protected me pretty well in the wilderness."

He came to stand in front of her, forcing her to look up into his craggy face. "It would not be Red Sticks and the ravages of nature he would need to protect you from, but men of power."

"Men like you?"

"Men like Jackson."

"But Jackson relies on his Cherokees. He will owe them a huge debt when this war is over."

Father sat down, leaning an elbow on the table, his expression and posture intense. "That is what they are depending on, but I happen to know that Jackson views most native people as less than human and most Cherokees as children. Not in terms of their fighting ability, but in terms of reasoning and their ability to govern themselves. He is much like Colonel Meigs in that. Only to Major Ridge have I seen him pay true respect. He is using them, Susanna. And Jackson is the least of it. There are many other forces—in Congress, in the highest places—who will not rest until the Cherokees are pushed out so that Georgia can expand."

Susanna swallowed, shaking her head. "Father ... there must be some hope."

He continued, his voice gruff but gentler. "Do you think it is what I wish? I would see the Cherokees living among us, honored for their contributions, their advances."

"I know some have already moved west, and it might be that the poor, the indigent, are relocated ... but farmers? Landowners like Charles Hicks? It could never be."

"Promises have already been made."

The fact that he whispered this truth wrought a shiver all through her frame. Susanna covered her mouth. Her hand shook as if she had palsy, and she couldn't look at her father as he continued, voice low, persuasive.

"What do you think will happen to the families of Cherokee men at that point? There is a chance even the mixed-blood families of white men could come under threat. Have you not thought this through, Susanna? Even guessed why I pressed so hard all these years for your match to a white gentleman?"

She shook her head again, and a tear ran down her cheek.

"It is the only way I can be guaranteed we will not lose Big Springs Bluff."

She turned her face toward him, fingers still steepled over her mouth. "You would put land above love?"

"Susanna. A man must have land on which to keep the family he loves."

Sobs broke from her chest. "Father, please, do not ask this of me."

He stood up, placing his pipe on the plate on the table. "My dear, I am not asking. I have thought it over and come to my decision. I will never allow you to marry Sam Hicks."

"I would rather live as a spinster all my life than wed a man I do not love!"

"Very well." His chest swelled with a deep breath. "I suppose you can inherit our family estate just as well as a spinster as a married woman. That would at least buy us some time. I will ask Bold Hunter to make ready to escort you back to Turkey Town tomorrow."

She shot to her feet, emotion strangling her reply. "I am a woman now, no longer afraid to defy you if I must. And I must when you are wrong. I will run away with Sam first!"

Father's imposing figure hardened until it appeared as an impenetrable wall between her and the world beyond. "No, you will not. I saw him go into the hospital this morning, and I decided it wise to move up his company's departure. They rode out just past noon. By now, he is miles away."

The next morning, Susanna adjusted her head covering to block the cold, early February wind whistling down Hines Mountain. Bold Hunter approached from the corral with their horses, giving her time for one last glance around the ramshackle frontier establishment known as Fort Strother. Hungry men, dirty men, injured men—they overflowed the stockade, representing a hundred needs she could help fill. But there were also proud men. Men who bent the others to their own egos and visions.

And nowhere in the fort was the one man for whom she yearned above all others.

The lack of goodbye was perhaps most painful of all. Anger stirred like a great horned beast at the thought of how her father had cheated them even of that. When she'd questioned him further, he'd not concealed the fact that McNair's men had received time for nothing but gathering their supplies before they'd been instructed to mount up.

Could they not have been given the comfort of parting words? Of thanks? The assurance of memory? Maybe even hope that the future would bring change. But, of course, that was exactly what

Colonel Moore had not wanted.

When he stepped out of the cabin, Susanna turned her back. She took hold of the saddle of the mare she would ride and waited for Bold Hunter to hand her up.

But someone called her name—not her father. Someone perhaps equally unwelcome. A quick glance showed that Dr. Hawkins hurried from the hospital with something in his hands, the ends of his black frock coat flapping.

"Miss Moore. Miss Moore, just a moment. Please, may I have a word with her?" He glanced at Bold Hunter, who nodded and stepped away despite Susanna's internal consternation.

Was he here to plead for her to change her mind? Having not seen him since the previous afternoon, she assumed her father had told him she'd rejected his suit.

Susanna took a breath and angled slightly toward him. Yes. Thank goodness. Regret rather than hope now lined his face.

She'd take the high road. It wasn't the doctor's fault she was not attracted to him. "I apologize, Dr. Hawkins. I should have stopped by the infirmary to say goodbye and to thank you for allowing me to help yesterday. As you can see, my father has decided it is time for me to return to Turkey Town."

"Yes, I heard. It is to you I owe thanks. I should have recognized your skill and employed it much earlier. I wish I could keep you …" When his voice trailed off, the implied meaning wrung her heart.

She extended her gloved hand to squeeze his arm. "I am sorry it was not to be. I did try."

"I know." He exhaled and stared at his leather shoes. "And I do not blame you. I am old and crusty and difficult to work with."

She smiled, warmed not only by his admission but by his consideration in communicating it in doublespeak. "You are an excellent physician and a good man, but my … attentions … lie elsewhere."

He nodded. "It happens in youth. It happened to me once, so

I should not expect otherwise of you." Sad awareness rippled his brow, and he held out the packet he clutched. "But would you be so good as to take these letters to my children at my sister's when you return?"

"Of course." Susanna took the bundle and tucked it into her coat. "I will visit the very next day after I return. I know how important news of your welfare will be to them."

"They will love that, even if it is only the one visit." Did he sound the tiniest bit hopeful that there might be more?

"I will do my best to answer all their questions."

"And now, you can tell them firsthand what it is like in the hospital."

"Yes, I can indeed." This was the most they had ever spoken and with the greatest ease. It must be because he was releasing her, and with far more grace than she had expected.

He moved away from her mare, folding his hands in front of him and bowing his head. "Godspeed, Miss Moore."

"Goodbye, Dr. Hawkins." Susanna nodded and gestured for Bold Hunter to return, but it was not he who stepped up behind her, but her father.

His voice rumbled in her ear as he rested a hand on her waist. "I know you are nettled with me, but I love you and would covet your prayers."

How could she withhold a proper farewell when he could be killed in the spring campaign? Even though bitter emotions still tangled her heart into a tight ball, she hesitated for only one of its contractions before turning and flinging her arms around him. But she couldn't contain the whimper of pain that passed her lips. "You said you would consider my happiness."

"And I did. I am." Father smoothed the side of her head with one of his large hands, the calluses catching in her hair. "I know you do not see it right now, but one day … you will."

Tears flooded her vision. She shook her head, pressing her

trembling lips together. If she attempted to speak again, she would sob. For so many reasons. So she turned back to her mare, gripped the saddle, and allowed her father to give her a leg up.

Bold Hunter nodded to him. "I will take her safely to her mother."

"I could use you at my side when we next ride out."

A grin split her stepuncle's broad, tawny face. "I will be back." Then he spurred his stallion forward.

Susanna had no choice but to follow him through the gates of Fort Strother, leaving her heart behind but taking with her the sure knowledge that, unlike Bold Hunter, she was never to return. Eagles soared on a current in the bright blue sky high above, and sunlight glittered on the rocky shoals of the Coosa. She followed the long ribbon of water with her gaze as far as she could see southward.

Bold Hunter circled back and pulled up beside her, his Cherokee words forming a frosty cloud. "The lieutenant said not to tell you goodbye, as they do in English, but *Do-na-da-go-hv-i*."

Susanna stared at him with widened eyes, her heartbeat accelerating. Sam *had* found a way to reach her in parting, to extend a thread of hope. She murmured the English translation. "Till next we meet."

CHAPTER TWENTY

On the morning of their departure from Turkey Town, Walani loaded them with provisions and gifts. The first hint of a smile tugged at Susanna's lips as her stepaunt and stepmother quarreled over the bounty. Polly knew those at Turkey Town, like all the people in the region, suffered from the deprivations of war. Jackson's army continued to demand sustenance long after the local residents' larders emptied.

George and Bold Hunter waited in the lane, holding the horses. She moved from the door of the cabin to her stepuncle, who carried a musket, a tomahawk, and two knives. "You look fearsome," she told him in Cherokee.

He would depart the same time they did, but for Fort Strother, not Hiwassee. George had expressed his displeasure at this parting of ways, though for entirely different reasons than Susanna. He'd unsuccessfully begged Polly to let him join the battle or at least assist at the fort, only acquiescing when she pointed out that he was needed as their protector the rest of the way back to Big Springs. Bold Hunter would be riding toward Sam as Susanna rode away, a fact that rent her heart. And she'd barely slept in the cabin where she'd kept picturing the two dead guards, the flashbacks eroding even her normal questionable level of emotional control.

Naturally, Bold Hunter frowned when Susanna swiped a tear from the corner of her eye. But she almost jumped back in surprise when, instead of berating her or turning a cold shoulder, he stepped forward and wrapped his free arm around her. She had to hold her breath to keep from breaking down.

In his grip, Susanna felt like Lulu the rag doll. He thumped her back ... a little hard. Much more of his affection and she might convulse.

George shook his head while Bold Hunter stiffened her spine with one final *thump*. *"To-hi-ya." Be healthy.* Or better translated for her, perhaps—*be strong*.

She squeaked out the question she should be able to ask her father. "Will you watch out for him?"

Bold Hunter nodded as he stepped away. "I will guard his back. He is young. But he will learn. And maybe one day, he will guard mine."

"Wa-do ... e-du-tsi." Thank you ... my uncle.

The expression of relation brought a rare smile to Bold Hunter's face, and that filled Susanna's parched heart with warmth.

Next was Nokassa, standing outside the door of the cabin, hair in the traditional two braids under her scarf, her hands clasped in front of her woven skirt. Oh dear. Susanna couldn't recall ever seeing her sport so long a face. If she cried ...

She tried embracing her cousin without comment, hoping her gesture would communicate her affection.

But Nokassa clung to her neck so tight she could scarcely breathe. "No say goodbye."

Susanna gave a little cough and managed to secure a modicum of relief. "I know, we say *Do-na-da-go-hv-i*."

Nokassa shook her head, her eyes glistening and lips trembling. "No. We not say that."

"What do you mean?"

Her cousin grabbed her hands, and her unreadable emotion blossomed into a wondrous smile. "No goodbyes. I go with you!"

"What—?" Searching for confirmation, Susanna turned to their mothers, who were coming out of the cabin. As though she needed it when Nokassa began hopping up and down.

Making the sign of a tear tracking her cheek, Walani frowned.

"You sad." Then her face, too, lit with a smile. "No one sad with Nokassa."

Susanna could scarcely pull her jaw up to enunciate her next question. She glanced back to her cousin. "But what about Culsowee?"

The girl scoffed, flicking her hand downward. "He wait."

Everyone chuckled but Susanna. Instead, she pulled Nokassa in with an arm around her neck and buried her face in her silky hair. Her sweet spirit did ease a fraction of the empty ache in Susanna's chest. It was true, no one brought her joy like Nokassa.

No one but Sam.

As much as she treasured her family's good-hearted gesture and the loving intentions behind it, was this really the best time for a visit? How long could she politely pretend that her heart wasn't missing?

With Susanna's departure, the colonel had moved back into his tent, leaving the small cabin for Dr. Hawkins and his wounded. That was a relief because Sam had no need to intensify the pain he carried in his chest. Reporting to his senior officer at that location would have stirred too many memories of the woman he loved.

He could only hope that the message he'd entrusted to Bold Hunter had been delivered and received as intended—to ease the shock and devastation she must have felt upon learning he'd been sent away so abruptly. To assure Susanna he would not forget his promise.

It would be hard to face her father—to reveal neither resentment nor desperation in front of him—but he'd agreed to accompany Captain McNair when he gave his scouting report, nonetheless. In the absence of John Ross, who had gone home on a furlough, McNair would need an interpreter. Anything for a morsel of information about Susanna or a shred of hope that Colonel Moore might change his mind.

However, as Sam stood at attention behind the captain with the winter wind snatching and shaking the tent flap, Moore acted as though he didn't see him. The burn in his chest did intensify after all. He ignored it, speaking English words over McNair's Cherokee, even though the colonel kept his eyes glued to McNair's face.

"The remaining Red Sticks have gathered with their women and children at a village on the Tallapoosa not far from Emuckfaw." McNair gave his report with legs planted shoulder-width and hands behind his back. "The National Creeks say it is called Tohopeka. The river curves sharply there around roughly a hundred acres of high ground, but the neck is barely over a thousand feet across. The village lies near the tip of this peninsula on a bluff, protected by steep banks."

Moore held up his hand. "The river here is wide?"

Sam answered without thinking. "Wide and deep, with a swift current."

He earned a glare of censure for his lapse. Sam bowed his head.

"How many in this village?" Moore played with a container of sealing wax as he made a point of staring at McNair.

This time, Sam translated the question and awaited his captain's reply.

"We counted maybe three hundred newly built huts. In the neck, they are constructing a log wall, around six feet high."

"No wall will stand long against our cannons."

McNair nodded. "When will we move against them?"

Sam expected the answer to call for an almost immediate return in the direction from which he'd just come. Strother had swelled noticeably in his absence, including the Thirty-Ninth Tennessee, army regulars in sharp navy uniforms and high-brimmed hats with leather cockades. Moore would need only await the return of his furloughed Cherokees. But the reply surprised him.

Moore shifted back in his camp chair. "We must receive fresh

8

munitions and supplies first, and our soldiers at the wharf must complete our boats to carry those supplies down the Coosa. Jackson is also arranging for army contractors to bolster our supply line at Talladega. This campaign must be the last. It must have no reason to fail."

"Yes sir. What are your orders, sir?" McNair looped his fingers through his sash.

"You and your men may return home for several weeks, Captain. I have requested the other Cherokees to report by mid-March." Moore rose to denote the conclusion of the exchange. "I ask the same of you and thank you for your extra service. You are my eyes and ears, McNair."

Sam's captain bowed his head, expressed his thanks, and pivoted for the exit. Sam started to follow, but an aching need stayed his feet at the door, requiring that he face the colonel as he took his seat. "Your family, sir ... did they make it home safely?"

Moore never lifted his gaze from the report uppermost on his field desk. "Your captain has retired, Lieutenant Hicks, and I do not believe I addressed you."

He despised answering rebuke with meekness, but it was a necessary means to an end. "Yes, but sir, I just—"

"As for my family, you have no need to inquire of them, for you will have naught to do with them in the future."

Sam's spine stiffened. "Colonel Moore, after the services I provided to you and yours at the expense of my own safety, you cannot find it impudent of me to—"

"Tell me, Hicks, do you believe there is some quality in you that supersedes Susanna's future security? Do you actually think you deserve her?" He fairly spat the question. Moore's gray eyes fixed on him, hot and challenging. "My oldest child. My only English daughter. My most prized possession?"

"Is she a possession, sir?" He clasped his hands in front of him and stood his ground.

"What pride, what selfishness!" Moore almost trembled in his righteous indignation.

Sam refused to digress, forcing out the rest of his query. What did he have to lose? "Or is she a person, with thoughts and feelings of her own? Do those count for nothing in your sight?"

He'd strayed too far. The colonel resumed a standing position, his fingers on his desk. "You are dismissed, Lieutenant. As much as the regiment benefits from your skills, it would be better for you not to return if you cannot put away your hopes of my daughter."

"I will return." His answer pushed through his clenched teeth, and he snapped off a salute. "And I will show you that I do deserve her."

This morning, the workers were clearing off land to expand the east cornfield. Susanna inhaled the tang of woodsmoke on the early March breeze. Hugging a post on the back porch, she closed her eyes. She could almost pretend she was back at Turkey Town or Fort Strother. If only—

"Susanna?" Polly's call from the garden forced her back to reality. "These onion buttons and beets will not plant themselves. Bring your gardening gloves and Nokassa and come."

"Yes, Mama."

Ever since Bold Hunter had delivered her back to Turkey Town in an emotional shambles and Polly had daily propped her up with Scriptures and tasks designed to preserve her stability—like this one, meant to get her outdoors—Susanna had forgone calling her stepmother by her Christian name. The time on the frontier had shown her what mattered. She might never convince her father to allow her to wed the man she loved, but sure as certain, she would call Polly the name she deserved from this point forward.

But where was Nokassa? Now that was the question.

Her lovely Cherokee cousin had accepted her invitation to make free with Susanna's wardrobe, descending to breakfast in a sprigged burgundy silk, a relic from Kingston days. She hadn't seemed to mind that such a gown should only have been worn to a formal dinner or dance. Instead, Nokassa had partaken of her eggs, bacon, and real coffee in the manner of an English lady. Much to Mammy Kate's consternation, she'd insisted on helping the servant wash and put away the pearlware and silver. Susanna had last glimpsed her angling to catch her reflection in a butter knife while Mammy Kate jangled the silver chest key on her chatelaine with her lips poked out.

Each new day at Big Springs Bluff represented an adventure to Nokassa. Her endless curiosity and exuberant exploration did help dull Susanna's sense of loss to a manageable ache. Hard work—outdoor work—also helped. Susanna sighed as she peeked into the empty parlor. No matter how busy she tried to stay, it was at night that the pain monster awoke to devour her heart all over again.

"Nokassa?"

"Here." The light, eager voice came from the library.

Susanna found the girl bent over Father's atlas, still wearing the burgundy silk, the contrast of rich coloring making her hair resemble a glossy raven's wing. "Mama sent me to fetch you. We must help her in the garden, then we need to take down the smoked hog and sew it up and whitewash it. You'll have to change that dress."

Nokassa seemed not to hear anything Susanna said. She glanced up, her finger hovering somewhere over Louisiana Territory. "This the land here?"

Susanna smiled. "Yes. Our land. America." She came up behind and redirected her cousin's focus to the border of Tennessee and Cherokee Territory. "We are here. Just below the Tennessee River. See?"

"The lines … be rivers? Oh!" Nokassa lowered her nose until it nearly touched the page. "Where my river? My town?"

"Mmm." Susanna twisted her lips to one side before pointing. "Turkey Town would be about here, on the Coosa. C-o-o-s-a." She followed each tiny letter with her index finger.

"It say that?" Wonder suffused Nokassa's expression, and her dark eyes glowed. She patted the chair next to her. "You sit. Show me your letters."

"You wish to learn English?"

An enthusiastic nod. "No Cherokee letters, so I learn English."

"Well …" Susanna blinked rapidly as her mind raced ahead. "I suppose you could sit in on the lessons Mama wants me to give to Sally and Molly."

"Oh yes! To read and write!" Nokassa grabbed her hand.

"And figure sums."

"What sums?" She dropped her grip and drew back with a suspicious frown.

"Adding and subtracting numbers."

Nokassa shook her head with as much vehemence as she'd just eagerly nodded it. "Oh no. No needing that."

Susanna laughed. "You might. You never know what changes may come to Turkey Town. To your life."

"I think … I not go."

"What?" Susanna's brows flew up.

Her cousin gathered her skirt in her hand, fingering the slick folds as her gaze drifted out the wavy glass of the window to the log smokehouse. "Better here."

How could she tell Nokassa that she couldn't remain at Big Springs Bluff forever? As a traditional Cherokee, she might not grasp that her welcome could expire. Susanna shifted, not wanting to offend the girl.

As if reading her mind, Nokassa's attention returned to her. "I know, I must marry. But maybe I wait … for a man like Sam."

The arrow of the mere mention of his name pierced Susanna's breastbone, and she sank onto the extra chair.

Nokassa patted the wrinkled muslin sleeve of her work dress. "Sorry. Did not mean to speak of."

"No, it's all right. As you can probably tell, he is in my thoughts constantly. But what about Culsowee?"

Nokassa's brow pinched in regret, and she released a weighty sigh. "Some Cherokee men ... know more."

"If you can picture living without him, then you should wait for someone like Sam. Because I ... I can't picture my life without Sam." She gulped down a knot in her throat.

"He will come for you." Nokassa squeezed her hand. When Susanna failed to respond with the expected lightening of countenance her cousin likely expected, she leaned in. "Trust me. He will come."

An insistent rapping on the window sprung them apart with squeals. They swiveled to find Polly's round face peering in with an uncustomary scowl. She gave an impatient swipe of her hand. *"Do-yi! Wi-di-tsa-lv-wi-s-da-si!"* Go out! Go to work!

As Polly stomped away, Nokassa looked back at Susanna, widened her eyes, and covered her mouth with her hand. Then they shared the first rich laughter Susanna had given herself to in months.

CHAPTER TWENTY-ONE

"John Woods, you have been tried by a court martial on the charges of disobedience of orders, disrespect to your commanding officer, and mutiny; and have been found guilty of all of them. The court which found you guilty of these charges has sentenced you to death by shooting."

The loud, bitter wailing of the prisoner—a private probably not quite eighteen years old—drowned out the reading of the remainder of General Jackson's written sentence. Sam ducked his head and crushed his felt hat in his hands, the mid-March wind whipping his hair across his face with a chill the noonday sun could not quite diminish.

The chaplain came forward to administer a divine service. Sam had no idea how any of the Tennessee soldiers assembled on the elevated ground in front of Fort Strother could hear a word he said. The angry rumbling of the crowd and the boy's blubbering only crescendoed.

His crime? Refusing to pick up bones the other militiamen had thrown on the ground after breakfast several days prior. When his officer had shouted at him, the foolish Wood—one would think if the general sentenced a boy to die, he'd at least get his name correct—had brandished his rifle before submitting. Jackson had offered the alternative of enlistment in the regular army to punishment, but already mutinous, the other militiamen had discouraged it. They never believed Jackson would order one so young put to death. And by the Thirty-Ninth, no less ... because the officers had signed a petition asking Jackson to spare Wood's life.

Such was the erosion of morale among the troops. Horrifying what hunger could do.

Sam couldn't stand to watch any longer. He made it halfway back to his camp before the shots sounded. His steps faltered as he paused, winced, then kept walking.

He found his father around a fire with Major Ridge and Ridge's brother Watie as well as several privates who leaned forward with attentive postures. Word of the sermons Captain Hicks repeated from the Moravian missionaries spread throughout the Cherokee Regiment. The men liked the miraculous stories from the Old Testament, and they admired the life of Jesus—His birth as a human baby, how He'd shared food with everyone, and how He'd died for others without complaint. Only the greatest of shamans could rise from the dead like Jesus did, the captain told them.

The concepts of living as a follower of Christ as presented in the New Testament offered greater challenges. This Sam understood all too well. He'd thought to find peace during his weeks at Fort Hill. In the past, he'd been able to channel anger or disappointment into a plan of action. But Colonel Moore had made it clear that no action on Sam's part would persuade him to consider Sam for his daughter's hand.

The situation was but one example of the white man's pride. His indomitability. Moore was like a boulder that would never be worn down, the settlers washing around him like a flood that would never recede until it reached the other coast. Why would Sam want to fight for such a man when the flood would soon drown his people?

Because he would never respect himself if he failed to prove himself as a warrior. So he was back in this miserable place, himself miserable. And growing more so by the day.

"One can ask the Christian God favors, but not the Great Spirit." Father leaned over the Bible open on his knee, speaking with fervor in Cherokee. "It gives me confidence in the face of the coming battle that God watches over me. You, too, can have this confidence."

Sam plunked on a stump, poking at the fire with a stick. Sparks flew up into the pale blue sky, drawing the gazes of the audience.

A private with deep-set eyes grumbled. "I do not know. Becoming like this Jesus does not sound natural."

"It is above natural. God Himself helps in this."

The young warrior shook his head. "God is not helping the white men."

"Many of them are not Christians," Sam muttered through tight lips.

The Ridge shifted, adjusting his matchcoat. "I cannot believe God will forgive all the bad things I have done if only I ask Him."

"Maybe you do not wish to humble yourself to ask?" Father made the suggestion with a slight twinkle in his eye, but his friend grunted and stood up, the others following his example.

"I will think on these things."

"You have been saying that for years."

Major Ridge waved his arm in a dismissive, downward slash before sauntering away.

"Have you any luck with your evangelizing, Father?" Crossing his moccasin-clad ankles, Sam leaned back for a swig from his canteen.

"The concepts are hard for them. For me too. I lie awake at night thinking of all the mysteries."

The reverence and awe in his father's answer brought Sam up short. He lowered his canteen, slowly capping it off. When had he lost the joy of salvation and the desire to please God that the missionaries had encouraged in him as a boy?

Father watched him. "I have never seen you so restless, my son. Of the two wolves we Cherokees like to say live inside each of us, you are feeding the wrong one."

"How do I feed the good one, when everything around me—everything going into me—is bad?"

"I know of but one way." Father lifted his Bible with both hands and laid the weighty book on Sam's thigh.

He sighed, chest tightening as he smoothed his hands over the filmy, precious pages. "I cannot stop hearing what the colonel said to me. He asked if I thought I deserved Susanna." At the memory, his previous remorse over his spiritual languor clenched into anger. "How can one man ask that of another? He called me proud—when he is the one who is proud!"

"You are right. He did not have the right to ask you that. But God does."

"What do you mean?"

Father cocked his head to one side, the silver in his hair glinting in the afternoon light. "Do any of us, before God, deserve anything?"

Sam froze for a moment as the insightful question illuminated the darkness within. Then he slumped. "No." The missionaries had taught him that no good came from the human heart apart from God's Spirit acting upon it, and he'd known by his own inclinations it was true. "But does God not want to give us good things?"

"Yes, but not always the same things we ask Him for." Father took out a whetstone and patiently began sharpening his long knife. "You seek peace?"

"Peace in the midst of war? What an idea." With the stick, Sam traced symbols in the dirt he'd once written in Sister Kliest's syllabary, the mental residue of a dormant dream. Then it came to him. He had a new dream. "Yet I do seek that very thing. In fact, I seek peace *through* war. I want our people to come out of this stronger. But what is more, *I* want to come out of this stronger. Not just a scholar, but also a warrior. I want the two wolves to lie together inside. In peace."

Father nodded, meeting Sam's eyes. "Then you cannot fight this war to prove yourself to the colonel. That is fighting from a position of weakness. You are sure to lose. Instead, you must forgive the colonel. If you fight, it must be what you believe is right before

God, asking Him to come alongside you to help our people. That is fighting from a position of strength."

Truth. The power of it never ceased to amaze him. It was what he had sought his whole life. The breath rushed out of him in a shaky sigh. "And Susanna?"

Father had never catered to his brooding, lovelorn silences as Mother had, patting his shoulder and making his favorite dishes, as though that would staunch his gaping wound. He stood up, pointing at the Bible as he clasped his blanket around his shoulders. "I leave you with that. I will rest now." He shuffled toward his tent, in a rare moment favoring his troublesome hip. Wasn't he even going to answer? Sam trailed his progress with an incredulous gaze.

Finally, at the tent flap, he turned back. "You must be willing to give her up, as Abraham was with his son Isaac. This will show you are open to receive whatever good gift God Himself may choose."

They could hear Polly call out from the yard even from where they sat in the kitchen, books and slates spread out on the table for late-afternoon lessons. "A letter! A letter!"

As Nokassa and Susanna's half sisters looked up from their writing assignments, Susanna stood and went to the window. She pulled the ruffled curtain back to spy her stepmother hastening up the lane, flapping an envelope while George scurried behind, laden with her packages from their trading post. Polly could get someone to deliver these things for her, of course. The colonel's wife's wish was the employees' command. But she preferred to maintain a close oversight on her own business, repairing there frequently and spending hours checking the accounts and talking with customers. Yet another reason Susanna admired her.

"Clear the table off." Susanna waved her hand, and as she went to the door, the others hurriedly marked their places and stacked their books.

"A letter from Father!" Molly, now eight, swung her legs from her bench, pumping as hard as if she sat on the swing Father had hung from the big oak tree in the yard.

"Maybe news of my father too. I make tea." Nokassa arose, added a stick of wood to the fire, and hung the kettle above the heat.

Maybe he will have news of Sam. "You use any occasion as an excuse to make tea."

"Hmm, well, I like." She smirked as she examined the tea chest filled with several varieties of block and loose-leaf teas, not the herbal infusions the Cherokees brewed from assorted plant parts. Nokassa did have a taste for the finer things of life, while Susanna had sought adventure and strength from the frontier. Funny how one always craved what one lacked.

Mama and George entered with a flurry of activity. As George discarded his burdens, their mother removed her bonnet and sat on the bench next to Molly. She handed her hat to her youngest daughter, who promptly placed it on her own head, smoothing her braids with a preening air. "News from your father." Mama spoke breathlessly as she opened the envelope. "I have waited to read it with you."

Susanna took a seat opposite her as Nokassa slid a pearlware cup prepped for hot water in front of her aunt, earning an appreciative smile.

"Do not wait on me, Aunt Polly. I listen." Nokassa stood behind her, hands folded and an eye on the kettle spout.

The cheerful crackle of the fire chased away the chill of early spring as Mama read aloud, pausing for clarification from Susanna on one or two of the more difficult English words.

March 23, 1814
Fort Williams on the Coosa River
My dear family,

I pray this letter finds you well, as I am.

We moved south from Fort Strother two days prior with about two thousand infantry, seven hundred cavalry, and a hundred mounted Tennessee rifleman. Our friendly Indians number five hundred Cherokees and a hundred National Creeks under Major William McIntosh. We journeyed about thirty miles before stopping to set up a new base command at this location. The ready lumber allowed us to construct a quick garrison while we await the arrival of our supplies coming downriver. To our consternation, there is no sight of the goods in Talladega that were supposed to have been delivered in advance by the army contractors.

Meanwhile, I have sent out the Cherokees to scout the area, and our engineers go ahead to widen the narrow Indian trails for our cannons and supply wagons. It will be fifty miles to the town of Tohopeka, where the enemy is gathered at a horseshoe bend in the Tallapoosa.

This will be my last opportunity to write you until after the great battle is joined. Pray for me and for our army, that victory may be decisive, that this land may be secured, and that I may return to you soon. With love,

Your Husband and Father

Susanna sat back from the table as her stepmother folded the paper, a sobering realization dawning. "Even if that letter traveled with the utmost haste by messenger to Fort Strother and on north, that battle has probably already been fought." She went ice-cold as she said it. The letter was like a bend in time.

Mama's gaze met hers, and with a subtle glance at the children, she gave her head a little shake. Father, Bold Hunter, and Sam, any or all, could be wounded or dead, but she must not display any fear.

Susanna sucked in her breath and stood abruptly, almost bumping into Nokassa, who approached from behind with the tea kettle. The girl gave a little cry and elevated the hot cast iron, clutching the handle with a rag.

"I am so sorry." Susanna scooted out of the way.

"It is all right. Let me pour your water for tea."

"No—thank you. I … need to go for a walk."

Concern furrowed Nokassa's brow. "You wish me to come?"

"No. Please, stay. Enjoy your tea." There was a time for companionship, and there was a time for introspection, and this was the latter.

"Do not stay gone long." A tinge of worry laced Mama's admonition as Susanna swung her cloak about her shoulders.

She headed not for her usual haunts along the river, but across the lane, into the forest. Polly would never have approved her walking alone there without an escort or a weapon, but Susanna needed the comfort of the trees, the rich, loamy smell of the awakening earth.

The promise of spring kissed the land. Pink, pea-like blooms dotted the redbud trees, flat clusters of white flowers the thorny mayhaws. White and pink dogwood blossoms glowed here and there among the sober, barren hardwood giants and the deep-green pines. Birds twittered and squirrels scampered in branches overhead, while soft sunshine filtered onto the forest floor.

The beauty did not ease the ache in her heart as she had hoped it might. Instead, anxious imaginings and relentless questions darted through her mind. Would her father resume his pressure for her to marry Dr. Hawkins upon his return? If he did not return, what would become of their family? How could they run Big Springs Bluff long-term without him? Would Sam come for her then—if he survived the war? And if he hadn't …

There would never be another man like him. She would never love like that again.

Darkness and tears clouded her vision, and she wept as she walked. The Scripture Mama liked to recite every evening as they tucked the little girls into bed came back to her, bringing a modicum of peace. *For God hath not given us the spirit of fear; but of power, and of love, and of a sound mind.*

Yet here she was again, wielding no control over her future. And that frightened her more than anything.

Suddenly, Susanna stopped and looked around. At some unknown point over the last half hour, she'd wandered from the deer trail on which she'd started. She had no idea where she was. Perhaps if she climbed that little ridge over there, she might gain a view.

But the top revealed only unmarked forest gently undulating in every direction. Her heart rate quickened. *Please, God, show me the way.*

Of course. West. She needed to go west. Picking her way around patches of rhododendron, she followed the rise toward the setting sun. Twenty or so more steps, and the ridge dipped to a trickling creek tributary. And there in the hollow, a bent tree that almost exactly resembled the one outside Fort Strother. It pointed in the direction the water ran, west, doubtless toward the river.

Gasping out a little laugh, Susanna skittered down the hill, the leather bottoms of her boots rolling on loose sediment. Relief flooded her soul as she acknowledged her heavenly Father's provision. She was most definitely not in control. But she believed in Someone who was. And if she believed His goodness, she also must believe He had a good future for her.

She sank onto the arm of the bent tree to catch her breath and to give thanks. Not only for His provision in this moment, but also for the prayers for safety He'd already honored at that horseshoe bend in the Tallapoosa River.

CHAPTER TWENTY-TWO

Sunday, March 27, 1814
Tohopeka, Red Stick Creek Territory, later known as Horseshoe Bend,
Alabama

The sun rose toward its zenith as the cannonade across the river continued, bombarding the wall that guarded the Red Stick village of Tohopeka. Sam crouched in the edge of the woods next to Major Ridge, his brother Watie, and Watie's brother-in-law, Charles Reese.

The Cherokee Regiment had been dispatched at six-thirty that morning to cross the Tallapoosa downriver and come in behind the town. Now, their main line curved along the bank facing the entire peninsula, with a reserve line in the woods behind. They'd picketed their horses to the rear before examining possible points of access to the huts on the other side of the river, in the teardrop of land currently between them and Jackson's cannonade of the wall.

"Over there." Reese pointed to the far bank. "Look. Log canoes pulled up in the mud beside those trees."

A private in his mid-twenties named *Tuq-qua*, The Whale, spoke up. "We should swim over and get them."

Major Ridge frowned, rubbing his jaw. "It is over a hundred yards across, and the current is swift here."

Not to mention deep and still icy this time of year, and the sparkling thread of water not peppered with rocks like the shallow ford at the *Oti Palin*. Sam shared his hesitation.

"We can do it. We are strong swimmers." Speaking over each other, Reese and The Whale remained firm in their insistence. "We could bring the canoes back and load the men."

Major Ridge glanced at Sam before his gaze slid past him to the tall figure of Colonel Moore. Spy glasses around his neck, he picked his way through the underbrush, returning from an inspection of the wall. Ridge shifted beside Sam. "The men do not wish to miss the action again. Will you see what Moore says?"

After only a second, Sam nodded. He hadn't spoken to the colonel since Susanna's father had ordered him out of his tent, but now was not the time to quibble over who conveyed messages. If someone didn't do something soon, the entire regiment might break loose. The tension in the ranks was palpable.

He skirted through the woods, approaching the senior officer before he could engage in conversation elsewhere. "Sir."

A flicker of annoyance crossed the man's face. "Yes, Lieutenant?"

"Major Ridge inquires if you could tell if the barrage is having any effect."

Moore shook his head and sighed. "I couldn't see much of the action from any point along our line, but Lieutenant Jesse Bean has about forty men on the small island across from the barricade. They passed word as best they could that it is not going well. Jackson's been firing the three- and the six-pounders for almost two hours now, yet the wall stands firm. There must be nigh a thousand warriors behind it, laughing as the grapeshot bounces off."

"Someone has to do something." The statement escaped under Sam's breath before he paused to measure it.

Colonel Moore shot him a dagger of a glance. "And I suppose that someone is you. Do you think an act of rash bravery will prompt me to offer my daughter's hand?"

Sam almost strangled swallowing down the reflexive urge to defend himself. He'd wrestled with his father's admonition during the march along the Weogulfga-Cussetta Trail, then through dense woods to Emuckfaw, that place of memories. Finally, last night, in the shifting dark of restless men and creeping forest things, he'd told God he would cease his demands. He wanted peace. He would do as God wanted. But that meant forgiving the colonel too.

"I spoke wrongly before. You were right, I do not deserve Susanna. But I do love her, and because of that, it would be impossible for me to ever give up the hope of her. That said ..." He heaved a breath and forced himself to meet the colonel's glower. "I respect your reasons for keeping her from me. I will not try to sway you."

"I am glad we finally see eye to eye."

That was certainly not true, and cynicism colored the colonel's tone, but Sam refused to even blink. He must remain focused, undistracted by emotions, be they good or bad. "I am here for my people today because my hope is that to fight with the Americans will be the best thing for them. They are restless. They want a part in this battle. Some of the men have spotted a long line of hollowed-out log canoes on the opposite bank, and they want to swim across and retrieve them."

The lines on Moore's face relaxed a fraction. "General Coffee gave orders that we are to remain here in case a band of the enemy approaches from behind. We are needed to guard the flank." One corner of his mouth drew up, and he trained his glasses on the bank opposite. "But the stalemate does need tipping."

A heartbeat passed during which Moore refused to look at him. But his meaning was clear. He could not countermand the order of his superior, but neither would he disapprove of someone who did. Someone not counting on an ongoing position in the armed forces. "I understand, sir." Sam saluted and turned to go back to the cluster of talking, gesturing Cherokees.

"Hicks?"

He glanced over his shoulder. "Yes sir?"

"*To-hi-ya.*" Be healthy. "You deserve to make it through this battle."

Heart pounding, Sam took that as a call to action. "You, too, sir."

Everything was about to change. He was about to change. Was he ready for this?

Minutes after he relayed the exchange with the colonel, the Ridge-Watie group formed a plan. Reese, The Whale, and Sam left their rifles with their friends while Major Ridge and Watie secured places behind fallen trees, ready to provide cover. Red Sticks patrolled the opposite shore to the rear of the village. If anyone spotted them, they could face a bevy of musket muzzles the minute they reached those canoes—lacking their own firepower.

Sam paused a moment on the bank of the Tallapoosa. No time to hesitate. Reese had already gone ahead, his head breaking the surface like a turtle's. He and The Whale followed, quickly out of their depth.

Swimming as the icy water surged around his shoulders, he gasped. Prickles of pain shot along his limbs. He didn't look back. Only forward. No one on the bank. Reese splashed harder as he forded the current. Relentless fingers of water tugged his own clothing, and he touched his knife to ensure that it remained secure. Put his head down and pushed on.

Finally, his moccasins regained footing on the river bottom. He angled upstream toward the canoes. Reese already had his hands on one, turning it around. Sam grabbed another.

The popping of musket fire jerked his head up. Down the bank, warriors took aim, smoke from their guns wreathing their red-painted faces, tattooed upper bodies, and roached hair.

Sam yelled to The Whale, who stood closest to their attackers. *"Ha-la-ta-du-ga a-ma-yi!" Get into the water!*

Too late. The man bent, clutching his left arm, red appearing beneath his fingers.

Splashing toward him, Reese offered The Whale a canoe, but he shook his head, staring blankly. He couldn't paddle, but he could ride. They couldn't leave him to the mercy of the approaching Red Sticks, although from the sounds of it, the Cherokees were holding them off.

Sam helped ease the wounded private into a boat, then climbed in behind him. Bending low, he paddled hard after Reese's canoe. A cold breeze—or were those bullets?—whistled past his ears. He clenched his innards tight to avoid shivering in his wet clothing.

The canoe barely scraped bottom before shouting Cherokee warriors swarmed him, lifting The Whale onto the bank and piling into his spot. One of the Watie men shoved Sam's rifle into his lap. That afforded someone else the opportunity to grab the paddles. Sam made no protest. The cold swim, followed by the frantic paddling while bearing the weight of the wounded man, left his arms and legs shaky.

Once they completed the return trip to the other side, the Cherokees fanned out, seizing canoes to ferry more men. Women and children fled from the nearest huts farther into the village as lead balls continued to zing across the river. From the village-side peninsula, they needed to help cover the relentless relay taking place. Sam and several others crouched in the greening thicket to ready their guns.

The rifled barrel of his 1803 Harper's Ferry flintlock might give better accuracy, but in moments like this, what he wouldn't give for the reloading speed of a musket. His hands shook with anxiety, with hurry, as he measured out powder, poured it down the muzzle, and retrieved a cloth patch to seat the bullet. Tamped it down with the ramrod. Too many steps. His jerky effort to slide the metal piece back under the barrel sent it bouncing in the underbrush. He felt around for it with his free hand, crumpling delicate violet wood sorrel until his fingers closed over the rod.

One of his comrades cried out from a canoe as a musket ball pierced his chest. Sam closed his eyes. The lives of those men rested partly in his hands. Men who included Major Ridge, Colonel Moore, Adjutant John Ross—and Captain Charles Hicks.

God, make me fast and accurate.

He returned the ramrod and primed the rifle with fine-grain powder. Closed the pan cover. Lifted the muzzle and shifted from behind his tree for a clear shot of a warrior aiming for the canoes.

A flash, a boom, a light kickback on Sam's shoulder, and the warrior fell dead.

Two Cherokee brothers from his company, slightly older than Sam, who went by the English names of Jake and Joe, both sporting a stripe of black war paint across the eyes, joined him under the trees. Together, they repeated the seemingly endless reloading and firing until as many as a couple hundred passed over the river and began to flow like an irresistible tide into Tohopeka. Smoke rose to the sky—the crude log cabins nearest him burning. Screams and sobs pierced the air.

Sam loaded his rifle one more time and, topping his powder horn, turned to the brothers. "What happened at Tallushatchee must not happen here. Will you come with me? Help get the women and children clear of the fire?"

Although their faces twitched with impatience—for they surely craved the thrill of combat—they nodded. Legs stiff from kneeling and crouching, Sam stood and ran toward the village.

As he approached the first cluster of cabins not yet aflame, two braves rounded the nearest dwelling, skidded to a halt, and leveled their muskets. All three Cherokees fired first. Jake and Joe fell upon their enemies to finish them with blades.

A woman in calico with her hair in braids came screaming from the cabin, trying to throw herself upon one of the vanquished men. Sam caught her. When he tried to hold her back, she drew a knife from her belt and lunged at him. It took only a flick to her wrist to disarm her.

He restrained her by the arms and spoke in her ear in soft Muskogean. "Please. You must submit. We will not hurt you, but these cabins are next to burn." He'd heard Major Ridge order those in the rear torched to drive the people toward the barricade, trapping them. The woman's pupils fastened on him, pinpoints of shock. He turned her away from the sight of the fallen warriors. "You have others in the house?"

She nodded, and Sam gave her a little push in that direction. He waited outside, instructing the brothers to check the next cabin. The woman returned with a hand on both a round-eyed young girl and a gaunt man with long, white hair.

Sam pointed. "Go to the edge of the trees. We will send others. You must sit together and not resist. Do not try to cross the river. You will be killed if you do. There are soldiers on the other side."

A long roll of drums thundered from the hill opposite the barricade. Sam jerked his gaze in that direction. Jackson must have seen the smoke from the town and comprehended the unplanned rear attack. "They are charging."

Jake and Joe hesitated, muscles tensing, bodies leaning toward the sound.

Sam shooed the prisoners to the trees as he addressed the two battle-hungry Cherokees. "Clear these cabins first. That's an order."

After sharing a scowl, the brothers darted to the next structure. They herded more women and children from the dwellings before Major Ridge's men arrived with torches. Sam sent the civilians to huddle with the others already at the tree line, away from the action. The Cherokees were moving as a large group through the village now, dispatching warriors, sounds of conflict calling them toward the wall. None would want to stay behind.

Just beyond another cluster of cabins, a flash of silver caught his eye. A familiar, tall figure. Colonel Moore, circling a warrior with his sword drawn. The brave feinted, then darted under the swing of the long blade to land a tomahawk blow to the colonel's ribs. Sam ran toward them as the sword dropped from Moore's grip. The colonel stumbled, clutching his bleeding side. His back to Sam as Sam closed the distance between them, the warrior weighted his weapon in his hand, the tension in his limbs testifying that he prepared to deliver the fatal blow.

Sam slowed and took aim. *Whoosh. Thud.* His tomahawk landed in the man's spine, dropping him to his knees. By the time Moore retrieved his sword, Sam stood over his dying opponent.

"Aren't you going to finish him?" Moore rasped the question from one knee.

"He *is* finished." Even as Sam spoke, the man hissed his final breaths into the dirt.

"Take his scalp?"

"No scalps." He and his father had made that agreement before the battle. They would do what they must, but no more. They didn't need physical relics to display their bravery, to bring them honor. Their actions alone would do that.

Moore pushed himself to his feet. "I admit to being thankful for your throwing skills."

Bending to wipe his blade on a patch of grass, Sam gave a solemn nod. He never took a man's life without a piercing concern for the fate of his spirit.

"You could have let that man kill me." The implication was clear, the rest of the statement unspoken but loud—*and the path would have been clear to my daughter.*

"That is not the way we do things." Sam hung his tomahawk on his belt and stepped closer to the colonel. "Where are Ross and Bold Hunter?" He'd thought both would stick to Moore's side.

"We got separated just before that warrior came at me."

At the spread of the crimson stain under Moore's armpit, Sam frowned. "You need to tend that wound."

"It is nothing. The men are leaving us behind." The colonel gazed toward the front of the village, where the din of gunfire and war whoops increased by the second. "More and more enemy braves are fleeing from the wall."

"You still plan to fight?" Untying his commanding officer's sash, Sam lifted his eyebrows. Moore glowered at him but complied by raising his arms with a little grunt. Sam knotted the fabric directly over the bloodstain.

"This will be my last battle, Hicks."

Sam met his gray eyes. "And I hope it will be mine."

"Then let us go face it."

They ran together for the wooded hills that lay between the town and the barricade, stopping to engage the enemy when necessary, eventually joining Bold Hunter, Ross, and the group of Cherokees. Fighting beside his countrymen, some non-thinking part took over, some deep layer blending training into an instinct that he'd not thought he possessed. But when they reached the wall, reason returned. And Sam hoped he'd never see again the horrors that spread before him.

CHAPTER TWENTY-THREE

Susanna pushed her bonnet back, allowing it to dangle from its strings as she raised her face to the April sun. She sat back on the feed sack Solomon had spread so the manure-enriched dirt of the garden wouldn't stain her work dress as she basked in the warmth on her skin.

"Your father not like that." Nokassa's teasing admonition came from the middle of the newly planted row of corn, where she mounded an earthen hill in the pattern of a Cherokee Three Sisters Garden. "He be angry if he come home and you brown as me."

"It would serve him right," Susanna muttered as she poked a hole at the foot of the corn plant and inserted a bean seed, pressing it down about an inch. Remorse instantly filled her. She just wanted him to come now, whole and healthy—she truly did. Every day without news increased her worry.

And here she'd thought she'd dealt with her bitterness over Sam. Like a noxious weed, though, it reared its ugly head from time to time. Mostly, she fought her own ongoing battle against unrequited longing. How many times had she given it to God? Yet sometimes it snuck up at night, trying to strangle her in silent anguish. At other times, it ambushed her in broad daylight, stabbing her with intense need.

"Well, I plant four … er, squash seeds while you do one bean seed." With a smug look, Nokassa covered her seeds with a thin layer of soil.

"Ah, but I am also pulling the weaker of the two corn seedlings as I go. Although … I always hate to. It seems … cruel somehow."

"Some things not meant to ... how you say ..." Pausing after scooting down the row, her cousin rolled her hand in search of the right word. "Keep alive?"

"Survive?"

"Yes. Survive. Some things we throw away."

Was her love for Sam one of those things? Did God will her to a life without love? Did He have some other purpose for her? Susanna struggled to imagine that anything could fulfill her as being Sam's wife would.

"Horses coming." Nokassa held her hand to the ground as if she felt it vibrating beneath her fingers.

Susanna frowned and stood up, brushing dirt from her skirt. She shielded her eyes and looked toward the drive. Her heart constricted as she breathed a name, for there was no mistaking that broad, upright figure. "Father."

"Who with him?" Nokassa scrambled to her feet.

For half a heartbeat, hope abducted reason. But the second mounted man was also too big to be Sam. Regret lumped in her throat, preventing reply, even as she rejoiced for her cousin.

"*My* father!" Nokassa started running.

Polly should be the first to greet her husband. Susanna darted to the kitchen. "Mama! Mama!" She scrambled to open the back door at the same time Polly did. Mama's wild eyes met hers. "Father is home."

"Oh! Children, come!" Mama called over her shoulder. Screams and yells sounded as George and the girls tumbled out the door, George's strong, long legs quickly outpacing even his mother's.

Susanna followed, picking up Molly when she tripped in her haste. By the time they reached the men, who had dismounted to embrace their families, Father had greeted all the others and extended his arms to embrace both her and Molly as one.

"My oldest and my youngest. All my sweethearts." Father kissed both of their foreheads, the combined scents of horse and smoke and leather—the smell of security—coming with him.

Susanna found herself weeping as all her anxiety and questions and fears receded. Whatever else happened, their family was together, and her father would protect and provide. He had assured her she could remain with George and whatever bride he took. She had a place forever here. These people and this land would be hers. Couldn't that be enough?

Father thumbed her tears away. "You must have prayed for me as I asked, for as you can see, God returned me safely."

"I did, Father. Were you not hurt?"

He shrugged away her inquiry. "Only a scratch. A little scar to remember the war by." He turned to wink at George, who now reached his chin in height. The boy was shooting up as lanky as the cornstalks.

"Is it really over, Father?" As Susanna hugged Bold Hunter, her half brother piped up and toggled on his toes. "Did you beat the Red Sticks?"

Father put an arm around Mama, drawing her to his side as he smiled at his son. "It really is over. General Jackson had a price on the head of Bill Weatherford, or Chief Red Eagle, who started the whole thing with the attack on Fort Mims. But the man walked right into Jackson's camp and turned himself in. The officers have resigned their commissions and headed home. All that remains is to negotiate the peace and the land settlement."

Susanna's smile faded. No matter how fierce the Red Sticks or how close their alliance with the British, she could not help but grieve for the loss of life and land. And wonder if their allies, their own family, might be next. She glanced at Nokassa and Bold Hunter. Imagining them sent away left a sour taste in her mouth and a bitter gall in her stomach. She couldn't entertain the possibility that her immediate family might ever be in that situation. And now was not the time to.

Now was the time to rejoice, but she had to know something

first. Surely, her father would not cheat her of the sparse assurance of Sam's welfare. She trailed him as the men began to lead their horses up the lane.

"Did ... *all* the officers resign their commissions and head home?" Her question came out so soft that when her father did not answer at first, she wondered if he had heard.

Finally, he looked back over his shoulder. "All the ones we know. They acquitted themselves bravely and earned the rest they will find with their families."

Susanna nodded as the warm comfort that Sam had survived, and not only survived but done well in her father's sight, wrapped around her heart. *Thank You, God.* If she submitted to her father's plans—and what other choice did she have?—it was a gift she could take out and treasure on lonely nights. But she would never imagine Sam with a wife and children. She would only imagine him as he was now, his heart bound to hers with a love no man could break.

Two days later, Nokassa opened the window and leaned out the frame, twilight glittering on the burgundy silk gown Susanna had gifted her. "They have lit the bonfires." When she turned back, cheeks flushed with anticipation and the ringlets Susanna had painstakingly created around her face bouncing, she had never looked more fetching. "A wonderful night to share joy in your father's return."

Susanna joined her at the window, the folds of her spring-green gown rustling. Servants and local residents already gathered around the two piles of winter's refuse in the field, laughing and drinking. Torches lined a rectangular, grassy space for dancing, and a local fiddler scratched off a few rusty notes. Even before he trailed into a song, her heart tugged, remembering—David Crockett and the Tennessee militia, and the man who'd walked beside her when she'd last heard a fiddle. Woodsmoke drifted to her nose. The setting sun pinked greening forests and fields, breathing of the promise of life … and she began to cry.

"What is wrong?" Nokassa put her hand on Susanna's shoulder, tilting her concern-lined face close.

"I can't. I can't do it."

"Do what?"

"Go down and pretend that I am happy."

"But you *are* happy. Your father home and the war over."

"Yes, and I thought that would be enough. I have told myself since Father returned that I would not say anything, that I would wait and pray he might change his mind, but I can't." Susanna wiped the tears streaming down her face.

Nokassa closed the window and straightened to look at her again. "What you going to do?"

"I am going on strike." Susanna placed her hands on her hips.

"On what?"

"On strike. A new word, but not a new idea. It's when you stop doing something that someone wants you to do to make a change."

"What you stop?"

"For now, I will stop pretending I accept my father's decision to keep Sam and me apart. He has already said local young men who fought in the militia and whom he wants us to meet are coming tonight. I understand if you want to meet them …"

Nokassa shook her head, returning to her native tongue but speaking slowly enough Susanna could understand. "I do not mind meeting them or maybe trying some of the dancing you taught me, but …"

"But?" Susanna prompted her, tugging her own heavy mass of curls tied with a silk ribbon behind her shoulder.

"Since Father came, I feel eager to go home. I miss my family and village."

"And Culsowee?" Cocking her head, Susanna quirked up one side of her mouth.

"Yes." Back to speaking English, Nokassa nodded, tucked her chin, and gave a coy smile. "I miss him … after all."

"If you leave with Bold Hunter tomorrow, I will miss *you* … sorely." Susanna drew Nokassa into an embrace.

"I will miss you too. I hope we visit."

The sadness in Susanna's heart told her that was not likely. At least, not for a long time. "You are always welcome here." She moved back, wiping fresh tears. "Now, I am going to find my father and beg him to excuse me from the party tonight on the grounds of my broken heart."

Nokassa's eyes grew huge. "He will not be happy."

"He will not, but at least he will talk to me when he understands that I mean business." In Tennessee, she'd heard of girls who had holed themselves up in their rooms or even quit eating to make a point to a strict parent. Hopefully, it would not come to that.

"Oh dear." Taking a few steps away, Nokassa twirled her bracelet in circles. That her normally bold cousin displayed that much anxiety testified to her increased awareness that authority flowed differently in families with white fathers. And her certainty that Susanna's rebellion could spark a flame. "I will pray for you."

Susanna gave a little laugh and headed for the door. "I will see you later."

She did not expect to encounter her father the moment her slipper hit the landing—yet there he stood in the foyer, conferring with Solomon, who held two wine bottles. And he glanced up and saw her before she could retreat.

"Ah, my dear. You look lovely! But you are early. I did not expect you and your mother and cousin for another half hour."

She descended the last set of steps, reaching for his hand as Solomon whisked into the dining room. The scents of roasted meat and rich sauces floating about would have tempted her stomach had it not been churning.

One of her father's brows rose with apparent suspicion. "What is this? This look of mourning? We're to have none of that tonight."

"You ask me to go against my own heart, then, Father." Susanna squeezed his hands, pleading for sympathy. And a quieter voice. In the manner of the Cherokees, early arrivals drifted in and out with the servants, searching for a cup of whiskey or a rib of pork. Susanna and her father were attracting stares, and her tears remained far too close to the surface.

Her hopes for a modulated response went unheeded. "Do not tell me you are still thinking of Sam Hicks. Did I not make my reasons that you could not wed him clear at Fort Strother?"

"Father, please." Susanna cringed and dropped her hands to her sides. "I must ask your leave. I cannot attend the party tonight."

As Mama rushed down the stairs—with a doe-eyed Nokassa tiptoeing along the wall behind her—Susanna cast her a pleading look. Pausing on the bottom step, her stepmother laid her hand on Susanna's shoulder as Father barked his response.

"You most certainly can, and you will. I will not have my own daughter shaming me by weeping in her room on the occasion of my homecoming. And what is more, you will welcome my special guest tonight and recompense him the honor and attention he deserves."

"What?" She whispered the word. Her father had been insensitive before, but how could he ask this of her? Making conversation and hanging on the arm of some stodgy old officer or influential businessman from Tennessee? Now, when he knew only one of the two men she'd longed to welcome back from the war had been allowed to return to her life? "What special guest?"

"The officer who likely saved my life at Horseshoe Bend." Father's gaze sought his wife's.

Susanna did not understand, but apparently her stepmother did. Mama nodded, her face controlled, as if she feared giving away any emotion. "I believe he is in the library."

Father seized Susanna's elbow. "Since you are down here, you can meet him now. But get hold of yourself. I would not wish on him the company of a weepy female. No, not even on him, though I admit, he can be trying himself."

"I-I don't—" Susanna's question cut short when Father tugged her along the hall. She locked her feet onto the rug. "No. You require too much. I will not be bartered like a horse or a slave. I will not be forced to keep company with men I have no wish to ... know."

Her protests trailed into silence as her father pushed open the door of the library. A trim figure in a dark tailcoat stood in the middle of the room, holding a thick book. When he turned, Susanna's buckling knees threatened her imminent collapse. It was a good thing her father supported her. Reason rejected the image her eyes attempted to communicate to her mind. Instead of heeding the cry of her heart, she turned to the man beside her, her voice quivering with fear—absolute terror she misunderstood what this meant or that she might even be losing her mind.

"Father?"

A faint smile lifted his lips. "When I told you at dinner yesterday that a foe had come at me and I lost my sword, well, I did not rally on my own. It galls a man of my age and experience to admit that, but it is true. Naturally, I invited the fine young man who came to my aid to my homecoming celebration."

A thick *clap* turned Susanna's head back toward the library. Sam slid the closed *Idea Fidei Fratrum* onto the table beside him and smiled at her. She could barely hear her father's throaty murmur for the blood rushing through her ears.

"Go to him, my Susanna. I have told him he can have you."

She saw then only Sam Hicks. The next moment she was in his arms. She wasn't sure which one of them moved or if both did, or if her father looked on or if he had given them the gift of privacy. But privacy they had need of, for Sam braced the side of her face with one hand and her waist with the other and cut off her cry of longing with the kind of kiss she'd dreamed of every day since she'd tasted it in the wilds of Creek Territory. Her mind blurred with impressions of his mouth and skin under her lips, his whispers between their meetings, spoken in Cherokee. *My love. My heart. My wife.*

Susanna froze and drew back, staring at him with her breath coming in little gasps.

He nodded. "It is true. Your father has agreed. If you will marry me, there is a reverend here. Tonight will be our wedding feast. Our wedding night."

When she sagged with shock, Sam's arms held her up. He looked over her shoulder and chuckled.

"I cannot believe it." Grasping his arms, Susanna pivoted to find Father, Mama, and Nokassa all peeking in the door with grins wreathing their faces. She focused on her father. "Did he really save you?"

Father nodded. "He did. The young man can throw a tomahawk."

Susanna darted a glance between them, searching for clues to verify such an abrupt change of circumstance. "This still doesn't make sense. Why? Why would you change your mind?"

Mama beat on her husband's arm and answered for him in a play-gruff voice. "Because he needed reminding that love is greater than land. He wrote to me of what the lieutenant did, and I reminded him. And he missed me enough that this time, he listened."

"Yes." The glower never lifted from her father's face. "I rode to Fort Hill before I came home. We would rather lose all we have than watch you mope away your life into spinsterhood." There was no denying the note of cynicism in his statement, but at the end, a corner of his mouth twitched.

"He *means* than see you miss the kind of love we share." Polly shook his arm and gave him a scolding stare.

Nokassa giggled, her hand over her mouth.

"Did you know about this?" Susanna arched a brow at her.

"No. Do you think she could keep a secret?" George poked his head around the doorframe. "Oh brother." At the sight of her in Sam's embrace, he rolled his eyes and disappeared. Susanna heard him say, "Come on, time to pike off," and he jerked Nokassa out of the door as well.

"Yes, husband, I think Lieutenant Hicks has something to say to our daughter." Mama gently tugged Father down the hall.

Alone with him at last, Susanna turned her face up to Sam's. "*Do* you have something to say to me?"

He ran his thumb along her cheek. "I love you, Susanna Moore."

What a joy and a relief to finally hear him say it outright. "I love you, too, Sam Hicks."

"If you are willing to risk everything for a future together, I would like nothing better than to call you my bride."

She placed her arms around his neck. "I am not risking anything. I am giving everything. To you, and to God." Susanna paused to seal his lips with a soft kiss, eliciting a gentle smile.

"Likewise." Her tender warrior, her learned lieutenant, smoothed the hair framing her face. "Our path to each other was not straight, but as sure as a bent tree gives direction in the wilderness, God brought us back to each other."

AUTHOR'S NOTE

After the Battle of Horseshoe Bend, Captain Charles Hicks of the Cherokee Regiment walked among the breastworks. He took no scalps. Rather, in English, then in Cherokee, he spoke the story of Jesus to the dying, the dead, and the listening Cherokees. He did this while members of the allied Cherokee-American armies stole bloody souvenirs from the Red Stick Creeks—an example that light can shine even in the deepest darkness.

Moments like these compel me to write historical novels. In the midst of the tragedy of the human struggle for land and survival, they give us examples of integrity among all people groups.

Charles Hicks was a real Cherokee chief, one of the leaders during this period of transition for his people who believed working with the Americans might allow the Cherokees to keep their land. Even though the Red Stick Creeks were the enemies of the Cherokee-American forces, it is easy to understand how they hoped alliance both among Native American tribes and with the British might afford them the same outcome. Many details I included in *Bent Tree Bride* about Charles were factual, including the massive size of his library, his work as an interpreter for US Indian Agent Colonel Return Jonathan Meigs, and his participation in the Red Stick War. It is always very tricky to include real historical figures in a fictional story. When generating conversation, I attempted to capture his manner and beliefs as closely as I could from research. I used one known quote when Hicks spoke of his faith: "*I lie awake at night thinking of all the mysteries.*" Too beautiful not to include.

Other real historical people who make cameo appearances in *Bent Tree Bride* are John Ross, adjutant of the Cherokee Regiment and future principal chief of the Cherokee Nation; George Guess/Gist/Sequoyah, who did indeed produce the Cherokee syllabary a few years later; and David Crockett, later famous for his death defending the Alamo during the Mexican War. Crockett participated in the fall campaign of 1813 against the Red Stick Creeks but missed the Battle of Horseshoe Bend because his enlistment had expired. He reenlisted later in 1814 and fought in Florida.

Another man who would later achieve fame at the Alamo did make an appearance at Horseshoe Bend. Young ensign Sam Houston was one of the first over the barricade at Tohopeka, taking an arrow in the thigh. I just couldn't figure out how to include him in my story since we were in deep point of view with Sam as he approached the wall through the town.

For my novel, Sam Hicks became a fictional son of Charles. His story actually begins in *The Witness Tree* (Smitten Historical Romance, September 2019), when he was a boy at the Moravian mission school at Springplace. Sam allowed me to embody the thinking of this type of Cherokee family without writing a non-fiction accounting, which has already been done so well.

Susanna's father, Colonel Gideon Moore, is a fictional character but is based upon Colonel Gideon Morgan, who did hail from the same area on the Hiwassee River, did marry a Cherokee woman, and did lead the Cherokee Regiment. Gideon Morgan's father, Gideon Morgan Sr., was a Revolutionary War vet who lived in a beautiful brick house-ordinary in Kingston, Tennessee. Pinhook Plantation, built in 1810, inspired the Moore family home of Big Springs Bluff in the actual Big Springs community.

My goal in writing *Bent Tree Bride* was to frame a riveting romance against as realistic a period backdrop as possible. Please keep in mind, there are gaps or straight-out contradictions in our historical record and our ability to understand it, so at times we have to make an educated guess about how something might have happened. For example, one source said that after being shot after swimming the Tallapoosa River at Tohopeka, The Whale was too dazed to get in the canoe for the return trip. Another source said his comrades helped him into the canoe. I made a guess that the Cherokees probably wanted to get him to safety, so into the canoe he went!

At other times, a fictional story needs a bit of tweaking. History records that John Ross stayed by the side of Colonel Gideon Morgan during the Battle of Horseshoe Bend. But I had a fictionalized Colonel Moore and a hero who really needed to help save him to get in his good graces! So Colonel Moore is facing an enemy alone when Sam comes to his aid.

You can read more about the real history from this period using some of my sources. *Trail of Tears: The Rise and Fall of the Cherokee Nation* by John Ehle; *Forging a Cherokee-American Alliance in the Creek War: From Creation to Betrayal* by Susan M. Abram; *Toward the Setting Sun: John Ross, the Cherokees, and the Trail of Tears* by Brian Hicks; *Jacksonland* by Steve Inskeep; "War of 1812 in Clay County, Alabama" by Don C. East; *The Moravian Springplace Mission to the Cherokees: Volume 1, 1805–1813*; and countless websites.

I hope you have enjoyed your trip to this unique portion of the War of 1812 as much as I have, and that the characters, their ideals, and their romance stay with you for a long time to come. Your online reviews mean the world to me and are part of what determines if my future stories can be published. Please visit me at https://deniseweimerbooks.webs.com, and I'd also love to connect on social media.

Monthly e-mail list: http://eepurl.com/dFfSfn
https://www.facebook.com/denise.weimer1
https://twitter.com/denise_weimer
https://www.bookbub.com/profile/denise-weimer